Come Back *to the* World

Other Titles by Catherine Ryan Hyde

Falling Apart and Other Gifts from the Universe
Michael Without Apology
Rolling Toward Clear Skies
Life, Loss, and Puffins
A Different Kind of Gone
Just a Regular Boy
So Long, Chester Wheeler
Dreaming of Flight
Boy Underground
Seven Perfect Things
My Name is Anton
Brave Girl, Quiet Girl
Stay
Have You Seen Luis Velez?
Just After Midnight
Heaven Adjacent
The Wake Up
Allie and Bea
Say Goodbye for Now
Leaving Blythe River
Ask Him Why
Worthy
The Language of Hoofbeats
Pay It Forward: Young Readers Edition
Take Me with You
Paw It Forward

365 Days of Gratitude: Photos from a Beautiful World
Where We Belong
Subway Dancer and Other Stories
Walk Me Home
Always Chloe and Other Stories
The Long, Steep Path: Everyday Inspiration from the Author of Pay It Forward
How to Be a Writer in the E-Age: A Self-Help Guide
When You Were Older
Don't Let Me Go
Jumpstart the World
Second Hand Heart
When I Found You
Diary of a Witness
The Day I Killed James
Chasing Windmills
The Year of My Miraculous Reappearance
Love in the Present Tense
Becoming Chloe
Walter's Purple Heart
Electric God/The Hardest Part of Love
Pay It Forward
Earthquake Weather and Other Stories
Funerals for Horses

Come Back *to the* World

A Novel

Catherine Ryan Hyde

This is a work of fiction. Names, characters, organizations, places, events, and incidents are either products of the author's imagination or are used fictitiously. Otherwise, any resemblance to actual persons, living or dead, is purely coincidental.

Published by Lake Union Publishing, Seattle

www.apub.com

EU product safety contact:
Amazon Media EU S. à r.l.
38, avenue John F. Kennedy, L-1855 Luxembourg
amazonpublishing-gpsr@amazon.com

ISBN-13: 9781662522406 (hardcover)
ISBN-13: 9781662522383 (paperback)
ISBN-13: 9781662522390 (digital)

Cover design by Eileen Carey
Cover images: © NDS Visuals / Shutterstock;
© Gerard Soury, grandriver, Kathrin Ziegler, ti-ja / Getty

Printed in the United States of America
First edition

Come Back *to the* World

Chapter One

The Sky Is Smaller Here

Amelia opened the door to her son's room and saw nothing but a lump under the covers. Even the boy's face was obscured. All she could see was the whiteness of his little fingers, holding the bedding up over his head, grasping the top of the sheet-and-blanket stack.

It filled her with an eerie sensation, because it reminded her of the way someone will pull a sheet up over a person's head when they've expired. Fortunately, she could see the blankets rising and falling with his breath.

"Jade," she said. "Time to get up and get ready for school."

For a moment, nothing. Then the boy's hands came down suddenly, bringing the blanket along. Flipping it back, revealing Jaden's face, torso, and arms, along with his Spiderman pajamas. He was frowning.

"Don't call me Jade," he said.

"What's wrong with Jade? It's just Jaden, but a little shorter."

"I don't think that really saves you very much time," he said.

He lay still for a few moments, blinking too much, his dark, curly hair almost comically disheveled. His face was lit up by a beam of light pouring through his bedroom window, and it took Amelia's breath away. Almost literally.

"It's just that Jade is a girl's name," he said.

Still he made no move to rise and dress.

"Unless it's just short for Jaden."

"But once you called me that to my teacher, and then she called me that in class, and all the other boys laughed at me later, in the hall, because one of them has a cousin named Jade. And she's a *girl*."

It struck her—not for the first time—that he might be taking more than the usual dose of teasing and bullying at school. He certainly showed enough resistance to going. But she had asked him many times if anyone was hurting him there, and he had always said no, and seemed to mean it.

"Okay," she said. "I won't do it again. Jaden it is. Now get up and get dressed, Jaden. The carpool will be here in twenty minutes and you need to eat your breakfast."

His big brown eyes met hers, melting her through and through.

"You're not driving carpool today?"

"No. Lissa Anne's mother is driving."

Jaden sighed.

"Too bad," he said.

"Seriously, honey," Amelia said. "You need to get a move on."

She let herself out of his bedroom and into her home office, where she quickly checked her email.

There were at least twenty new messages, but most were junk, or predictable communications—things she had been expecting, and that were not especially important. Only one looked unusual.

She sank down into her desk chair.

It was from Richard and Carla Jacobs, a couple she had spent a fair amount of time with for several years, but only before her separation. She had not seen them since, because they were Mark's friends much more than they were hers. Mark had shared a dorm room with Richard for their four years at the university, and in the classic "marriage goes awry" scenario, there had never been any question regarding on whose side they would fall.

So the very fact that they were contacting her felt like a thing out of place.

She opened the email.

It was a photograph.

They had sent her a photograph of an older woman choosing mangoes at an outdoor market and placing them in what looked like leather saddlebags draped over her arm.

"Amelia," it said. "We just got back from vacation in a very remote spot in Mexico. Eastern Baja, on the Gulf of California. A little town called Santa Rosarita. Do you know it? Touristy but small and out of the way. We saw this woman and we were just sure it was E. L. Swann. Actually, I was sure. Richard, not so much. But we had to show you. To see if it really was her. If anyone would know, it's you. Hope you are doing okay."

Yes, Amelia thought. *If anyone would know, it's me.*

But she did not know, which set up a troubling knot in her belly. Because it was important, and she wanted it to be true. But she didn't know.

It would have been fair, though probably not utterly beyond debate, to call herself the country's foremost authority on the author E. L. Swann, who had not been seen for forty years. Still, forty years is a long time, and people's faces change as they age. It's hard to match a forty-four-year-old face with its eighty-four-year-old counterpart.

She pulled up the image and zoomed in on the woman.

"Possible," she said out loud.

But, really, what were the chances? They seemed so small and inconsequential compared to the much greater chance that this older woman simply bore a passing resemblance to the author.

She shook her head as if to dismiss the whole line of thought, then jumped up and stuck her head into the kitchen.

No Jaden. His cereal had not been touched.

She walked back to his room to find that the small blue ripstop-nylon tent his father had given him had been fully assembled on the bed.

It made her wonder how he could have put it together so fast. Or had she been thinking about that email longer than she'd realized?

"Jaden," she barked.

She didn't want to lose patience with him. Then again, he didn't make it easy.

The zipper of the tent moved, pulled down slightly from the inside, and she saw one of his brown eyes peering out.

"I don't want to go to school," he said. "I don't feel good."

"Tell me what's wrong."

He never exactly answered the question. He took the conversation in a different direction.

"Second grade is hard," he said.

"Your grades are terrific, though. Are you really having trouble keeping up with the coursework?"

"No."

"Then in what way is it hard?"

This time he didn't answer at all.

A moment later, before she had figured out the best way to go forward from that place, she heard the honk of the carpool driver. So she *had* been preoccupied with that email longer than she'd realized.

"And now it's too late," she said quietly.

She walked out of her son's room, out the front door, and down the stairs to the street, where she told Lissa Anne's mother that Jaden was late yet again and she should go on without him. That she would drive him to school herself.

They ended up walking, because it was only seven blocks. And it was down the steep hill rather than up, which made for a better pace going toward school. And Amelia had figured that, traffic being what it was, it might even turn out to be faster than driving.

Jaden walked beside her, his shoulders slumped forward, angular shoulder blades showing through his T-shirt just above his sagging backpack in a way that looked so inexplicably vulnerable it broke her heart.

"It's pretty today," he said, extending one skinny arm to point to the bay.

They were walking down a hill that would have been bizarrely steep in any other city, and was pretty darned steep even by San Francisco standards, and they had a view of Alcatraz Island and the hills of Marin County beyond. The sun glinted off the bay, and a haze of fog hung at the horizon, and the boy was right. It was a sight.

"It is. It's why so many people think this is a beautiful city," she said.

"Did you know some people don't even live in a city?" he asked her.

"I did know that. Yes."

"This girl Hazel at school, her father lives in Montana now, and he says it's better than any city."

Amelia knew Hazel's mom. She had separated from her husband within a week of Amelia's separation from Mark. Twice they had gone out to a neighborhood pub to first share, and then drown, their sorrows.

"'Better' is a matter of opinion, though," she said.

"He says it's better because the sky is bigger. But I can't quite figure that out. I mean, isn't the sky the same size everywhere?"

"I think he means it seems bigger. Probably because there's nothing blocking it. No buildings or power lines or whatever, and probably you can see down to the horizon in every direction."

"I've never been anyplace like that," he said, sounding wistful. Then again, everything he said on the way to school sounded wistful.

"I guess not."

"I've mostly never been outside the city except when we went to Muir Woods and Mount Tam."

"I guess we'll have to go someplace, then."

"When?"

"When school gets out."

"Eleven days," he said, making it clear that he was counting.

They stopped in front of his school and stood at the bottom of the stone steps, and Jaden sighed.

"You can manage for another eleven days, right?" she asked him.

"Yeah. I guess."

"Can you tell me anything about why you're not liking school?"

At first he only shrugged, his eyes cast down to the sidewalk. Then he looked up and caught her gaze, and held it.

"Did you like school when you were me?"

She could only assume he meant when she was his age. She quickly decided to tell him the truth.

"I'm afraid I really didn't, no."

He gave her an expansive shrug. It was clear that he didn't quite have the words to draw the parallel. But it was also clear what he meant.

He hesitated another moment. She moved in his direction and started to bend down, but he blocked the move with one stop sign of an extended hand.

"No kiss," he said. "Someone might see."

Then he trudged up the stairs and disappeared inside.

Amelia did not go straight home. Instead, she stopped by the bank where her friend Leon had recently taken a day job in IT. They had worked together at a small independent local paper before the publication had gone belly-up the previous year, and she had only seen him in person a handful of times since, though they texted and emailed regularly.

He was just trotting down the stone steps as she arrived.

He stopped cold when he saw her, seeming more than a little bit shocked.

Amelia was immediately filled with a sense that she should not have come here.

She had always known that Leon had something of a crush on her, if that was the right way to put it, though he had kept a respectful distance due to her marriage. But her marriage was essentially over, and to come seek him out in person now might convey the wrong impression.

"Amelia," he said.

He walked down and stood two steps above her for a moment, and they regarded each other.

When she'd last seen him, his hair had been shaved close to the scalp, but he had grown it out and was wearing it in twists, dangling onto the dark skin of his forehead. His eyes looked hopeful but also a bit guarded behind his narrow wire-rimmed glasses.

"Weird time of morning to be leaving," she said. "Actually, weird time of morning even to have gotten in yet."

She had expected to have to wait for him.

He smiled a crooked smile and seemed relieved by the break in tension.

"There was something I needed to do before everybody else got in," he said, in that deep, familiar voice. He had been a comfort to her at the paper, a friend and confidant in what had felt like a hostile environment. And now, on this confused and disconnected morning, he was all of that again. "But I haven't had my coffee yet. So now I'm going to go do that."

He stepped down to her level and they walked off along the downtown street together.

She said, "I guess I was wondering if you could tolerate drinking coffee and having your brain picked at the same time."

"I guess I thought that already went without saying," he said.

Funny, she thought, how often they talked about it out loud without ever really talking about it out loud.

They sat outside in the cool morning, drinking their coffee drinks alfresco as the downtown work crowd strode by.

"How's Jaden?" he asked, after a tentative sip.

"He's good. He's . . . different. Not from how he ever was. I mean . . . more like from the rest of the world. He's absolutely, one hundred percent himself."

"Not sure if you mean that as a good thing or a bad thing," Leon said.

"No. Me neither. I mean, I adore him. And who he is . . . I'm all for it. I just worry the world's going to beat him down. You know the world."

"Yeah," Leon said, his voice wry and downbeat. "We've met."

They sipped in silence for a minute or two. Amelia was braced for him to ask about Mark. He never did.

"What did you want to pick my brain about?" he asked after an awkward time.

"Oh. Right. Well. You know more about apps and software than anybody I know. I had some questions about aging apps."

"Aging apps?" He sounded unfamiliar with the concept.

"The kind you use to see how someone will look as they age."

"Oh. Predictive aging. Got it."

"You know anything about that?"

"It's not exactly my field of expertise, but I know a little something about pretty much everything out there. What do you need to know about them?"

"That's a good question," she said, realizing she should have thought this out better and more fully. "I guess . . . how accurate they are, and if some are better than others."

"Is this for some kind of freelance story?"

"Maybe. I mean . . . if it pans out. Which at the moment doesn't feel likely."

"Okay. Here's what I know. The whole concept is a bit inexact at best. Sometimes they get it pretty right, other times it's way off. I suppose some people's aging is just more predictable than others. But on balance I'd have to say, if this is a serious project . . . the world is full of free phone apps for the purpose, but as hit-and-miss as they are, they're more for entertainment purposes. At least in my opinion. Modern AI does a better job. It's more and more the go-to these days. I know the police are using AI for predictive aging. I still talk to Frank Buckley now and then, and he just solved a cold case. Not entirely on an AI-aged image, but it sure didn't hurt."

"But this is not police work."

"No. But he's a friend."

"You really think he'd do that as a favor?"

"He wouldn't have to do it on department time. I can't see the harm in asking."

Amelia dug her phone out of her purse, wondering as she did if she had a photo of E. L. Swann in her photo app. But the more she thought about it, the surer she was that she didn't.

"I think the photo I need is on my computer at home. I'll email it to you."

"Don't bother," he said. "I know where to find a picture of E. L. Swann."

Her eyes came up to his and their gazes locked.

"How did you . . ." But it didn't seem worth going further in that direction. Of course he knew her well enough to know that there was only one person—not seen for decades—she would be looking for. Everybody who knew her did. "Never mind. I guess I'm more obvious than I realized."

He took a long sip of his coffee, staring out toward the bay.

Then he said, "Here's what I don't get. Why just now?"

"What's the point of trying to figure out what she looks like forty years later if you have no eighty-four-year-old woman to try to match to it? I needed a sighting."

"This is probably a stupid question," he said. He stalled for a long time, as if examining the question carefully for stupidity before asking it. "But I guess if anyone would know, it's you. How does she still manage to be such a legend forty years later? Or is that one of those things no one can answer?"

"There's a level at which it's unanswerable, I guess. But there are clues. Her book is still taught in just about every English lit class, every year, so new generations keep learning about her. But I think it's more the J. D. Salinger effect."

"They both have initials instead of first names?"

He tossed it off jokingly, but she let it go by.

"No, silly. They're reclusive. They insist on not being found, so everybody wants to find them. It's a challenge. People are just like that. She would have done better saturating the media until people got tired of her. Everybody wants to crack an enigma."

"Then I guess my next question is . . . why did it take so long to get a sighting? If she's such a legend."

"Yeah, but she's a legend *author*. That's different from being a famous movie star. You can garner an awful lot of fame in the literary world without people knowing your face. Especially someone like her who refused to do publicity. Then again, other people might have seen her before this and just not have known to come tell *me* about it."

"Not sure who else they *would* go to about it. You're the expert."

"They'd go to no one," she said. "The average person would wonder but probably go to no one. Just see it as a curiosity and then move on with their lives."

While Jaden was washing his hands for dinner, Amelia got a text from Leon.

It was an AI-generated image of an eighty-something E. L. Swann with the caption "What do you think?"

She brought it up as big as she could on her phone, but wasn't sure what she thought. So she saved it into her photos along with the image of the old woman buying mangoes in Santa Rosarita, and transferred them both onto her home office computer. The big one, with the seventeen-inch monitor.

She brought them up side by side and stared at them for a long time. Longer than it should have taken Jaden to wash his hands, though she'd forgotten about that.

She still wasn't sure what she thought.

The angle wasn't helping. The image of the woman at the market showed mostly the left side of her face, while the aged headshot of the author showed her looking directly into the camera. There was a resemblance. No doubt about that. But enough of one? Amelia really didn't have enough evidence to make a reasoned conjecture.

Her cell phone rang in her shirt pocket, and she pulled it out and saw Leon on the caller ID. She touched the screen to accept the call.

"What do you think?" he asked.

She touched a button on the screen to put the call on speaker, setting the phone down by her keyboard.

"I was just trying to decide. Just sitting here going back and forth about it. And I guess I think . . . it could be her. And also it could not be her. I really can't make a highly educated guess with what I've got in front of me, but if I had to just go off and make a wild guess I'd say fifty-fifty. Equal chance it is and is not her. Or if you want to get all quantum physics-y we can go the Schrodinger's cat route and say, since we don't know, that it simultaneously is and is not E. L. Swann at the exact same moment."

"You do have a unique way of looking at things," he said.

"I try."

She gazed out the window for a moment while neither of them spoke—at her city view, such as it was. Five years earlier she and Mark had responded to an ad for this apartment—the downstairs of a duplex—because it claimed to have a Golden Gate Bridge view. In reality one could see most of a single upright between buildings, along with a few yards of cable. But it was a neighborhood known for a good school, so they'd taken it anyway. She stared at the rust-red metal in the distance for a few moments, hoping Leon had better thoughts than she did regarding the right way forward.

He was the one to break the silence.

"But I'm thinking it puts you in a position where it's just enough of a chance that you have to go find out."

Jaden showed up in her empty office doorway suddenly.

"When are we *eating*?" he asked, his voice slightly judgmental. "I'm *waiting*."

"Be right in," she said.

"Hi, Jaden!" Leon said, obviously having heard the boy in the background.

"Hi, Leon!" he chimed, and then disappeared again.

Amelia sat a moment longer, then sighed deeply.

"Yeah," she said. "That's the position I'm in all right."

Chapter Two

Dad's Friend Makes Mac and Cheese

She waited eleven days, until school was out, before bringing it up with her son.

Jaden was picking at his dinner, which was breaded, oven-baked chicken. Something he usually liked.

She opened her mouth to suggest the trip, but he spoke before she could.

"How come we never have mac and cheese?" he asked, frowning at his food. His face was tilted down, sending spills of brown curls across his forehead and over his eyes.

"I guess I just think it doesn't have all that much in it for a growing boy. Nutrition-wise, I mean."

"But it's *good*," he said. "Christine makes mac and cheese."

"Christine?" she asked. But, although she'd never heard the name before, a place in her gut already knew. It sent a pang of stress shooting through that tender place, but she ignored it.

"Dad's friend."

"Oh. I didn't realize Dad had a friend."

"Doesn't everybody have friends?"

"Not everybody. Most people, though. Does Christine make real macaroni and cheese? The kind where you grate real cheddar cheese into a homemade sauce and bake it in the oven with buttered breadcrumbs on top? Or does she just make the kind from the box?"

"From the box," he said, brushing hair away from his eyes. "But it's still real."

She almost suggested a haircut, but she suggested it regularly, and he never wanted one.

"See, I especially don't think that has any nutrition for you," she said. "It's just bleached white flour and that powdered-flavor packet that might not even have actual cheese in it. I'm not sure. I mean, I've read the ingredients on that box, and I'm still not sure. I try to give you food that helps you grow."

"But it's *good*," he repeated, whinier this time.

"Okay, if you want I'll make real macaroni and cheese this week."

"I like the box stuff better."

"You've never had my real macaroni and cheese, so you can't possibly know which you like better."

Jaden sighed, but didn't answer.

It struck her then that he had completely derailed her plan to ask about a trip to Mexico. So often it happened that way, with Amelia simply following along helplessly as he led her on tangent after tangent.

"What would you think about a trip out of the city?" she asked him.

His eyes came up to hers, and he ate a big bite of chicken, as though her question had caused him to forget that he was boycotting it.

"What kind of trip?" he asked, his mouth still full.

"You said we never go out of the city. Somewhere with a bigger sky."

He swallowed hard, clearly not having done a thorough job of chewing. "We could go to Montana," he said.

"Actually, I had a special place in mind. In Mexico."

"What's in Mexico?"

"Us, I was thinking."

"I mean what can you do there?"

"Lots of fun stuff. I've been looking at it online the last few days. It's right on the Gulf of California, so it's a beach town. So there's swimming, and boating, and fishing, and snorkeling—"

She meant to go on, but he stopped her there.

"What's snorkeling?"

"It's where you swim with your face in the water, but with a mask and a breathing tube, and you look at all the fish."

"Do they eat people?"

"The fish?"

"Yeah. Do they?"

"No, they aren't nearly big enough for that."

"Are there sharks?"

"Actually I was reading about how there's this really nice place to go snorkeling that's protected by a coral reef. Kind of far from where we're going, but it might be worth it. There are all kinds of colorful fish there because the sharks can't fit through the coral. So the fish live there because it's safe, and that means the people are safe too. But if you don't like snorkeling there's parasailing, and we can rent a Jet Ski, and we can even ride a horse on the beach."

"We don't have a horse."

"We can rent one."

"Oh. But why can't we go to Montana? Why does it have to be Mexico?"

"Because I have this story I need to follow up on in this little Mexican town."

"Oh," he said again. He sounded disappointed. As though it had been only a matter of time until she revealed a motive that had nothing to do with him, or fun. "I guess that would be okay. How long would we be there?"

"I'm not really sure. Depends on how my research goes. At least a week. Maybe two. But probably not two. Probably I'll just find out it's nothing."

"Won't Dad be mad?"

His words twisted into Amelia's gut. Yes, Mark would be mad if Jaden wasn't available for their agreed-upon weekend visits. And it wasn't the first she had thought of it. But most likely they would be back in time.

"We'd just have to work it out with him," she said. "Maybe arrange for you to spend more time with him when we get home."

Jaden picked at his food a little more, staring at his fork as he stabbed the chicken.

"Is the sky big there?" he asked, forgetting or ignoring that she had already said it was.

"Very big," she said, her mind filling with the images of Santa Rosarita she had seen online.

"I guess that would be okay, then," he said.

She called Leon later that night to tell him she really was going to do it.

"Too late?" she asked when he answered the phone.

It was a little before ten.

"Not at all."

"Good. I just got Jaden down to sleep."

As she spoke, the cell phone in the crook of her neck, she poured herself a glass of wine and took it to the padded seat of her big bay window.

"Seems late for him," Leon said.

"He's all excited because school is out, and now he's even more excited about going to Mexico. And he wasn't going to get to sleep anyway, so I let him stay up and watch TV with me."

"So you're going."

"Yeah. That's what I called to say. That and thank you. For doing that favor for me with the picture. I keep going over what I said about it when you sent it to me, and I can't recall saying thank you. Apologies for the oversight."

She leaned forward and opened the window on one side of her, letting the breeze of a summer night into the room. Feeling it flow across her bare arms and feet.

"I wasn't too worried about it," he said. "The situation was distracting. When were you thinking of going?"

"Pretty much straightaway."

"You know you need a passport for Jaden, right? That takes time."

"Yeah, I've been looking into that. He needs a passport to *fly* to Mexico. But by land or sea a birth certificate will do. Don't ask me why. So we're going to fly to San Diego and rent a car. The insurance is murder when they know you're taking it over the border, but there are rental places down there that are pretty much set up for that. It's not far south on Baja at all. It's only a six- or seven-hour drive once we get into Mexico."

"How long do you think you'll stay?"

As she briefly avoided answering, Amelia watched fingers of fog drift in from the bay, obscuring what little of the bridge she could see from home. But it was beautiful in its own way.

"As long as it takes, I guess. Until I find her or convince myself it's not possible."

"And Mark is okay with that?"

The question hit her like a fastball to the belly. She breathed deeply once before answering.

"I haven't told him yet."

"Oh."

"I actually thought I'd wait. As long as possible. Like . . . I'm picturing calling him from the plane right before the cabin door closes. And if he gives me a hard time, I can say, 'Oops. Flight attendant just said all devices in the off position.'"

She sat still a moment, waiting for his reaction. It was an ill-advised plan by any measure, so she did not expect to like what she heard next.

"Wouldn't that just make him madder?"

"Yeah. Probably so."

"Why, then?"

"Because then he can't talk me out of it."

"Wouldn't it be easier to just be someone who can't be talked out of it?"

"Leon," she said, "if I were somebody who could do that, I wouldn't be in this situation to begin with. I would never have been in a bad marriage and I wouldn't be in a nasty divorce now. He just wears me down. He's like a fire hose of argument. I never manage to stand up to it. It just sweeps me away every time."

She stared out at the fog for a long time, or at least what felt like a long time, while he—presumably—gathered his thoughts.

"Please promise me you won't go back with him this time," he said.

"Don't worry. We're way beyond that."

"And I don't mean that in a self-serving way," he added.

"I didn't think you did."

"It's just that you're such a strong woman and it seems like a shame for anyone to put you in a position where you can't handle yourself in a fight."

Amelia said nothing because she could think of nothing to say. He was right, which only made it harder.

"When you get back . . ." he said, his voice full of a hesitation a stranger might not have noticed. And she thought, *Here it comes.* ". . . Maybe we can have dinner."

And she thought, *There it is.*

Apparently she took too long to answer, because he said, "Never mind. Got it. That silence said it all."

"No, I was just gathering my thoughts," she said.

"Which I still think I won't like."

Again, she did not produce words fast enough.

"I understand if the interracial thing is an issue," he said, "and I don't mean that in any way that's personal to you. I know you're not prejudiced. But it's such a weird moment in our world. It's like putting a political bumper sticker on your car these days and then every time you go out there you're half expecting your windshield to be smashed in. It's a vulnerable feeling. Believe me, I get it."

"No, it's not that. Not even a little bit. Ninety-five percent it's just this separation being so fresh, and the divorce not even being final, and me being so completely discombobulated . . ."

He jumped into her pause.

"I always thought that word was weird. Discombobulated. Not weird bad. I'm not criticizing you for using it. Kind of weird fun, if that makes sense. Because it has such a crazy sound to it, and because it has no antonym. Nobody ever says they're feeling combobulated. Ever notice that? I realize I'm off on a weird tangent, and that I'm talking about nothing, and that I can't stop talking about nothing, and I think it's because I'm bracing for the other five percent and thinking it will hurt."

"No," she said. "I really don't think it will. It's that you're such a good friend. You're so steady, and you've always been there for me as long as I've known you, and I value that. And I guess I just wonder if we'd be putting that on the line."

This time it was Leon who was slow to answer.

While she waited, she realized it was also that she didn't think of him that way, though she had no intention of saying so. She'd always thought he was handsome, in a bookish sort of way, but not really her type. Then again, she thought, Mark was exactly her type. And where had it gotten her, other than into the middle of an acrimonious divorce?

"It's just dinner," he said.

He said it quietly. Not challengingly. Not sounding like he wanted to talk her into something. He sounded almost as though he was offering some reassurance.

"That's very true," she said. "It's just dinner. And I'm making a big deal about it for no reason at all. I'll call you when I get back."

"You'd better. I want to hear what you found."

"If it's interesting I won't wait till I get home to tell you."

"What if the woman in the photo was just visiting as a tourist?"

Another baseball to her tender gut. For reasons she could not sort out, it had never occurred to her. She had always assumed that E. L. Swann had chosen a very out-of-the-way spot to settle, and lately she had entertained the idea that Santa Rosarita might be that place. She had never pictured the reclusive author going on vacation.

"Then . . . I guess I just see if I can find someone who knows what hotel she was staying at and see if I can match her with the name she's using now."

"Right," he said. "Good luck."

But by the time she'd hung up the phone it was dawning on her just how much luck she would need. So much more than she had been thinking. And what she had been thinking had been enough of a long shot anyway.

She briefly wondered if she was crazy to go down this road. But she didn't wonder for long. Because it didn't matter. Because she was going to do it anyway.

Chapter Three

Coming Back Down to Earth

"Everybody talks like people are all squished together on planes," Jaden said, swinging his legs wildly in his window seat. "And like there's no room. But this feels great."

"That's because I used up all my frequent-flier miles upgrading to first class."

"First class is better?"

"Much better. Hang on a second. I have to call your dad."

She pulled her cell phone out of her pocket as a line of passengers streamed by, mostly headed for the coach section. Now and then someone's bag smacked her on the shoulder or leg, but she said nothing.

"Why do you have to call Dad?"

"To tell him we'll be gone for a while."

"I thought he already knew."

"He'll know soon enough," she said.

She touched "Mark" in the contacts of her phone, and then the call icon.

Her heart hammered as it rang. Five nerve-jangling rings. Then the call went to voicemail, and she breathed as though she hadn't truly breathed in days.

"Mark," she said. "Sudden change of plans. I have this really important story to pursue in Mexico. Could be big. Jaden is with me. Not sure when we'll be back but probably in time for your weekend. I promise to keep you posted."

She quickly ended the call.

"I thought he already knew," Jaden said again.

"He knows now."

"Not really. He might not have listened to the messages yet."

"Anyway, he'll know soon enough."

There was a subtext to the whole exchange. Jaden was seven, but he wasn't stupid. He knew what made his father mad.

Not a minute later her phone rang, and she glanced at it just long enough to see Mark on the caller ID. She powered off the phone and let it go to voicemail.

"Who was that?" Jaden asked.

"Nobody important."

"Was it Leon?"

"No. It was nobody."

"Why were you talking to Leon the other night?" Jaden asked.

"I talk to Leon all the time."

"No you don't. You text him and email him but you don't talk to him."

"He did me a favor to help me with this story. You like Leon, right?"

"Sure. Leon's great."

A flight attendant came by to offer to refill her champagne and to offer Jaden more orange juice and warm mixed nuts.

"We're going to Mexico," he told her.

"Sounds like fun," she said, her face caught up in a smile that was clearly a job requirement.

"When do we get to Mexico?"

"This flight doesn't go to Mexico," she said. "It goes to San Diego."

"Then how do we get to Mexico?"

"We're going to rent a car," Amelia said. "I told you that, remember?"

"Oh. Maybe." He directed his attention to the flight attendant again. "We're going to ride a horse on the beach. Even though we don't have a horse. We're going to borrow one."

"Rent one," Amelia said.

"What's the difference?"

"When you have to pay somebody to borrow something like a horse or a car or a house, that's renting."

"Do you like horses?" the flight attendant asked, filling Amelia's champagne glass.

"I don't know," Jaden said. "I never met one before. But I've seen pictures of them, and they look nice. They're pretty."

"I'll go get you some more nuts," she said.

Meanwhile Amelia's nerves still jangled from her close call. From almost having to talk to her ex. She wondered if having to imagine what he might have said was even worse than it would have felt to hear it.

Jaden gazed out the window as the plane taxied backward, away from the gate. For a long stretch, all she saw was the back of his head.

When he turned to her, his eyes looked alarmingly wide.

"The man who drives the plane," he said. "Oh, maybe not a man. I don't know that. The person who drives the plane."

"Flies the plane," she said, halfway registering that so far the pilot was driving more than flying.

"Flies the plane. What do you call that person again?"

"The pilot."

"Right. I knew that."

"There are actually two. A pilot and a copilot."

"Do they . . ."

But then he looked out the window and seemed disinclined to continue the thought.

"Do they what?"

He looked back at her, his eyes less wide but no less intense.

". . . know how to do this?"

"Oh yes."

"I mean, do they do it a lot?"

"Many times a day," Amelia said. "And there are years of training involved before they even get to fly people like us around."

For the moment, he seemed unconvinced.

"I know they know how to get it to lift up off the ground," he said, using his hands to illustrate. "But what about when it comes back down again? Do they know how to do that so it doesn't hurt?"

"They are absolute experts at that," Amelia said, as reassuringly as possible.

"Have you been in a lot of planes?"

"Dozens," Amelia said.

"Has it ever hurt to come down?"

"Not once."

He turned his gaze out the window again as they lined up for a turn on the runway. She tried to put an arm around his shoulder as a gesture of support, but he shook her off again.

"I'm fine," he said. "I was just making sure."

When the wheels touched down—gently—he turned to her again, his face much more relaxed. He said one word and one word only.

"Whew."

When the flight attendant announced that electronics could be turned back on, Amelia powered up her phone.

Mark had not left a voicemail.

He had, however, sent a very brief text.

It read, "Two words, Amelia: parental rights."

She slipped the phone back into her pocket and tried to turn her mind forward to the adventure ahead.

"Where were you thinking of crossing the border?" the young man at the car-rental desk asked her.

Amelia was unclear as to whether he was engaging in idle chitchat or expressing genuine professional concern.

"Just . . . right here. Just south of here."

"But then you're going over to the eastern side of the Baja peninsula, right?"

"Correct."

"Do you mind if I give you a piece of advice?"

The man could not have been more than twenty-one or twenty-two, and wore his blond hair straight up and spiky on top, shaved short on the sides. For some reason she found his extreme youth intimidating.

Meanwhile Jaden clung to her, one of his small hands clutching the top of her back jeans pocket, clearly intimidated by the bustling airport crowds.

"Yeah," she said. "I guess that would be okay."

"Don't."

"Don't go to Mexico?" she asked, aghast and a bit angry.

She had already finished the rental process, and had paid a lot of money for additional insurance, and it was way too late in the game for this type of advice.

He smiled, seemingly more professionally than genuinely.

"No, go to Mexico. But don't cross the border here, at San Ysidro. Do your west-to-east miles of the trip while you're still here in the US. Drive from here to Calexico, and cross the border there into Mexicali. Then you'll be on the 5, and it will take you nearly straight down through San Felipe, and then all you have to do is cruise down the shore. And the 5 is a good road."

"It sounds like you're saying the road from Tijuana to Ensenada is not a good road?"

Jaden tugged hard on her pocket.

"I have to go to the bathroom," he said.

"Can it wait just a second, hon?"

"Yeah, but before we get in the car I have to."

"That's a good road," the car-rental guy said. "Very good. It's just like driving in the US except the billboards are in Spanish. But then you have to cross the peninsula west to east. And that's the road I'm advising you to avoid. Parts of it are good. Parts of it have potholes on a level you probably haven't experienced before. And then there's a twenty-five-mile stretch that's unpaved. It's slow going, and if you bottom out or flatten a tire, it's remote out there. You're going to feel very alone in the event of any kind of mechanical failure."

"Oh," Amelia said. "Thank you. That's definitely welcome advice."

"And there's a nice office in Calexico where you can stop and get your FMM cards," he said, referring to the tourist card that served in place of a visa for visitors to Mexico.

"I already got them online."

"Better yet."

He smiled that professional smile again and handed her the keys, which he seemed to have been pointedly withholding.

"Have a nice trip," he said.

On the walk to the bathroom with Jaden, Amelia's mind spun. Almost literally, from the feel of it. She had very nearly made a mistake that could have put her and her son in the middle of a tough situation.

It made her wonder what else she should know but didn't.

She took him to the ladies' room, because no way was she letting Jaden go into an airport bathroom alone. She announced that a seven-year-old boy was coming in, but, predictably, no women objected.

As she waited just outside the stall for him, Amelia considered abandoning the trip.

Maybe it was *too much* of an adventure.

If she had left Jaden with Mark, she would not have thought twice about proceeding. But she was responsible for his safety. And all this to chase after a woman in a picture who probably wasn't E. L. Swann.

Maybe she should just turn around and go home.

But she had come all this way, and rented the car. And if she drove it home, that was probably an eleven-hour drive. More than she dared bite off in one day.

No, the only way out of this impasse was forward. She could talk to the authorities at the border, or to the staff at the hotel. They could help her be sure she was doing things in a smart way.

She had promised Jaden a fun vacation outside the country, under a big sky. And she was going to deliver.

Still, it left a big, jangling hole in her gut, the kind of hole that only walking into the unknown can create.

—

Jaden stared outside the car in varying directions as they approached the border crossing.

It was not quite what Amelia had expected, though she really hadn't known what to picture. She mostly saw a lot of temporary construction and lane control, with the intimidating-looking border wall on one side.

Amelia was trying not to let her son see that she was nervous. But Jaden was taking it all in, and he probably knew how she felt despite her attempts to put a cheerful face on it. He was perceptive that way.

"It doesn't really make sense," he said.

It was the first thing he had said in many miles of travel.

"What doesn't?"

"That it's another country over there."

She mulled that over for a bit, hoping to get a sense of what he was trying to say. But nothing came clear.

"Okay," she said. "You know there are other countries besides the United States."

"Sure, I know that. But I could see if you had to get on a plane and cross an ocean or something like that. But this is just like . . . it's like this line. On this side, us. On that side, Mexico. And it even looks like a different country over there. You can kind of see the difference. But why? It's just a line."

While they spoke, she inched the car forward, merging lanes and stopping at red stoplights that turned into green advance lights.

"I'm still not sure what part of it doesn't make sense," she said.

"Like . . . how do they know where to put the line?"

"Borders are . . . well, they're fought over. People fight wars to claim land. Land is very valuable."

"Did we fight a war to get the line put here?"

"Yes, but a very long time ago. This used to be Mexico, this part of California."

She pulled up behind the last car in her lane that had not yet crossed. Two border guards spoke briefly to the driver at his open window, then waved the car through.

"Let me do the talking," Amelia said. "Just answer questions like where you were born and where we're going. Don't tell them I'm a journalist. Sometimes that's a sticking point between countries."

"I don't know what that means," he said, sounding uneasy.

But now Amelia was pulling up, and slowing, and it was too late to teach him, and she wildly questioned why she hadn't discussed it with him on the long drive from San Diego. And she realized she was nervous, even though she had done absolutely nothing wrong. It was more of a free-floating fear of the guards' abject authority over her, even though that fear existed independent of any specific reasons.

Then the guards waved her through. Literally just signaled her to keep driving.

She pulled away into the town of Mexicali and sighed, releasing all that meaningless tension.

They drove along streets in the sprawling town, past box stores, and dirt lots, and road construction, and long rows of billboards with the occasional one in English. They passed more than one big red Coca-Cola truck, and lots of gas stations with names she did not recognize.

Highway 5 to San Felipe was well marked, with overhead signs indicating what lane she should use.

"I think I know what you mean, though," she said.

"About what?"

"About the border just being a line that doesn't make sense. I mean, if you flew over it in a plane you wouldn't see a line. You wouldn't see the difference between one country and the next. The whole thing is kind of . . . I want to say 'arbitrary,' but that's a big word for a little guy. It means something that's just kind of . . . chosen for no special reason. The best way I can think to describe it is to call it more of a 'construct' than a real thing, but that must sound confusing to you, too. A construct is like . . . it's like a thing that only exists because we all agree to act like it does."

"Huh," he said.

And for a mile or two, he said nothing more.

Then, as they were heading out of Mexicali, he added, "So I was right."

"Yes," she said. "You were right."

As they got farther outside of town, the buildings all but disappeared. The land was strangely empty and flat, with big light-colored patches, as if the soil were more sand than dirt.

And then, just like that, there were hills. High mound-like hills that looked unformed and loose in their construction, as if the dirt or soft stone of them was sliding off, or just about to. And the sand was definitely sand, but not flat. It formed drifts and dunes, little hills in front of the bigger hills.

And there was nothing much out there besides the hills.

For a moment she found it troubling. She thought, *If this is the road to take because the other road is remote, what must the other road look like?*

Somehow if felt more unnerving to be someplace that felt like no place at all in light of the fact that it was not her country.

But then she reminded herself that countries were mostly a construct.

Jaden, who she'd thought was asleep, said, "This looks like a desert."

"Oh, it's definitely a desert."

"I've never been in a desert before."

"Well, we're here to try new things."

He powered down the window and hung his head out, hair blowing wildly, peering up at the sky. The wind that came through the window was so hot it felt like a blast furnace.

"That's a very big sky," he said, pulling his head back inside.

Just as the water came into view, Amelia remembered something very important she had forgotten to tell him.

"You have to remember not to drink the water," she said.

"How can I not drink water? We're going to be here for days."

"We have to ask for bottled water. All the hotels and restaurants have it, because everybody from the US wants it. And you have to brush your teeth by pouring bottled water into a cup. And you have to keep your mouth closed in the shower."

"Why?"

"Because the water can make you really sick. Diarrhea and throwing up. Really miserable. Tourists have a name for it. They call it Montezuma's revenge."

"I don't know what that means."

"Actually," she said, "I'm not sure I do either."

They drove in silence for a time, breathing in their first views of the Gulf of California.

"The water is pretty," he said. "*That water*, I mean."

"It really is."

"But I have a question about the other water. That you drink. How can it be different on this side of the line? How does it *know* to be different on this side of the line?"

"It's not that the water is different, I don't think. I think we have a different kind of water-treatment plants in the US. We dump a bunch of chemicals into our water, which might not be all that good for us in the long run. I don't know. But it kills these little organisms that would make us sick. I guess if we'd been drinking water with no chemicals all our lives, the organisms wouldn't make us sick. But our bodies are just not used to it."

"What's an organism?"

"Like a little microscopic bug."

"Ick," Jaden said, making an exaggerated face. "I definitely won't forget."

When Amelia arrived at the hotel in Santa Rosarita, it was already dark. It was impossible to take much of a measure of the town. Clearly there was a main drag, one lane in each direction, and a spill of moonlight on the water told her it ran very close to the beach.

When she pulled into the parking lot and opened her driver's-side door, she could hear the gentle lapping of the water on the shore.

Jaden was fast asleep.

She moved around to the passenger's side, unclipped him from his seat belt, and carried him into the lobby over her shoulder in a fireman's carry.

The hotel was not exactly what she had expected.

Somehow she had pictured a kind of plush luxury that would feel familiar to her. After all, it catered to tourists, and mostly from the US. Instead it was . . . old. Not in a bad way, though. Classically old. Dark wood-beam ceilings with hand-painted floral designs, and a tile floor that had clearly been washed an almost infinite number of times over many decades. It was lovely, and had a lot of character. It was just not quite what the website photos had led her to expect.

The young man behind the desk looked up and smiled as she carried Jaden in.

"Do you speak English?" she asked hopefully.

"Oh, yes, ma'am," he said, his voice heavily accented but clear. "Of course we do here."

"Good. Thank you. Not that I should expect you to. But my Spanish is pretty rusty. Pretty bad. I took two years of it in high school. It's just insane how little we remember."

He smiled again. If it was a professional smile, a requisite for his employment, he was doing a good job of selling it. Or maybe he was just a nice young man.

"Sí. Yes, ma'am. People forget. But we will understand you here, and you will have what you need. I see your little one was not able to stay awake for the trip. Do you have a reservation? I hope so, because we have no free rooms."

"Yes, I made a reservation. Amelia Booker."

He pecked around on his computer for a few seconds.

"Ah, yes, ma'am. We have your room. It's a very nice room. It has a patio with a gate that opens right onto the beach. I think you will be happy there."

"I have a couple of questions," she said.

She jostled Jaden slightly while retrieving her phone from her shirt pocket. He did not wake up.

She opened the photo app and navigated to the photo of the older woman buying mangoes at the outdoor market. She brought it up to the full size of the screen.

"By any chance do you know this woman?"

She held the phone in his direction.

The young man frowned at the screen for a moment and shook his head.

"No, ma'am, I don't know her. But I have to tell you, I only came here a few weeks ago from Michoacán to take this job. I don't know too many of the local people yet. When you get up in the morning I'll be off shift, and a man named Guillermo will be working. He has lived here for many years, and maybe he can help."

"Thank you," she said, and took her room key. It was not a key card. It was an actual key.

"There was something else?" he asked.

"There was?"

"You said you had a couple of questions."

"Oh. Right." She shook her head as if to clear it, suddenly realizing how exhausted she was. It hit her like a wave. A tsunami. It left her feeling slightly disconnected from the scene. "I read online that you can rent horses and ride on the beach."

"Yes, ma'am. When you wake up in the morning, go out to the street and turn south. You'll see a hitching post a few blocks down, between buildings, on one of the short streets that go down to the sand. If you go too early there might not be horses yet. They might still be in their pastures or their barns. But by . . . maybe . . . nine o'clock, someone will be there with horses."

"Wonderful. Thanks."

She moved to leave, slightly unsteady from her fatigue, then stopped and turned back to him.

"Is there bottled water in the room?"

"Oh yes, ma'am. Always. And if you need more, just call the desk."

"Thank you."

She carried Jaden to their room.

She unlocked the door, stepped inside, and turned on the light.

The room was simple and old, but pleasantly charming. Tile floors, white stucco walls. A dark, heavily knotted wood ceiling with beams painted white and then hand-painted with that same floral design.

There were two twin beds, covered with spreads in an old-fashioned brocade.

She gently laid Jaden out on one bed, pulled off his shoes, and covered him with the spread from the other bed. It was plenty warm in the room. A little too warm, really, even this late in the evening.

She walked to the patio doors and, after figuring out how to undo the latches, opened them out wide to let in the slightly cool evening air. She stood a moment in the doorway, watching the moonlight shimmering on the water.

For possibly the hundredth time that day she wondered if this whole thing was just an elaborate wild-goose chase.

She took out her phone and texted Mark.

"I understand," she typed. "And I'm not trying to deny you your rights. We should be back by the time you're supposed to have him for the weekend. I promise to keep you posted."

She hit send, then powered down the phone before finding out if he would quickly respond.

She moved back inside, locking the patio doors, and lay down on the free bed. Sleep took her almost immediately.

Chapter Four

Señora Steinbach, a Skinny Mare, and a Very Big Donkey

When she opened her eyes it was wildly light in the room. Enough to make her wince.

Jaden was standing at her bedside, staring at her.

"You're sleeping a lot," he said.

"Right. I know. Sorry." Her mouth felt papery-dry from sleeping with it open, and her eyes felt grainy. "I think I was just really tired from all the driving."

"Okay, but please get up now, because I'm hungry."

"Okay." She sat up and rubbed her eyes. "How long have you been up?"

"Hours!" he whined.

"What did you do all that time?"

"I sat on the patio. I wanted to go out on the beach but I didn't think I was allowed to on my own. And I changed my socks and my underwear. And I brushed my teeth."

"Good for you," she said, swinging her legs around and planting her sock feet on the cool tile. "You remembered to use the bottled water to brush your teeth, right?"

The long silence that followed seemed like answer enough.

"Oops," Jaden said.

Probably not two minutes later she was fully dressed and hustling into the lobby, towing Jaden by one hand.

"I feel fine," he said.

The middle-aged man behind the reception desk looked up. And he must have seen the worry in her eyes, because he said, "Trouble, señora?"

"My son forgot to use bottled water to brush his teeth, and now I'm worried about him. Do you think I should call a doctor? Is there a doctor?"

"Sí, señora, there is a doctor that will come very quick from San Felipe if you need him. But maybe it is too soon?"

She stood a moment, letting her thoughts settle.

She looked at the man's name tag. It said "Guillermo." It sent her mind in a different direction, but she dragged it back again.

"You think he might not get sick?"

"I feel fine," Jaden said.

"Just from brushing the teeth, maybe not so much. Or maybe not at all. I am not a doctor, señora, and I'm not giving to you that kind of advice. I'm just telling you that most people, even with small children, maybe they will wait and see. Maybe they will watch very good. Very close they watch the child. First sign of sick, you can call and the doctor will give your son . . . the pills. What in English do they call the pills?"

"Antibiotics?"

"Sí. Yes. Antabiotics. Or maybe he won't even need that. If it was just the brushing of teeth."

Amelia breathed deeply for a moment, and tried to let the whole thing go. She knew it might return. But, for the moment, she fully realized that she had allowed herself to flip the switch into panic mode over an emergency that might never happen. And even if it did happen, it hadn't happened yet.

"If you want the doctor," Guillermo said, "you say so to me and I will get him here very right away."

"Thank you," she said. "Where would we go to get breakfast? Is it right here in the hotel?" Then she looked down at her son, hovering close to her right hip. "Are you okay to have breakfast?"

"I feel fine."

"Sí, señora, you just go down that hallway. Very nice room to dine that looks out over the water. It is no charge. It's part of what you pay for your room."

"Thank you," she said again. She slipped her phone out of her back jeans pocket. "The young man from last night says you've lived in this town for a long time."

"Sí," he said. "I'm not so good with the bigger numbers in English but since I was a boy."

She pulled up the picture of the possible E. L. Swann.

"Do you know this woman?"

He stared at the phone for what seemed like too long a time, and shook his head. Almost wistfully, it seemed. Almost with regret.

"Nobody *know* her," he said. "Not really. Not *know*. But I see her. She comes down once a week to buy from the market. Fresh things. For anything else she have a girl to work for her but she likes to go to the market herself. She lives in that very big house on the hilltop. You will see it. You can't miss. She likes to ride down on her donkey for the market."

"A donkey?"

"Sí, señora."

"She rides down on a *donkey*?"

"Yes, the road is not so good. You would not want to go there in a car. Every year more of it washes away, and nobody is fast to fix. Probably she could afford to fix it, but I think she likes it this way so nobody ever tries to go up. She has something else, one of those things with four wheels. I don't know what you call in English. It will go anywhere. But she prefers the donkey."

Amelia stood a moment and let that sink in. Was it a deal-breaker? she wondered. Did it completely rule out the E. L. Swann possibility? Would a person go from being a storied part of American literature to riding a donkey down a hill into town to buy her produce? Would E. L. Swann be part of such a thing?

The first answer that came back in her head was: How would Amelia know? How could anyone know? Other than the fact that the author was known for being brusque and depressive, it wasn't as though anyone actually knew her. The second answer was that in the realm of human nature, nothing was ever truly impossible.

"Do you know her name?"

"Sí. Yes. She is Señora Steinbach."

For a fraction of a second Amelia felt a letdown. As though he had been about to say her name was E. L. Swann. But it had been obvious all along that the author was living under some kind of pseudonym, or her whereabouts would have been unearthed decades ago.

"Then maybe we'll drive up and see," she said out loud.

"Oh no, señora," Guillermo said.

"Oh, that's right. The road is not suitable for cars."

"But more than that, señora. She is very private person. Unless you know her, I think she will not welcome you. I think she will not be happy if you go."

"Okay," she said. "Thanks. We'll think about it over breakfast."

And she turned and headed toward the dining room, still clutching one of Jaden's hands.

"Are we going up there?" he asked, peering up at her face.

"Probably. Yeah."

It wasn't as though she had ever imagined E. L. Swann throwing her arms wide at the idea of being found.

"But we don't have a donkey. Can we rent one?"

"We could walk up. Unless you're not feeling well."

"I feel fine. But you said we could ride horses on the beach. Can't we do that first? Before the work stuff? You said we'd have lots of fun here."

Amelia pulled in a deep breath and sighed it out again.

"Okay. First breakfast, then horses. Then the house on the hill."

She would have been tempted to say it nearly killed her to commit to that chronology, based on the feeling it left behind as it moved through her. Knowing that the author she'd spent her life studying might or might not be sitting in a house on a hill over where they were about to eat breakfast was almost too much to bear.

She had to know.

But she had promised Jaden lots of fun activities.

It was one of those sacrifices you make only for your child. For anyone else that level of restraint would be utterly out of the question.

She stopped briefly. Turned back to Guillermo, who looked up questioningly.

"I thought donkeys were too small to ride," she said. Actually she more or less shouted it, because they were all the way across the lobby by then.

"Oh no, señora," he called back. "People, they are riding donkeys all over the world. Besides. It's a very big donkey."

They stepped out into the already warm morning and began walking down the main road together, hand in hand.

There were a lot of goods for sale. To phrase it mildly.

There were open-air food stands, mostly closed, and an almost comical number of souvenir stalls, mostly open.

She looked to the west, up and over their corrugated metal roofs. Up to the hill behind town. Guillermo had been right. One couldn't miss that big house. It seemed to be on a huge property, surrounded by a stucco wall. Something stirred inside her, wanting to go up there immediately—whether the resident would welcome her or not.

She pulled her attention back to the present.

Each time they passed a cross street—though the word "street" made them sound fancier than they were—she could see the water of the gulf at the end of its narrow, sandy dirt trail.

"You feel okay?" she asked her son.

"I feel fine," he said. "It sure gets hot here, though. It doesn't get this hot in San Francisco."

"We're a lot farther south."

"I don't really like hot."

"I guess I don't either. But we can always go in for a swim later."

Then they looked left and saw a horse. Just one.

The horse was a dark bay color, standing saddled and tied at a hitching post on the sandy road. It did not look especially healthy or fit. Its ribs showed, its neck was oddly narrow and thin, and there were hollows in front of its hip bones.

A man Amelia took to be the owner was sitting on a blue plastic milk crate nearby.

They walked up to the beast, Jaden pulling backward against her hand.

"What's wrong?" she asked him, stopping to accommodate his fear. "You wanted to meet a horse."

"I didn't know they were this big."

"You didn't know horses were big?"

"I didn't know they were *this* big."

"You've seen pictures of horses."

"Things look smaller in pictures."

"Haven't you seen horse pictures with people in them? Standing next to the horse, or riding on its back?"

"Maybe. But maybe the horses looked smaller because the people were on top. Not way down on the ground like this, looking up."

The man lifted his head to address them. He wore a thick mustache and a battered brimmed hat. Like a cowboy hat, but rounder.

"Mirabelle is a very gentle mare," he said. "You can go up to her. She would never hurt nobody."

Amelia moved a little closer, and Jaden tentatively followed.

She reached one hand out and touched the horse's dusty neck.

The horse reached out with her nose, low and in Jaden's direction. She stopped a foot or so from him and blew air into his face through dilated nostrils. He reached out and stroked her long face, and she held still for him to do so.

"Oh, he's nice," Jaden said.

"She," Amelia said.

"How do you know she's a she?"

"The man said she's a mare."

"I didn't know what that meant. I just figured she was a horse."

"A mare is a girl horse."

"How can she be both a horse and a mare?"

"Well," Amelia said. "You're a person and a boy. I'm a person and a woman."

"Oh. Right. I get it."

Amelia turned her attention to the owner.

"Are there more horses coming later?"

"Why do you need more?" he asked, sounding both chiding and disappointed. "Mirabelle is the best one in all of Santa Rosarita."

"But there are two of us."

"She can carry you both."

"Are you sure? She looks so thin."

"She is very fine and strong. Here. I will show you. Put your foot in the stirrup and I'll help you up. And I'll hand your little son up to you."

But for a moment Amelia only looked at the horse, entertaining her own doubts.

"First I need to know how much."

"Twenty dollars US for half an hour. You come back late, you pay me another twenty. You bring her back all sweaty and blowing because you ran her too hard, you pay me double."

"We wouldn't run her too hard."

He held the thick wooden stirrup out to Amelia and she found herself putting her left foot into it, despite still having doubts.

The man put his two big hands at her waist and helped propel her up into the saddle. Next thing she knew Jaden was being swung up onto the pommel of the saddle in front of her. She wrapped one arm around his waist as he settled.

"Whoa," Jaden said, looking down at the sandy dirt.

"Twenty in advance," the man said.

"I still have questions."

"What do you need to know?"

"Like what if we get out on the beach and get our directions turned around? What if we can't find our way back here?"

"You don't have to know," he said. "She knows. Always she will choose to come back. You have to steer her forward, away from here, if you want to go away from here. When you want to come back, just give the mare her head. She knows the way."

Amelia sighed out her doubts—or tried to, anyway—and dug into her jeans pocket for a twenty, which she handed to the man.

Then they all just sort of . . . stood there.

"Now what?" Amelia asked.

"You have to kick her."

"I don't want to kick her."

"Don't kick her," Jaden said, still looking down to judge the distance to the ground.

"I don't mean kick her like hard. I mean give her a nudge with your heels."

Amelia pressed her heels to the horse's sides. The mare flinched a bit, as if that had been unexpected. Then she moved toward the beach.

They stepped into the sand, which gave and sank under the horse's hooves. It was slow going for her, and Amelia could feel that it was work. And she felt guilty.

"What did he mean 'give her her head'?" Jaden asked. "Doesn't she always have her head?"

"It means give her a loose rein and let her go where she wants to go. Not steer her with the reins and the bit."

"What's a bit?"

"It's a piece of metal in the horse's mouth."

"Ouch," Jaden said.

They rode along in silence for a time.

Mirabelle made a beeline for the water's edge, where the sand was much more tightly packed. Her hooves still sank in, but not as deeply. Amelia turned her head and watched the trail of deep hoofmarks quickly fill with water.

Jaden leaned forward and patted the horse's neck.

"I think this is hard for her, because it's both of us," he said.

"I could get down and walk if you're really worried about her."

"Yes," he said. "Please. She says it's hard."

Amelia reined the mare to a stop and sighed. Then she swung her leg over the mare's hindquarters and dropped onto the beach. She took hold of the reins and led the mare along the wet sand.

The mare met her gaze with a look Amelia could only classify as grateful, though she immediately accused herself of reading too much into the eye contact.

"Thank you," Jaden said. "I don't think that man feeds her enough."

"She does look thin."

The water of the gulf looked turquoise in the morning sun, and Amelia could see the irregular shapes of the land mass on the other side. Apparently Jaden saw it too.

"What is that?" he asked, pointing with an exaggeratedly extended arm. "Is that an island?"

"No, that's mainland Mexico. At least, I think it is. I could be wrong."

"What's mainland?"

"Like . . . the part of it that's not the Baja peninsula." Then, anticipating the next question, she said, "A peninsula is a long, narrow piece of land jutting out into the ocean. And it's what we're on right now. Then there's the gulf in between, and then there's mainland Mexico."

They walked in silence for a while longer, Amelia glancing up at the house on the hill every few seconds. Letting her attention drift to where she really wanted to be.

"What do you keep looking up there for?" Jaden asked.

"That's where that lady lives. The one I need to talk to."

"You want to go there."

"When we can, yes."

"Then let's go there."

"We've only had the horse out for five or ten minutes."

"So? He didn't say we couldn't bring her back early. We paid for the time, so if we want to use it to let her take a break, we can do that. Right? I think we should go get her something to eat. And then go up there to the house. What do horses eat?"

"Grass and hay, I think."

"There's no grass around here. Where do you buy hay?"

"No idea. Maybe we could find a market and get some carrots or apples. And come back and give them to her."

"Yeah," Jaden said. "Let's do that."

The man who owned the horse drew back his sleeve and looked at his watch when he saw them coming.

Amelia noticed that two more saddled horses were now tied to the hitching post. If they looked better fed than Mirabelle, it was not by much.

"That was eleven minutes," he said when they were close enough to hear. "Did you have trouble?"

"No, no trouble," Amelia said.

"Because Mirabelle never makes no trouble."

"Then why did you ask if we'd had any?"

"Because when you left you were riding and now you are on the ground."

"Oh. No. That was my decision, to get down. My son wants the mare to rest for whatever's left of the time we paid for. And he wants to give her a snack. Can she have a snack?"

He pushed his hat brim up and back at an angle and considered Amelia, as if she must have an agenda he had not yet unearthed.

"If it's a thing a horse can eat, then yes, I suppose."

"We were thinking apples or carrots," Jaden said as Amelia lifted him down and set him on his athletic shoes in the sandy dirt.

"She can have that, yes. Not so much that she gets a stomachache. But maybe two apples or a bunch of carrots."

"Don't rent her out to anybody while we're gone!" Jaden said, pointing at the man in a way that seemed to be intended as domineering.

Amelia worked hard not to smile at his bravado. The man did nothing to cover up a smirk.

When they got back from the little open-front market, the mare was still there. Resting.

Jaden broke each of the carrots into several small chunks and dropped them into a rubber feed bin for her. She lowered her head immediately and began to chew, the crunching sound resonating through her bony jaw.

Jaden wrapped his arms around her neck as she ate, and the mare seemed not to object.

"He has a feeling for animals," the man said to Amelia. "Doesn't he? Has he always been this way?"

"Strange as it will sound to say," Amelia said, "I have no idea. This is all news to me."

—

As they walked back to the hotel in the gathering heat, Amelia said, "Have you always had feelings for animals?"

Jaden shrugged expansively.

"Don't know," he said. "I don't really know very many. I know I like dogs, but you won't get us one."

"You know they don't allow cats and dogs in our apartment."

"What about a horse?"

"That would be a hard no," Amelia said. "From the landlady and from me."

—

They sat in their rental car at the bottom of the big hill, looking up at the imposing estate. The dirt road was every bit as bad as Guillermo had indicated, dangerously pocked and rutted, and ravaged by erosion.

"I don't think we should walk up there now," she said.

"Why not? You said you really wanted to go."

"I do. I really, really do. But it's getting hot. And I don't want us to go without lunch when we're expending that much energy."

"We just had breakfast."

"But it's a long walk up there. I'm not sure how long it will take us. And also I want to take a little bit more time to be sure you aren't about to get sick."

"I. Feel. *Fine!*"

He shouted the last word at her, clearly irritated by her concern.

Just for a moment she was hit with a wave of regret. She should have come here to Santa Rosarita alone. She should have dropped Jaden at his father's and done what she needed to do, when she needed to do it. Granted, she had used the excuse of a much-needed vacation for her son as a way to justify the whole project. But she could have taken him somewhere fun later in the summer and done this alone. All that would have been required of her was the courage to openly state that she was going to pursue this E. L. Swann thing against ridiculous odds, no matter what anyone thought about the effort.

"I guess we could go after lunch," Jaden said.

"I think it'll be too hot then. I think we should spend the afternoon swimming and snorkeling, and then if you still feel fine in the morning we'll go."

She shifted the car into drive and headed back in the direction of the hotel, nursing a feeling of something being pulled out of her gut. It was the surrendering of something she had been holding as really important. At least, she surrendered for a brief time.

Even that was hard enough.

Chapter Five

When Bad Things Happen to Good Terraces

Amelia woke much earlier the following morning.

Jaden was awake, but still in bed.

Their eyes met.

"I feel fine," Jaden said.

—

The walk up the hill was many times longer and more strenuous than Amelia had estimated. Now, in the middle of it, she figured it was about a mile at a surprisingly steep angle. And though it was only about eight thirty in the morning, it was already hot.

She brushed sweaty hair off her own forehead, then off her son's.

She had brought one small bottle of water from the hotel. Already it was almost gone.

"You doing okay?" she asked him.

If he had said no—if he had asked to be carried—they might have had to go back down. It was hard enough for Amelia to carry herself up the steep slope.

Fortunately, Jaden was more stoic.

"Pretty okay," he said. "It might be nice to stop and take a rest, though."

They stopped and sat in the middle of the steep dirt road, their knees drawn up to their chests to brace against gravity.

Amelia looked over at Jaden's face and it looked a bit too red. She had slathered him up with sunscreen, but now she made a mental note to buy him a sombrero at one of the souvenir stands. Certainly they were not in short supply.

They looked out over the Gulf of California together, Amelia surprised at how high they had climbed.

"Wow," Jaden said. "You can see a lot more of the . . . what did you say it was over there?"

"The mainland. But I was guessing. It could be an island."

"Whatever it is, you can see a lot more of it from up here."

A long cloud scudded by in an otherwise clear sky, briefly blocking the morning sun. Amelia closed her eyes and sighed, delighted by the sudden coolness. Then it drifted away again and she winced into the light.

"Okay," Jaden said. "Enough rest. Let's keep going."

By the time they approached the stucco wall of the property, they were both struggling. The water was long gone. They were both drenched in sweat and panting audibly.

They stepped up onto a long, ornately tiled pathway that led from the terrible road up to the gate.

The gate had a stucco arch over it, covered in brightly colored bougainvillea, from which hung an iron bell. A long rope dangled from it, extending to a spot Amelia just barely might be able to reach.

They stepped up to the gate and stood a moment. For a time, Amelia did not reach for the rope.

"Why are you scared?" Jaden asked.

He always seemed to know.

"I don't know. Maybe because Guillermo said she doesn't want anybody here. Maybe because I want this to be the author so much, and the dream stands or falls here. If I came all this way for nothing, this is the moment I find out."

"It wasn't for nothing. It was so I could see a big sky and ride a horse on the beach."

"Right," Amelia said. "Of course. My mistake."

She reached up and pulled the rope.

It was a huge, heavy bell, and it required quite a strong pull to move it. But after a couple of tries she was able to tip it enough that it let out a mighty clang. It made them both jump.

While she waited—while nothing happened—Amelia wondered if that huge clang could be heard all the way down in town.

They stood in silent anticipation for a minute that felt like an hour.

"Maybe ring it again," Jaden said.

Amelia took hold of the rope again and produced another mighty, ear-assaulting clang.

Before she could even let go of the rope again, the gate swung open.

Behind it stood a short, plump woman in her eighties. She had leathery, sun-worn skin and long, thin white hair that trailed down both sides of her face. She was unmistakably the woman in the photo. She was not unmistakably E. L. Swann. She might have been the author. But seeing her in person was hardly all the evidence Amelia required.

Still, she bore a strong resemblance to the AI-aged image Leon had sent her.

She looked fiercely angry. So much so that Amelia instinctively backed up a step.

"Whatever you're selling," the woman said, "I don't want any. Now go away."

Her voice was whiskey-rough and deep, like that of a longtime drinker, or smoker, or both.

"I'm not selling anything."

"In one way or another you are. You obviously want something from me, or you wouldn't have walked all the way up here. And I want no part of it. Who are you and why are you here ringing my bell?"

Amelia instinctively put one hand on Jaden's shoulder and drew him closer, as if to protect him. Clearly, though, this small woman's wrath was directed at her and not at her child.

"My name is Amelia Booker," she said. "I spent more than a decade in academia, though it's not what I do now. But I taught American literature at the university level. Most would say I'm the number one authority in the US on the author E. L. Swann."

Amelia watched the woman's eyes narrow suspiciously as she spoke.

"I don't even know who that is," she said.

Amelia felt the letdown in her gut, though she was not a hundred percent sure she believed what she had just been told. She had noticed the older woman averting her eyes ever so slightly before answering.

"She was . . . is . . . one of the greatest American authors of all time. I'm surprised you haven't heard of her."

"The greatest based on what?"

"The popularity of her book. And its critical success."

"All that for just one book?"

"Yes, only one. After the success of her debut novel she retreated from the world and went into seclusion. Nobody has known where she is for about forty years. Or if anybody knows, they're not talking. Her publisher must know, because they send royalty checks somewhere. But it's not as if no one ever tried to get them to spill the information."

Amelia did not mention that she was one of the ones who had tried.

"Interesting story," the woman said, though her tone made it clear that she had not found it so. "I have no idea what it has to do with me."

A long moment of silence fell.

Amelia was weighing the idea of just saying it straight out: that she suspected the woman standing in front of her was E. L. Swann. But the woman might slam the gate and go inside and give her no more chance to explore the idea.

But if she didn't say that, what would she say?

Jaden saved the day.

He took a couple of steps forward and tugged at the hem of the woman's loose white linen overshirt.

"Excuse me," he said in a mousy, polite little voice. "Is it okay if I ask you for a glass of water? It's really hot, and it was a really long walk up this big hill, and we're really thirsty."

Señora Steinbach turned her gaze down to Jaden.

Amelia watched her face soften.

"For *you* . . . ," she said, in a clear dig that Amelia felt in her gut, "yes. You're a very polite boy. You don't see that much anymore. You can come sit on the terrace and I'll bring you each a glass of water and you can drink it and rest a minute before you go. But then you have to go, and never come back here again."

She stepped back from the gate, and Amelia tentatively stepped onto the property, clutching her son's hand. She made a mental note to verify—without offending their host—that the water they were served was bottled, or filtered in some way.

Señora Steinbach disappeared through the open doorway into the house. She did not indicate the terrace where they should wait, but it was obvious. It was just to their right. It was done in beautiful decorative tile work, and adorned with hanging potted plants and beige linen umbrellas for shade.

She led Jaden to a couple of wooden-slat lounge chairs, and they sat nervously on the edge of one, staring down over Santa Rosarita, surrounded by three cats who wandered around, weaving among their legs.

The view was stunning—quite literally. The morning sun cast a dusty quality of light on the water. Not only could they see the whole town and a big swath of mainland or island, but they could see miles up and down the beaches of the eastern Baja coast.

There were boats out on the water, and tiny ant-sized figures riding Jet Skis. And in one dramatic burst of color, a speedboat was towing a bright parachute that flew over and behind it.

"What *is* that?" Jaden asked, reaching down to pet an orange cat as the others scattered.

"I think that's the parasailing I read about. They put you in a harness dangling from that parachute, and then when the boat gets going fast you go up really high."

Amelia heard herself speaking as if removed from her body and brain. Her attention was entirely absorbed by the identity of the woman who would soon reappear.

"Huh," Jaden said. "Is that fun? Or is that scary?"

"Probably both."

"Can we do it?"

"Sure. If you want."

She waited a strange length of time for some kind of excited reaction from him, but nothing happened.

In her peripheral vision, she saw Jaden stand suddenly.

"Uh-oh," he said in a low, breathy voice.

Then he let out a sound she'd never heard him make before. It sounded like the bellow of pain from a wounded animal. A fierce groan.

She glanced over just in time to see him bend forward at the waist and project vomit an amazing distance, spraying it seemingly everywhere. Onto the beautiful tile work. Onto the end of the wooden lounge. Onto two of the potted plants. Possibly on the orange cat, though it might have skittered away owing to a near miss.

He straightened up, wiped his mouth on the short sleeve of his T-shirt, and looked at her with abject misery in his eyes.

"I feel sick," he said.

Señora Steinbach, if indeed that was her name, stood in the open doorway from the living room, holding two cold, sweaty glasses of water and surveying the unfortunate scene.

"Oh dear," she said.

"I'm sorry," Jaden said. "I couldn't help it. It just happened. I got sick."

"We're so, so sorry," Amelia said. "I feel terrible about your terrace. I'll clean it up."

Jaden wilted back down onto the edge of the lounge chair, as if half sitting and half passing out.

"I'll have Marta take care of it," Señora Steinbach said. She handed Jaden one of the glasses of water and towered over him, her energy scolding yet protective. "You drank the local water, didn't you?"

"I brushed my teeth with it," he said miserably.

"Yes, that can be enough."

"She told me not to, but I forgot."

"Well, let's get you into the house and we'll call the doctor."

Amelia's brain tried to fly in two directions at once. On the one hand, they had just been invited into the house, where they would likely have to wait for the doctor a long time. It was a remarkable and unforeseen opportunity. On the other hand, her son was sick and in misery, and she felt terribly guilty for even fleetingly glimpsing it as an opening.

Instead she only said, "Aren't you afraid the house is a mistake? All your nice things?"

"We'll put him in the guest room. The bed is very near the bathroom. I'll get him a trash bin or a bowl in case he can't make it there in time. Come along now. Carry him in. I need to call the doctor."

Amelia hoisted the boy up onto her hip and looked directly at the older woman, who looked away.

"This is very kind of you," shc said.

It seemed to enrage her host.

"It's not kind," she insisted in a loud and angry voice. As if Amelia had accused her of something terrible. "It's just what has to be. He can't go back into town on foot. He's sick. Now come along."

Amelia watched her spin around and head into the house, where she almost ran smack into a young woman in a white apron, her dark hair pulled back in a ponytail.

"Marta," the older woman said. "The boy was sick on the terrace. Take care of that, will you please? You can get most of it off with the mop and then hose it all down well. Come let me know when you're done, please. I'm going to call Dr. Torres, and have him come out and see to the child. I'll have him call when he gets to the bottom of the hill and you'll have to go down on the gator and bring him up the road."

Then she marched past the young woman into the house. Amelia had to hurry to keep up.

"You have a gator?" Jaden asked her, his voice both weak and full of wonder.

"Yes," she said. "Do you know what it is?"

"It's a big dangerous green animal that swims."

"No, not that kind of gator. Not the animal. It's a four-wheel-drive utility vehicle."

"Oh," he said.

Amelia knew that he likely did not understand the concept of a utility vehicle. She also knew he was probably too sick to want to ask more questions.

As she moved through the living room, following her host, Amelia's eyes scanned along the floor-to-ceiling bookcases. They were the kind with a sliding ladder to allow one to access the top shelves.

Something caught her eye.

It was a photograph in a silver frame. But it was not hanging on a wall. It was propped up, easel-like, in front of the books on an eye-level shelf.

It was a photo of a young girl standing next to an enormous white swan. The girl wore a short, robin's-egg-blue dress with white leggings, and her haircut looked as though it had been done with a bowl. Her gaze was downcast, her eyes partly closed. She had one arm draped carefully behind the swan's neck.

That was when Amelia knew.

She knew she could never prove it, and she knew the woman she was following might never admit it. But in that moment, she knew it.

She was following E. L. Swann through her home.

"What are you looking at?" her host asked, startling her. Only then did Amelia realize she had stopped in her tracks without even knowing it. The author's gaze followed hers to see if she could answer her own question. Amelia wasn't sure if E. L. Swann knew it was the picture that had caught Amelia's eye, or if she grasped the full significance of the moment. But she suspected so. "I didn't invite you to look at things in my house, so stop doing that. Now bring the boy into the bedroom before we have another unfortunate accident."

"Don't put him down yet," Swann said. "Just hold him a minute."

She hurried out of the room and came back with a sheet of thick, clear plastic, the kind Amelia's mother had used to cover the good sofa to save it from children. She spread it out on the bed in a grand flapping motion. Then she took a blanket out of a chest at the end of the bed and laid it on top of the plastic. To make it a bit more comfortable for her son, Amelia assumed.

"Now you can put him down," she said. "I don't mean to be indelicate, but bad things are going to start coming out from both ends of the boy soon enough."

"Don't put me down," Jaden said. "Take me to the bathroom very fast."

Amelia did, and got him there just in time for E. L. Swann's prophecy to come true.

"Close the door," he said desperately when she had gotten his shorts down and had him up on the toilet.

She reached back and began to close it, but he quickly made it clear that she had misunderstood him.

"No, I mean with you out."

"Oh," Amelia said, surprised and slightly hurt. "You sure you don't need me?"

"Mo-om," he whined, turning the word into two syllables. "I know how to do this. I've been doing it myself for a long time."

She sighed, and stepped out of the bathroom, closing the door behind her. She stood just on the other side of the door, close enough to hear him if he changed his mind.

Meanwhile she heard the voice of her host filter in from another room.

"Yes, it's Ella Steinbach," the voice said. "I need the doctor out as soon as possible."

At the sound of that name, a fierce tingling struck in Amelia's gut and rose all the way to the base of her throat.

"No, I'm well," the voice continued. "But I have these . . . visitors. The unwanted kind, I'm afraid, but the boy is just a little slip of a thing and it's not his fault his mother dragged him up here. I can't just send him down the hill in this kind of shape. He seems like a nice little guy." Pause. "Yes, waterborne. Apparently. Have Dr. Torres phone up from the bottom of the hill and I'll send Marta down to fetch him in the gator." Another brief pause. "Thank you."

A silence followed, and Amelia had no idea if her host had hung up the phone or not.

Seconds later the older woman stepped into the room, startling them both.

"You're not in with him?" she asked, her voice dripping with judgment.

"He wouldn't let me be."

"Oh, he's at that age, is he?"

They waited in silence for a moment. It was a tense silence that felt like some kind of stalemate to Amelia. She had been leaning her back against the closed bathroom door, and Ella was now leaning her back against the wall by the open door of the guest bedroom.

Amelia couldn't help noticing that they both had their backs up against something, and it struck her as a fitting metaphor for the moment.

When the weight of the air between them grew unbearable, Amelia rapped gently on the bathroom door behind her.

"You okay in there?"

"Yeah," Jaden's pained, tentative little voice called back.

"Why aren't you coming out?"

"I just keep feeling like the minute I do I'll have to run right back in."

"Got it," she said. "Take all the time you need."

Her eyes fell on the older woman again, and for a moment their gazes locked. Then Ella looked away again.

"I know you don't want me to say this is kind of you," Amelia said. "I tried that once and it seemed to make you angry. But I hope I can just say that I very much appreciate how you're not throwing me out to carry him a mile down a steep hill while he's getting sick from both ends."

"*He* doesn't deserve that." Once again the older woman put just enough emphasis on the word "he" that Amelia could feel the sting of her intention.

They stood awkwardly for a moment, Amelia trying to decide how brave she felt. But how often did an opportunity like this one come along? Once in a lifetime if you were brilliantly lucky. Never for most.

"Your name is Ella," Amelia said.

"How do you know my name? I'm quite sure I didn't tell you."

"I heard you talking to the doctor just now."

"Oh. I see. So you're both an intruder and an eavesdropper."

Amelia let the sting of that sentence move through her, hurrying it along slightly. She reminded herself that she had never expected, if she were lucky enough to meet her hero, that E. L. Swann would treat her kindly.

"This author you claim to know nothing about," Amelia said, "though most people know her name quite well . . . Her pen name was E. L. Swann, but she was born Ella Lynne Carmichael in Saint Paul, Minnesota."

"And?"

"I just thought it was an interesting coincidence. Ella is not a very common given name."

"Maybe not these days," her host said, studiously avoiding her eyes. "But when I was young you couldn't throw a pebble into a group of girls without hitting an Ella."

They stood in that strained silence for a moment, as Amelia tried to decide whether to push right up to that magical, invisible line. She had no idea how long they would be allowed to stay, and that influenced her choices.

"When Ella Lynne Carmichael was a young girl, she fell in love with a big white swan that lived in a local park," Amelia said.

"Sounds a bit unnatural."

"No, I don't mean it like that. She loved it the way children love their pets. She kept pestering her parents to take her to the park to visit the swan, who I guess in time grew fairly used to her. She'd been given a little Brownie camera for her birthday, and she took photo after photo of the swan, and when it began to allow her to come close, she would hand the camera to her parents and get them to take portraits of her with it. She didn't do public appearances, which is why people don't tend to know her by sight. The author photo from her novel, *The Third Labyrinth*, is really the only photo most people have to go by. But she did do a couple of interviews with journalists by phone, and she told one of them that when it came time to take on a pen name, she decided to use the opportunity to pay tribute to that swan. She added the extra N to make it a bit more sophisticated and less of an obvious reference to an actual waterfowl."

Still looking down at the tile floor, Ella said, "Based on what you've just told me, I get the impression that this author you keep going on about was always reclusive, even before she decided to disappear entirely."

"Sounds right," Amelia said.

"I wonder then," Ella said, bringing her eyes quite boldly up to Amelia's, "why everyone couldn't simply respect that. If she wanted to be left alone, why couldn't people just leave her alone? If they loved that damn book so much, then they might have acknowledged that she'd given them something."

"Oh, I think most people who read *The Third Labyrinth* agree that she'd given them something."

"And if all she wanted was to be left alone, why couldn't they give her that in return? It really doesn't seem like too much to ask."

Their eyes remained locked during this exchange, and it stung, but Amelia did not look away.

She was opening her mouth to answer when Jaden opened the bathroom door behind her. The sudden lack of support almost unbalanced her and caused her to fall over backward, but she caught herself.

"Whew," Jaden said. He wobbled unsteadily toward the high bed, and she helped him up. "I feel really, really bad. What were you two talking about out here?"

Once again Amelia opened her mouth to speak.

Ella beat her to it.

"Oh, your mother was just telling me more elaborate stories that have absolutely nothing to do with me." She moved several steps over to an upholstered wing chair and sat, crossing her legs at the knee, her face guarded and firm. She turned her attention to Amelia. "Now, I don't know you nearly well enough to leave you alone in my house, and the doctor will be at least an hour and a half, so I suggest we talk about something entirely unrelated. That is, if you insist on talking at all."

Chapter Six

If You Won't Take It, They Have to Keep It

Marta came in after a time with a small glass of ginger ale and a cool cloth for Jaden's forehead.

Amelia thanked her extravagantly, knowing as she did that her gratitude hinged partly on the young woman caring for Jaden and partly on her breaking the awful, tense silence.

She helped her son sit up slightly, propping pillows behind him.

She held the glass of ginger ale to his lips and he took a sip. She offered it again, but he pushed it away, shaking his head bitterly. He didn't say straight out that he knew he couldn't hold it down, but it went without saying.

As she pressed the cool cloth to his forehead, he opened his eyes fully and looked directly at Ella, seeming alert and engaged for the first time since the bug overcame him.

"You have a *donkey*?" he asked her, his voice full of wonder.

"Why, yes. I do. How did you know I have a donkey?"

"The man at the hotel said you did. He said you ride him down into town on the days when there's some kind of market."

"That's true. I do."

"That must be nice, to have a donkey. I wish *I* had one. What's your donkey's name?"

"I call him Francisco."

"I would like to meet a donkey named Francisco."

"Well. I'll tell you what. When you feel well enough to go out there, I'll introduce you to him."

"Thank you!" he said, his voice deep with gratitude and wonder. "That would be so nice of you!"

Amelia looked up at the author for the first time in a long, uncomfortable time. She was still sitting in the wing chair with her legs crossed. She did not return Amelia's gaze because she was busy focusing on Jaden.

In her eyes was a softness Amelia had not seen before. But more than just a softness. Some sort of reaching. As though Ella was trying to reach out through her eyes to connect with the boy in some kind of meaningful way.

She saw in that moment that E. L. Swann had begun to fall in love with her son. Not the way grown-ups fall in love with each other, of course. More the way Ella Lynne Carmichael fell in love with a huge, wild swan.

They waited for the doctor in a pained silence for another ten minutes at the least. It's hard to go ten minutes without talking to the person sitting right across the room from you, Amelia noted. Especially when she's your hero and you've been wanting to meet her for most of your life.

She decided to try a scrap of small talk.

She'd been staring at a cat that sat lazily on the ornate dresser, staring back. He was a huge cat, probably over twenty pounds, with a long, luxurious coat in a mottled sable color. His eyes were a dazzling color of green.

"That's a beautiful cat," she said.

Ella snorted in a way that sounded derisive.

"Don't think he doesn't know it, too."

Something hit Amelia's stomach in a way that made her flinch. A bad memory.

"Oh. I'm sorry I forgot to say this earlier. There was so much happening at once. I think it's possible that Jaden might have thrown up on one of your cats."

She watched the author's face but didn't see much reaction.

"Which one?"

"Slender. Orange. Shorthaired."

"Marta!" Ella called, startling her.

The young woman bustled into the room.

"Sí, señora?"

"Go find Soolie, please, and see if she needs a bath."

"Sí, señora."

She hurried away again, and Ella turned her full, burning gaze onto Amelia.

"Well, you're honest," she said. "I'll give you that much."

It wasn't much. But, as she had come to expect that E. L. Swann would give her nothing at all, Amelia was happy to take it, and felt grateful for what little she got.

"With your permission," Dr. Torres said, standing up and turning to face Amelia, "I'd like to give him injectable antibiotics. This is because . . . well, maybe you will know why. If we ask him to swallow a pill . . ." He gestured with his hands, a pantomime of something rising back up and out the mouth.

He was a man of about seventy, with a creased face and hair going white at the temples, and he had a look and a manner that put Amelia at ease.

"Of course," she said. "Yes. I understand."

"Oh no," Jaden said weakly when he saw the hypodermic. "I have to get a shot?"

"I'm afraid so," Amelia said.

She came to his bed, walking around to the other side so as not to crowd the doctor. She sat on the edge and held her son's hands tightly.

"You know why, right?" she asked him.

"Yeah. Sort of. But I hate shots."

"But you're so good about them."

"But I hate them."

"This is a very thin needle," the doctor told Jaden. "Not so bad, we hope. If it hurts, it will only be for a couple of seconds."

He swabbed the boy's upper arm with what Amelia assumed was alcohol. Amelia squeezed her son's hand as the needle slid in, and he tensed up and squeezed back. Too hard, really. Hard enough to hurt. When had he grown so strong? she wondered.

Then the doctor was applying an adhesive bandage, and it was over.

"In about twenty-four hours you should feel quite a bit better," the doctor told Jaden. "Just rest until then." He raised his gaze to Amelia. "I'm going to give you a bottle of cipro. A wide-spectrum antibiotic. Some call it 'the traveler's friend.' Some people never travel outside their own country without it. Wait twenty-four hours and then give him one every six hours. Try to be very faithful about the timing. And give the whole course, no matter how much he tells you he feels okay."

"Oh, you *know* my son," she said.

The doctor smiled slightly.

It was the first light moment in a very long time.

"He is a seven-year-old boy. What more does one need to know?"

He rose to leave.

"What do I owe you?" she asked him.

But he waved her words away.

"A favor for Señora Steinbach. If you are a friend of hers, then you are a friend of mine. When he says he's ready, give him something very bland to eat. Dry toast, maybe. And try to keep him hydrated as best you can."

As he walked out of the room, Ella, who had been hovering in the bedroom doorway, caught her eye. Then she looked briefly over her shoulder as if to assure herself that the doctor was out of earshot.

"There," Ella said. "See? I saved you some money by not correcting him and telling him you're no friend of mine. Now you'd better hurry."

"Hurry? And do what?"

"I assumed you'd want to go down the hill with them. Marta can take you back to your hotel."

Amelia felt the words like something collapsing in her gut. This was it, then. The long-sought-after experience was over. It felt devastating.

But Ella was not done speaking.

"If you're going to be here overnight I figured you'd want to get a change of clothes for you and the boy. Toothbrushes. Pajamas. The chances of him soiling himself are pretty high, so maybe even bring two pairs of pants and two sets of pajamas for him. We'll be fine here while you're gone."

"Oh. You're going to let us stay?"

"Well, I wasn't going to. But then I went and shot off my mouth and told him I'd take him out to meet Francisco when he's feeling well enough. I didn't really think about what I was committing to when I said it, but I said it, and I'm not going to break a promise like that to him now. He's not well enough to go out back yet, so obviously he's not well enough to go all the way down the hill. Now hurry up before your ride leaves."

Amelia only stood, noticing that her feet were planted oddly wide apart. As if having to stand her ground against something formidable.

"Why are you just standing there?" Ella asked. "Why are you looking at me like that?"

"I'm just . . . not used to leaving my son alone."

Ella straightened her spine and grew slightly taller. She placed her hands on her hips.

Once again they each had their back up against something, Amelia thought. But this time it was in the figurative sense only.

"You're not leaving him *alone*, you're leaving him with *me*."

"Okay. Let me rephrase, then. I'm not used to leaving my son with complete strangers."

Something in Ella's eyes seemed to burst into flames. The author had a fiery temper. That was no surprise.

"Are you saying I can't be trusted?"

"Not an hour and a half ago you told me you were going to sit right in this room and stare at me until the doctor came, because you didn't know me nearly well enough to leave me alone in your house. If you don't know me well enough to trust me with your inanimate belongings, I'm not sure why you think I'd automatically trust you with my only child."

She watched the fire flicker and die in her host's eyes.

"That's actually hard to argue," Ella said. "I guess I'll have to put a point up on the scoreboard in your favor for that comeback. Look. It's your decision. But I would never hurt him, and I can't very well lose him. We're not going anywhere. We're just going to sit right here and talk. The whole trip will take you twenty minutes, tops. And if he soils his clothes you're going to be awfully glad you did."

Amelia broke her gaze away from the author's eyes and looked to her son.

"Are you okay here with Señora Steinbach for a few minutes while I get some things from the hotel?"

Jaden shrugged. "Sure. Why not? We'll just talk."

But talk about what? Amelia wondered. She wasn't sure if the blackness of E. L. Swann's sophisticated worldview was the best thing for a seven-year-old boy.

Then again, clothes that had not been soiled from sickness were another meaningful priority.

"Fine," she said, and walked out into the hall. Then she stopped. Turned back. Stuck her head into the bedroom again, and addressed their host. "Oh, and for everything that happened before that last little dustup . . . thank you."

"Oh, just go," Ella said, and waved her away with an utter lack of patience.

She met up with Marta as the young woman was driving the gator out from behind the house. The doctor was waiting just outside the gate.

Marta stopped to let her climb in.

"You want to go to your hotel?" Marta asked.

"I think so," Amelia said, not climbing in yet. She had fallen back into doubt. "You think it's okay to leave the boy with Señora Steinbach for a few minutes?"

"Oh sure," Marta said. "She likes him. She hates everybody, but she likes him. I can tell."

"So she likes children."

"Oh no. She hates children. She just likes him. Get in."

The gator was green, and had a roof for shade, but no windshield or windows. It was just open. Like a big golf cart, but beefier, and clearly built to deal with much rougher terrain. It had heavy-duty netting that clipped into place with seat-belt-like buckles where most vehicles had doors. It had four seats. Marta was indicating the passenger seat beside her, but Amelia thought it would show more respect to leave that seat for the doctor, so she sat in the back and clicked the net "door" closed behind her.

They picked up the doctor and bounced down the hill, Marta steering around deep ruts and potholes.

The doctor turned around and looked into Amelia's face.

"Don't look so worried," he said. "It happens all the time with visitors from other countries. It will usually pass on its own, but why let him be miserable for longer than needed? He will be fine, I'm sure."

"Thank you, Doctor," she said.

She didn't bother to tell him that the waterborne illness was not, at the moment, her worry. In fact, she had briefly forgotten that Jaden was sick. She could think only of the fact that she had left him alone with someone who had a long-standing reputation of being the most disagreeable woman most people had ever had the misfortune to meet.

—

As she raced out of the hotel lobby with one small bag of their belongings, she passed Guillermo at the reception desk.

He looked at her, then out at Marta, waiting on the noisily idling gator just outside the front door. Then back at Amelia.

"I have no idea how you managed that," he said. "But . . ." He formed a fist and used it to bump himself in the chest, in the general area of his heart. "Much respect."

—

Marta dropped her at the front door of the house and drove away to park the vehicle.

Amelia opened the unlocked front door and walked inside.

As she drifted down the hallway to the guest bedroom, she heard them talking.

"I tried not to cry," her son said. "I tried so hard. I just squeezed down really, really hard and I said to myself 'I won't, I won't,' but then a little bit came out. And they laughed and laughed and then they started imitating me crying but much worse than the little bit I did. And not just right then, either. They kept doing it for years. They always called me Jaden Booger, but then after that they started calling me Boo Hoo Booger."

"Oh," Ella said. "That's unimaginative. Though not as mean as some of what you just told me. Thank you for reminding me why I despise little rug rats so much."

"What's a rug rat?"

"A child."

"You don't like me?"

"Of course I like you. I'm talking about most children. You're different."

"That's what everybody says."

Amelia made her footsteps as light as possible, and paused as close to the door as she dared.

"In a world where people are a blight on the landscape," Ella said, "it's a very high compliment to be different than most."

"I didn't get the land part," Jaden said. "But I guess you mean people are bad."

"That's exactly what I mean."

A moment's silence.

Then Ella said, "May I give you a piece of advice? There's an old story about the Buddha. I'm not sure if it's true or not. Do you know who the Buddha was?"

"I think I've heard that name."

"He was a prophet. An enlightened one. They say he was once speaking to a group, and a young man verbally assaulted him."

"I don't know what that means."

"It means something like the adult version of calling him Jaden Booger."

"Oh. Got it."

"The Buddha said to the young man, 'Son, if someone declined to accept a gift, to whom would it belong?' The young man said it would continue to belong to the giver. The person who had offered it. 'Yes,' said Buddha, 'and I decline to accept your abuse.' Now, I realize that's a pretty adult concept, but I wonder if you have a sense of what it means."

"I think so," Jaden said. "I think . . . Wait. I have to think about that for a minute." A few seconds of silence ticked by. "I think it means that if the kids at school try to give me something bad . . . something I don't want . . . if I won't take it then it has to be theirs."

"You're a very smart little boy," Ella said.

"But how do I not take it? If I say no, I don't want that, they'll just laugh at me."

"No, you don't say it out loud. You don't say anything. You just . . . don't take it on. You don't believe it. The problem is not that they *say* you're not as good as they are, it's that after a while you start to believe it. You think the fact that all the kids say it means it must be true. But that's not what it means at all. Really it just means that they found someone who seems willing to believe it. Just smile a little to yourself and go on your way, and know that they're only trying to make you feel small because they're afraid it's really themselves who are small. After a while they'll see they're not getting to you. And if they're not getting to you then it's no fun for them. There's no payoff. They'll get bored after a time and find somebody else to pick on. Does that make sense to you? Is that something you can understand?"

"I think so," Jaden said.

Nothing more was said for a time. Amelia began to consider letting them know she was back.

Before she could, Ella spoke again.

"Do you tell your mother how badly you're being picked on at school?"

"Um. Not exactly. She asks me if anyone there is hurting me, but they're not *hurting* me. So I say no."

A sensation like heartburn formed in Amelia's chest. Or maybe heartbreak would be a more accurate description.

"But they *are* hurting you," Ella said. "They're hurting your feelings and making you feel terrible about yourself."

"Oh," Jaden said. And paused. "I didn't know I got to count that."

The sentence moved through Amelia like a dull sword.

She backed quietly away from the doorway, because the conversation had been so important and so profound that she did not want them to know it had been overheard.

If they said more to each other, she was purposely too far away to hear.

She moved quietly into the living room, where she stared at the image of Ella Lynne Carmichael and her beloved swan at close range.

Then something to the right of it caught her eye.

It was a very old hardcover copy of *The Third Labyrinth*. Amelia would know that dustcover over that book spine anywhere. It would jump out at her from across a room.

Looking over her shoulder to be sure she was alone, she gently pulled the book free. It was a first edition, she saw from the copyright page, with shelf wear at the corners of the dust jacket and the book itself. It was unsigned.

It didn't prove anything, she knew. But it did seem telling that the woman who claimed never to have heard of the author E. L. Swann had a first edition of the book in her library.

She flipped a few pages, and felt a coldness strike her all over.

Someone had taken a proofreader's blue pencil and edited the finished book. Words were marked for deletion. Pairs of words were marked for reversal. Paragraphing was changed and line breaks added or removed.

She flipped through the book and did not see one page that did not have at least half a dozen proofreader's marks.

She quickly closed the book so she could put it away before she was discovered. Then she paused, and almost left it out on the coffee table instead. It would be a way to force the discussion.

But Jaden was still sick, and they were invited to stay for a day.

Maybe there would be better moments to force her host to do anything she clearly did not want to do.

Chapter Seven

The Night Sky in Three Dimensions

It was a couple of hours later when Ella stuck her head into the bedroom to see how the two of them were doing.

"Oh, he's asleep," she said.

It was almost two p.m., Amelia was hungry, and she'd begun to wonder if being a guest in E. L. Swann's home included being fed in any way.

"Yeah, he's been out for about an hour. I think between the stomach bug and the hike up here, the morning just wore him out."

"I was going to offer you both lunch, but let's just let him sleep. He's probably not ready to hold anything down yet anyway. I was just going to offer so as not to seem cruel."

They stood regarding each other for a moment, Amelia trying to figure out if lunch had just been snatched from her as well.

"Well, come on, then," Ella said.

Amelia followed her out to the now clean terrace, where Marta—she assumed—had set out a beautiful lunch: huge, shallow bowls of avocado gazpacho with a basket of crusty bread. The round wooden table was set with linen placemats and fresh flowers, and shaded by one of the standing umbrellas.

"Thank you for this," Amelia said, and sat, placing the tan linen napkin in her lap.

"Everybody has to eat. Oh, and remind me. When he wakes up, I have some electrolyte drink. I get it for myself for the crazy hot summer days. We have to try to get some of that into him so he doesn't get dehydrated. Even if he only holds it down for a few minutes, we have to try. Anything he can hold on to is better than nothing."

They ate in silence for several minutes. Amelia was watching the parasailing boat leaving a long wake on the gulf waters, and wondering if this was the worst moment in the world to bring up the edited book.

Before she could decide, Ella slammed her soup spoon down into her bowl. It made a mighty clang that startled Amelia.

"Oh, just go ahead and say it!" she barked.

"Say what?"

"I have no idea, but I can tell there's something on your mind, and that you're holding back because you think I won't like it. Go on and get it over with."

Amelia wondered if she was really that much of an open book. Could she have lived this long with no poker face at all, but without anyone pointing it out? Or did E. L. Swann read minds? Or was it the more likely scenario, that the author was simply more perceptive than most?

Amelia noticed her own hands shaking slightly, and wondered if Ella had noticed that as well.

"When you were talking to Jaden today, I wanted to leave the two of you alone. Not interfere. I like to look at people's libraries."

"Okay. And?"

"And you have a first edition of E. L. Swann's book. And I just thought it was interesting, because you claimed you'd never heard of her."

"Oh. Well." Ella averted her eyes slightly and stumbled over her words. "People give me books all the time. I put them on the shelf. I don't read them all. Sometimes I barely look at them."

Amelia continued as though no explanation had been offered.

"And because I thought it was interesting, I picked it up and looked inside. I know that might make you angry, you being such a private person. But it's a published book. It's not like reading your journal. I figured it would be exactly the same as every other copy of the novel, and so there would be no expectation of privacy. It looked like a first edition, and I just wanted to see if it was. But once it was open, it wasn't like all the other copies. And I think you might know how."

"I'm sure I have no idea what you're on about," Ella said.

Her gaze remained cast out over the gulf, as if something were happening out there that hadn't happened on any other day.

"It was edited."

"Aren't all books edited?"

"I mean by hand."

She waited, but the author did not reply. She only kept her eyes glued to the view.

"E. L. Swann had a reputation for being absolutely obsessed about editing. She seemed to find it impossible to stop. She only wrote the one novel, as I said, but before that she had several stories published in a handful of prestigious literary journals. In a magazine interview she did by phone, maybe forty years ago, she confessed that when the finished copies arrived in the mail she'd sit down with a blue pencil and keep editing. She never told anyone she did the same with *The Third Labyrinth*, at least not publicly. So I guess I might be the only person who knows. Well. Two people know, at least. And I believe they're both sitting at this table."

She waited for a reply. She might only have waited for a couple of dozen seconds, but it felt unbearably long. Her heart pounded. She remembered learning in school that Einstein had simplified his theory of relativity for the nonscientific mind by saying that an hour sitting on a hot stove is not the same length as an hour sitting on the couch with a pretty girl.

Amelia was definitely sitting on the stove.

The author's clawlike hand landed on her arm and squeezed hard enough to hurt.

"I let you come onto my property because your son needed a drink of water. I let Dr. Torres think you were my friend so he wouldn't charge you for the house call. I'm letting you stay until the boy is well enough to be driven down the hill in the morning. I'm feeding you lunch. I never do all that for *anyone*. Would you agree that offering me something in return would be good form?"

"I'm in your debt," Amelia said. "Absolutely."

"Don't tell anyone where you found me."

That resonated for a moment. It had surprised Amelia so completely that she needed time to respond.

"I didn't think you'd own it that fast," she said. "Or, actually . . . at all."

"Honestly, what difference does it make? You think I'm E. L. Swann, and you have compelling reasons to think so, and whether I say you're right or you're wrong you'll still tell people where I am. And my life will be ruined. I have a life here. I live in peace. If you spent most of your career studying my work, you must feel you've gotten something from it. Give me this in return."

They sat still and quiet for a moment. Then the author withdrew her hand, seeming to notice suddenly that her grip was too panicky and intense.

"Let me write an article about you," Amelia said. "A really thorough, in-depth article. I'll start right out by saying that I will not be divulging your whereabouts."

"Somebody knows where you were going."

"I don't think so," Amelia said. "Wait. Let me think. I told my friend Leon I was going to follow a tip about you, but I don't think I told him the name of the town. I must have said Mexico, because we got into a discussion of whether I needed a passport for Jaden."

"Mexico is too much for anyone to know. But, more importantly, who gave you the tip?"

"These friends of my ex-husband. They were on vacation in Santa Rosarita and saw you buying fruit at the market."

"Then they'll know where you found me."

Amelia took a minute to think that over.

"Okay. Here's what we'll do. We'll both sleep on it, and think about whether we're missing any threads that might lead to you. Meanwhile I'll tell my friends the tip led nowhere. I won't present the article for publication for at least a couple of months. Maybe more like three. And before I do, I'll tell everyone I got another unusually viable lead, and I'll take Jaden on another little vacation. He wants to go to Montana. If anyone can't keep a secret, people will be looking for you in Montana."

Ella did not respond immediately. She stared down at the table, her brow furrowed.

"I suppose that might work," she said. "But it feels like a form of blackmail."

"What does?"

"I have to say yes to this, or you'll tell people I'm here."

"I never said that."

"But you would. To pressure me to do it."

"I wouldn't. I owe you a debt. I will *not* disclose your location, even if you say no to the article. You're right when you say I owe you that much."

Ella looked confused for a minute, as if she were adding up numbers in her head and couldn't arrive at the right total.

"But there's no other reason I would do it," she said after a time.

"I think there is," Amelia said. "I think you have something to say to the people you ran away from. Think about it. I was only a few minutes in your house when you told me the people who got something from the book should be willing to leave you alone if you ask them to. You have reasons for keeping the public away. And I hope you'll take my word for this: They don't know it. They think they're doing great and you're just reclusive. They do *not* see the thing from your side. They have no idea what they do to make life unlivable for a person who was thrust suddenly into the limelight."

Ella seemed to take her time before answering, and before she could, they heard Jaden's voice.

"I threw up again."

They both turned their heads to see him standing in the living room, looking out at them. He looked pale and a little shaky.

"Did you make it to the toilet?" Amelia asked him.

"Yeah."

"Good boy. Come on. I'm going to put you back to bed."

She hurried into the living room and scooped him up.

"Will you sit with me?" he asked her.

"As soon as I finish my lunch. You want to try some dry toast?"

He shook his head vehemently.

"What were you two talking about?" he asked.

"Very complicated grown-up stuff."

"Why is being a grown-up very complicated?"

"Honey," she said, "I've been asking myself that question ever since I became one."

Amelia woke at a little after two in the morning. She rolled over, reaching out a hand to Jaden to be sure he was okay. She figured once she had located him, she would feel his forehead for signs of fever.

She never located him.

She sat up abruptly and turned on the lamp beside the bed.

Jaden was gone.

She swung her legs wildly over the side of the bed and ran out into the hallway.

The plan was to open doors until she found Ella's bedroom, in an effort to see if her host was missing as well. Meanwhile a panicky voice at the back of her brain was telling her she would not find Ella either.

That the author had quite literally kidnapped her child. That, feeling blackmailed, she had now found a way to blackmail in return.

She never managed to finish the plan.

Before she could open even one door, she heard soft voices from the terrace. The living room doors stood wide open into the night, and she quietly moved closer.

When it was clear that one of the voices was Jaden's, she breathed freely and began to settle her heart.

She sat in a deeply upholstered chair just inside the doors, off to one side so they would not notice her if they turned around. She leaned over slightly to better see the terrace, and, as her eyes adjusted to the light, she could see the dim, inexact shapes of their figures. They were lying on the wooden lounge chairs and seemed to have their faces turned up to the sky.

"We don't have stars like this in San Francisco," Jaden said. "Well. We have stars. And they're like this. But there aren't this many."

"Actually there are," Ella said. "There are the same number of stars everywhere. You just can't see them as well."

"Oh. I get it. Like the way the sky is bigger here or in Montana, but it's not really bigger, it just doesn't have so many big buildings getting in the way."

"Well, something similar to that. But in this case it's not about your view of the stars being physically blocked. It's about the city lights. Cities are very bright at night, and all that light washes out the dimmer stars. The darker the sky, the more stars you'll see. I could have moved to a city. Cities are a good place to disappear, because nobody keeps tabs on their neighbors. But I wanted to be somewhere with a dark sky. I look up at the stars and the planets and it's . . . maybe you won't understand what I mean by this, but it's my spirituality."

"I don't know that last part," Jaden said.

He sounded relaxed. He sounded like he must be feeling at least a little bit better.

"Spirituality . . . ," Ella said, "it's . . . a little bit like religion, but in other ways it's not like it at all. Religion is more like thinking there's a man with flowing robes and a long white beard in the sky, looking down on us. Spirituality is about the idea that *something* is out there. Something bigger than us. Bigger than all of this. And not necessarily just lumps of planets, either. Maybe some kind of intelligence or order. Does that make sense?"

"I think so. But aren't the stars sort of just lumps?"

"Oh no. They're very much alive. New stars are being formed all the time. Old stars are dying in these massive explosions. Supernova explosions. Nuclear reactions are going on out there in space. And our lump of a planet has life on it, so who's to say some of the others don't as well? But none of that is even the point. The point is that we look at the stars all wrong, and if we look at them properly it fills us with this sense of wonder and awe, and that's what I mean when I say it's my spirituality."

"I want to look at them right," Jaden said. "What am I doing wrong?"

"I'm guessing you're looking at them as if they're two-dimensional."

"I don't know what that is."

"Flat. Like a painting. We look at the stars like they're a flat background over our heads. But really we're looking out into space. And it goes on forever. Well, it has to, doesn't it? Otherwise what would be on the other side? Some of the stars you're looking at are millions of light-years away. Tens of millions. If you have a medium-sized backyard telescope, some of the things you can see in a really dark sky are as much as, say, eighty million light-years away. So let's pretend you can travel at the speed of light. You can't, but let's just pretend. Those stars are so far away that you'd need a million lifetimes to travel to one. But even that is only if you can travel at the speed of light, which is impossible. Only light can do that."

"So the trick is to look like you're looking out at the distance."

"Exactly. And then suddenly you realize that the universe is so big. And that we're so small. And you start to understand that the things we think are important are just too small to matter. We've built this whole world around thinking our needs and our egos matter. And then you look out at objects millions of light-years away, and you just know that can't be true. And that's what I call spirituality."

They were quiet for a long time. Several minutes.

Then Jaden said, "Honestly, most of what you just said I didn't understand. But I got the part about looking out at the stars like it's not flat like a painting. And just for a minute I think I could feel what you were saying. Even though I don't really get it with my head."

"I'm not sure anybody really gets it with their head," Ella said. "It's the feeling we're after."

"Can I have some more of that sports-drink stuff?"

"Of course."

Amelia saw and heard Ella stand and head for the house. Seconds before she stepped into the living room, inches from where Amelia sat, Amelia tried to warn her.

"Don't let me startle you," she said quietly.

It did not work out at all.

Ella jumped wildly and let out a strangled noise of surprise.

"More like scare me to death," she said, one hand on her heart. "Don't tell me, let me guess. You woke up and your son was gone."

"Exactly."

"He was wandering around in the kitchen, looking for water. There was plenty by his bed, but he didn't know that because he didn't want to wake you by turning on the light. He said he couldn't sleep, probably because he slept through so much of the day. I was in the kitchen having a cup of tea."

"You couldn't sleep either."

"True. I couldn't. But, figuratively speaking, I've been sleeping on what we talked about."

"The interview?"

"What else?"

"And?"

"Don't rush me," the author said. "I hate to be rushed. Now, if you'll excuse me, I have to go get some electrolyte drink for your son."

When Amelia woke in the morning, Jaden was gone again. This time she didn't panic.

She rose, dressed, and found Ella out on the terrace. The older woman was standing, hands in the pockets of her loose white linen pants, staring out at the view.

Alone.

Then Amelia panicked.

"Where's Jaden?" she asked, trying and failing to mask her fear.

"Oh, he'll be by here in just a minute," Ella said.

They stood looking out at the striking vista for a few seconds. Amelia was trying to form her next question into words.

Before she could, Jaden came into view. He was riding on a donkey.

He was still in his pajamas. His feet were bare. The donkey wore an adult-sized saddle, and its tooled-leather-covered stirrups flopped free, much too long for Jaden to reach. He wore no helmet or other protective gear.

He gripped the saddle horn tightly with both hands.

He waved at her as he went by, his face beaming. Then he quickly returned that hand to the job of gripping the horn.

They disappeared around the house for another lap.

"He's in his pajamas," Amelia said. "He's riding in his bare feet. He's never ridden before in his life except one time when I was leading the horse."

Ella clucked her tongue and dismissed Amelia's worries with a shake of her head.

"I can understand why you'd be concerned about your son suddenly riding an equine. But this is not just any equine. This is Francisco. Francisco is a legend. He carried both of Marta's children before they were old enough to walk. If he thinks they're not well balanced, he'll stop. I've even seen him shift his weight to help them get balanced again. He's like a child's nanny. Except . . . you know. Male."

"Like a manny."

"A what?"

"Never mind. Is he even feeling well enough for this?"

"The donkey or the boy?"

"My son," she said firmly, not knowing if her host was kidding or not.

"He swore he was."

"Okay, but . . . look. I know you think very highly of your donkey. But if something spooked him, my boy would go flying."

Ella smiled. Almost laughed, but not audibly.

"You really don't know donkeys," she said. "Horses spook. If a coyote or an aggressive dog goes after a horse, the horse will take flight, run for its life, and never look back. If the same coyote is foolish enough to try that on a donkey or a mule it will find itself stomped to death. Why, I've even known people who put a donkey out in the pasture with the horses to protect them from predators."

Jaden and Francisco wandered by again, and again Jaden grinned and waved before they disappeared from view.

"And look at that," Ella said. "It makes him so happy."

"I can't argue with you there," Amelia said. She paused, then dove in. "Did you think any more about my proposal?"

"I've thought about nothing else."

"And?"

"First, tell me something. What do you think is the most dangerous aspect of your article's publication? For me, I mean. What do you think is the slip most likely to give away my location?"

Amelia thought for a moment. Wrestled with herself for a moment more.

"I shouldn't say," she said at last. "Because I really want this. I should say I see no issues at all. But I want to be fair. Truthfully . . . I'd have to say it's that little boy who keeps going by here on a donkey."

"Once again, you surprise me with your honesty."

"Why is it a surprise? Did I strike you as a dishonest person?"

"Not you personally. Don't make it all about you. People are dishonest, in my experience. Did you tell him I'm E. L. Swann?"

"No, I didn't even tell him I was looking for her. I mean you. I just said I was following a story."

"Then as far as he knows, I'm just Señora Steinbach. I'm not who you thought I was, but I was very kind and welcoming when he got sick at my house. Right off the bat that will prove to everybody that it couldn't possibly have been me. The only bump I see is that I don't think you can take him on that second trip to Montana in a few months to follow a pretend lead. Because he'll see that you don't meet anybody there. He'll know it's a ruse."

"Okay, fine. I'll leave him with his father."

"And I think you should wait longer than two or three months."

"Okay. I was just thinking I wanted to take Jaden away again while school is still out for the summer. But if he's not going . . . tell you what. It's June. I won't submit the article for publication this year."

"Where would you publish it?"

"Remains to be seen. I'm a freelancer. But everyone will want this. I can pretty much take my pick."

They stood in silence for a few moments. Jaden rode into view again, this time at a lazy jog. And this time he was literally laughing.

Amelia didn't want to push her host for an answer. She knew from years of story-submission experience that a yes takes longer than a no, and if you insist on an immediate answer you might not be giving the person time to get to yes.

"Marta will take you to your hotel," the older woman said, finally. "Get all your things. Check out. There's no reason to pay for the room when you'll be here. We'll see if we can knock this out in a couple of days."

Amelia opened her mouth to offer an excited, positive answer. The author did not allow her the chance.

"Do *not* thank me. I'm doing this under duress. I'm still not your friend and I still resent your coming here and mucking up my peaceful life. But, since you know what I don't want anybody to know—what I've been able to keep to myself for forty years and thought I had in the bag until you came along—I'm going to do what you want and try to stay on your good side. Yes, I admit there'll be a certain satisfaction to it. But it's a risk. Well, it's a risk either way. That's the problem. So let's just hurry up and do this thing before I change my mind."

Chapter Eight

Leave Me on the Ground, Please

Amelia set their packed suitcases by the hotel room door and sat down on the edge of the bed with her phone.

She texted Richard and Carla Jacobs first.

"Interesting lady," she typed. "She's hosting us at her house. I might even do a story about her. You know, expatriate with a compelling life history. That kind of thing. Alas, she is not the author E. L. Swann. Thanks for the tip all the same."

She copied and pasted the text and sent the same message to Leon, changing the word "tip" to "help." The feeling was different, though, because she hated to lie to Leon. But she had promised.

Amelia knew that most people's typical version of keeping a promise was to tell only one or two trusted people and swear them to secrecy. But that's not good enough, she had long believed. Because they will do the same. And the people they tell will do the same.

She had never lied to Leon, but in this case she simply had no choice.

Then she took three very deep, noisy breaths and called her ex-husband.

Just as the call was about to go to voicemail, he picked up.

Amelia froze, and said nothing. For one panicky moment she almost hung up the phone.

"Do *not* hang up," he barked.

She held still and silent a moment longer, wondering how he could have known.

"I wasn't going to hang up," she said.

And, because it was Mark, she felt little or no guilt over lying to him. It was a survival tactic with him. Or, anyway, it felt like one.

"Where are you?"

"I was following a tip from your friends Richard and Carla. They thought they had an E. L. Swann sighting."

"*Our* friends."

"Get serious," she said. "Until this, neither one of them has said two words to me since our split."

"People have to sort out their loyalties."

"Yes, and they sorted them into something that underscores my original point. But this is a stupid thing to argue about, Mark. It turned out not to be E. L. Swann. But I'm following a different story down here. This Friday will be impossible. I'd have to beam us home. But I still think I can get back in time for you to pick him up next Friday."

A long silence fell.

Then Mark said, "How sure?"

"Eighty percent."

"Why did you even take Jaden with you? Why didn't you drop him off with me?"

"He'd been complaining about how we never get outside the city."

"Christine and I took him to Big Sur last month."

Amelia ran a hand across the brocade bedspread in silence, waiting for the sting to settle.

"He didn't tell me that," she said after a time.

"It's not okay that you took him on a trip without asking me."

"But it's okay for you to have a girlfriend in the house with him and not run that by me? Is that what you're saying? And taking him to Big Sur is not taking him on a trip?"

She could feel her energy coiling in her chest—feel it rising to do battle with him. With it came that familiar sinking feeling. Because he always won.

"I don't want to fight with you," he said. "But you're missing my weekend, and so I want him for Thanksgiving."

"That doesn't sound very—"

"And if you're not back next Friday and I miss a second weekend with him, then I want him for Christmas," he said, before she could finish.

"That's entirely unreasonable."

"Take it or leave it."

She held the phone to her chest for a moment and tried to breathe. And thought, *No wonder I left this man. But why didn't I do it much, much sooner?*

It was a bad trade he was proposing, unless she was actually trading Thanksgiving and Christmas for a chance to interview E. L. Swann. And she was. And she might even get back by the following Friday.

Then she felt a stab of regret, imagining herself telling Jaden she might miss those holidays with him. She had felt the stab often lately, as it would soon be time to break it to him that Christmas with both parents at the same time was a thing of the past. If she had to, she would provide the most lavish Christmas Eve imaginable and lean heavily on the fact that it meant two Christmases for him.

Better yet, she'd get back on time and wouldn't have to.

"Fine," she said. "I'll keep you posted."

She hung up before he could say more.

"I am so very sorry, señora, to have to say I can't refund you for tonight," Guillermo said. "It's not as much notice as we require. The other nights we won't charge."

"It's not a problem," she said. "I understand."

"You need someone to help with your bags?"

"No, it's fine. I can take them."

She hauled them out the door and onto the street, where Marta waited in the noisily idling gator.

As they drove off, Amelia looked back to see Guillermo and two waiters standing outside the lobby doors, watching them go.

"They are shocked," Marta said. "Because nobody goes up the hill, and even if somebody ever does go up, they don't stay up."

Amelia held her hat down to keep it from flying away as they breezed through town and up the road to the grand estate.

She looked back one more time as they neared the hilltop.

The three hotel employees now looked like ants, but they were still there. Still watching.

"Where's Jaden?" she asked her host.

Ella was sitting in an oversized, overstuffed chair in the living room, her plump legs folded underneath her in a way that looked uncomfortable. She had been reading a hardcover book, but she looked up when Amelia spoke.

"He went back to bed. He woke up this morning in fine fettle and insisted on meeting the donkey, and he swore he felt great. And he doesn't seem to still be throwing up. But he's not well yet. He hit the wall pretty fast with the riding. When he faded he really faded."

"I'll have to wake him up in an hour for his antibiotics."

"Unless he's up by then on his own."

"I'm just going to look in on him quickly," Amelia said, "and then I'm hoping we can get started. I'd like to get home by late next week at the latest."

"Why the big rush?"

Amelia felt a blast of surprise, along with a sinking feeling about Thanksgiving and Christmas.

"You're the one who said we could knock it out in a couple of days."

"Oh, but it's so much fun to have him here. But . . . okay. Sure. Go look in on him and then I'm willing to answer some questions. I mean, not so much willing, but . . . I said I would. I committed. So I will."

Amelia walked quietly down the hall to the guest bedroom, where she eased the door open. Jaden was asleep on his back, mouth wide open and eyes twitching.

She found her host again in the living room, slipped her phone out of her pocket, and set it to record. She placed it on the coffee table between them.

"Full disclosure," she said. "I'm recording this."

Ella set down her book.

"You're not recording this," she said.

She didn't sound as though she was saying Amelia was not *allowed* to record it. She seemed to be arguing with the very idea that any recording was happening.

"I *am* recording it," Amelia said.

"Do you have some kind of hidden recording device? Because I don't see a tape recorder anywhere."

"I'm recording it on my phone."

"You're joking."

"You didn't know phones recorded?"

"I did not."

"Do you have a cell phone?"

"I do. It's not the very newest model."

"It's a smartphone, though, right?"

"I'm not sure what that means."

"It's not like an old flip phone, is it?"

"It does flip open. But—listen. We're already off on a tangent. I wasn't raised with these gadgets, but I'm not a total Luddite. I can make a call and check my email, and I buy things online on the computer. But why do you need to record it? Why can't you just take notes?"

"Two reasons," Amelia said. She shifted uncomfortably in her chair, because she was about to be honest again. The kind of honesty her host found unexpected, and that might even put Amelia's goals on the line. "One of the reasons is for you and one of them is for me. If I scribble a bunch of notes, I won't be able to write as fast as you talk, and I'll have to summarize. And then when I go to write the article, there's a chance I'll misquote you slightly without meaning to. This way I can listen to exactly what you said as I write. More than once if necessary. And I can promise you I'll get everything exactly right."

Ella pulled her legs out from under her, stretching out her sock feet and leaning almost menacingly in Amelia's direction.

"And the 'you' part?"

"I have to have some kind of proof," she said.

That just sat on the table between them for a moment. They both appeared to be looking at it.

Amelia said more.

"I'll be claiming I met the author and got her to do an interview, but anybody can say that. And because I'll be refusing to say where I found you, I won't have evidence to confirm that I didn't make the whole thing up."

"So you're saying there are voice experts who can verify that it's me."

"That's exactly what I'm saying."

Amelia awaited her answer for what felt like several minutes, watching Ella stare in the direction of the bookcase. It definitely felt like sitting on Einstein's stove.

"I suppose I can't think what that would hurt," her host said at last. "Go ahead and ask me a question."

Amelia experienced something like a sigh, but it was only on the inside of her and could not be heard.

"I'm going to start with the most obvious one. The question that I imagine most of your readers would ask you if they could. You left the world without a trace forty years ago . . ."

"Why?" Ella asked, before Amelia could get there.

"Yes. Why?"

"I had my reasons."

"I hope you're prepared to say what some of them are. Otherwise this is going to be a painfully boring interview."

"I don't have a high opinion of people," Ella said.

"Are you offering that as a reason?"

"Yes. I wanted to live someplace where I could stay away from people."

"Marta is here."

"Marta works for me. That's entirely different. I'm her employer. I pay her a salary and she lives on that salary. If I tell her I need quiet, she'll be quiet. Try that with someone who's not on the payroll."

"So your genuine preference is to be alone."

"Oh, but I'm not alone. Not at all. I have Francisco and the cats. And you know what's great about them? They never think they can define me, and they never talk to me when I'm trying to read. They don't know I wrote that damn book, and if you had a way to tell them I doubt they'd be impressed."

Amelia leaned over the coffee table and checked to be sure this was all being recorded. She was suddenly intensely aware that she was hearing E. L. Swann explain her sudden departure, and that it was an opportunity she'd never expected to have. She'd never thought she'd even get to *read* the E. L. Swann "why" story, and now here she was about to write it.

And yes, she had known this for hours. But now it was happening, and it felt intensely real.

"Talk to me about the thing you said . . . about the animals not defining you. Who defines you?"

Ella looked up into Amelia's face, apparently genuinely surprised.

"Everybody," she said.

She seemed to think it should have gone without saying.

"Defines you how?"

"When I go into town here, I'm a person. Just a person. People judge me by whether I'm polite or whatever. Which I'm not, so let them think what they want. But the people who read that book, they think they know me. They've already decided who I am. And they've never even met me."

"An author does put a lot of herself into a book, wouldn't you say?"

"I would say . . . I'd say an author puts one very small aspect of herself into a book. And then people read the book and they believe they know that author. As if that one tiny little aspect is the whole of her. I find that irritating. But then, I really hated people to begin with."

"Hate's a strong word," Amelia said.

"People are a strong challenge," Ella replied without pause.

Amelia held still and silent and tried to pull her thoughts together. Tried to find a road that might lead the interview where she wanted it to go. As it stood, she felt as though she were chasing the author down a twisted path.

"Did you have negative experiences with reviews or criticism? Was that how things took a bad turn? Though, honestly, *were* there even bad reviews of *The Third Labyrinth*? I don't remember any."

Ella shook her head.

"Not major reviews, no. They were all good. But there were some who didn't like it. Of course. Every book has those who don't like it. But no, that didn't disturb me. Like the book, don't like the book. That's all normal stuff. No, my problem was with the ones who adored the book. The ones who thought I changed their lives. That's what I had to get away from."

Amelia could feel her brow furrow and her face twist slightly.

"Isn't that the good part?"

Ella laughed bitterly.

"Well, I know one thing. You're not a novelist."

"I'm not," she said.

It was a statement tinged with regret, because she had always wanted to be. But she had a child, and a need to earn a living. Life had intervened.

"Did you *want* to be a novelist?" Ella asked.

Amelia was left to wonder if she was being too transparent again.

"Why do you ask that?"

"Oh, I suppose because it's been my experience that everybody and his brother thinks they were meant to write a book."

"Can we get back to *you*?" Amelia asked, trying to shake off an irritable sensation. Once again the author was running things. Leading her in circles. "Tell me why it was a problem for you that people adored the book and thought you changed their lives."

"Two problems," Ella said, without hesitation. "One, they're putting me on a pedestal. I don't want to be on a pedestal. Just leave me on the ground, thank you very much. No one wins when anybody puts anybody else on a pedestal."

"I thought it was good for the pedestal person and bad for the people on the ground."

"You thought wrong. It's equally bad for everybody."

"I think people will need some clarification on that point."

"Fine. I'll give you an example. Years ago I was doing an interview for a newspaper, and I said this perfectly simple little thing. I don't remember the exact wording, but I was being critical of someone I felt—with good reason, mind you—had behaved badly. Well. This was back before email. This was back when people would send an actual letter to your publisher, and your publisher would forward it on. More than two dozen people wrote to me and told me they were disappointed in me. For what? For being aggravated with someone. But now . . . tell me. Is there a single human being on the planet who never gets aggravated with anyone? It's called being a person. But I was told that I had let them down by not being better than a person. I was their inspiration, so my job was to be inspiring. And nothing else. Everybody in the world gets to have a bad day, but not the great E. L. Swann. No. She must be all things to all people at all times. Does that sound enviable to you?"

"I suppose I see your point," Amelia said. "Thank you. This is good." She hadn't even meant to say the last bit out loud. It had just happened. "But keep going. Please. You said there were two things."

"Did I?"

"You did. See, this is the value of recording. But I think I remember this one well enough. You said you had two problems with the people who loved the book and felt it changed their lives."

"Oh. Wait. Where was I going with that? Oh yes, I remember. They think I have what they need. They read the book, and they find something in it. Something they've been looking for. Something that has eluded them up until that point. But what they don't realize is that I only triggered something—something that was in them already. I can't put anything into their psyche that wasn't already lying dormant in there. I can't inspire uninspired people. If you don't believe me, hand the book to an uninspired person. They'll be just as cynical when they set it down, believe you me. But the readers who adored it don't get that. They think I have something they want, and that they didn't have it until I gave it to them. And so they track this elusive something back to me. I've always said, 'Try not to be the person who has what someone else wants.' Like a poor Indigenous people whose ancestral home is sitting on valuable mineral rights. Once the searchers find out what's under there, they'll tear your life apart for their own gain. The readers who thought I changed their lives believed I had something inside me that they needed. And the problem with that, of course, is that they have to tear me apart to get at it."

"Whoa," Amelia said.

It dawned on her in that moment that she had not entirely "gotten" the author's departure herself. She had told E. L. Swann that her readers just assumed she was reclusive, and that they didn't get what they might have done to drive her away. But Amelia had not understood, either.

And, without realizing it, she had not expected the author's reasons for leaving to be well thought out, and to make perfect sense.

A movement caught her eye, and she looked up to see Jaden standing in the open archway to the living room, rubbing his eyes.

Amelia reached over and stopped the recording.

"You're awake," she said.

"I guess so."

"How do you feel?"

"Medium."

"You want something to eat?"

"No. I want to go see Francisco. And I want you to come, because I really, really want you to meet Francisco. He's the best donkey there ever was, and don't ask me how I know, because I never met any other donkeys. But I know. I just know."

"I'll go, but you have to take your antibiotics first."

"Ugh. Is it a shot?"

"No shot. You just have to swallow a pill."

"Okay then. I guess."

Amelia turned her attention back to the author.

"You okay with taking a break?"

"He makes a good point about the donkey."

"We're not done, though. I hope you know we're not done."

"Oh, honey," Ella said. "We haven't even begun."

They hurried across the terrace together, Jaden pulling her along roughly by the hand. He took her down a tended dirt path that seemed to curve around to the back of the house.

Amelia glanced over her shoulder to see if her host was following, but saw no one behind her.

"He lives back *here*," Jaden said.

When she turned to look ahead of her again, she saw a paddock made of split rail fencing surrounding a small stucco shelter with the same tile roof as the house.

"Francisco!" Jaden called. "Where are you? I brought my mom. I told you I wanted you to meet her."

The donkey stuck his head out of the shelter to look around, his comically long ears swiveling at their bases like radar devices.

He turned his nose to the sky, opened his mouth wide enough to show his teeth, and let out a noise that seemed alarming at first. It started out as a deep squeak and morphed into a full-on foghorn of sound, modulating in the animal's throat and rising and falling with his great gasps of breath.

They stepped up to the fence and so did Francisco.

He had a gray coat with a much lighter muzzle, and a curved, well-fed belly. His withers were marked with the characteristic dark cross.

"Hello, Francisco," Amelia said. "I've heard a lot of good things about you."

He reached out with his muzzle and seemed to snuffle the air in front of her face at close range. It made his nose appear delightfully and exaggeratedly large to her. She could see his velvety nostrils flare and twitch as he took the measure of her. His eyes were visible from that position, though one more than the other, and Amelia felt a strange sensation that the animal was trying to make a genuine connection.

She reached out a hand and stroked his long face.

"I think you're right," Amelia said in the direction of her son. "I think this is one very fine donkey."

"Told you," said a voice behind her.

She spun around to see Ella standing fairly close.

Jaden slipped between the rails and hugged the donkey around one of his hairy legs, and Amelia stepped back to stand by the author, close enough that they could speak without being overheard.

"You know," Ella said, "we can't go on with the interview until he's asleep again. He'll hear too much."

"Unless he's totally occupied elsewhere. I wonder if Marta would look after him."

"Marta has her hands full as it is. I think you need to settle in for the long haul."

"I suppose," Amelia said, feeling her dreams of holidays with her son slip away and disappear. It hurt to have them pulled out of her.

"You want to get it right, don't you?"

"Of course. Of course I do. But one question while he's too far away to hear. Why do you ride a donkey into town when you have the gator?"

"Look at Francisco," Ella said. "Really look at him, and then tell me he's not better than that noisy, oversized golf cart."

Amelia looked at the donkey for a time and said nothing.

"But you can't write about that," Ella said.

"Why can't I?"

"It's too much of a clue. It screams Mexico, or somewhere outside the US, and then everybody will be looking for sightings of an old woman riding a donkey into town."

"Right," Amelia said, feeling disappointed. It was a great note to the story—an intensely real visual that would have come alive in the reader's mind. "I guess I didn't think about that."

"And there could be other things you didn't think about. So you'll have to show me the finished piece. I need complete editorial approval before anything goes anywhere."

Amelia felt herself bristle at the suggestion.

"You realize no decent journalist would ever grant that."

"And *you* realize that this situation is utterly unique, and that you will grant it to me anyway."

"Yes," Amelia said, and sighed deeply and audibly. "I do realize that."

Chapter Nine

Two Unforgivable Questions

"When people don't know who I am," Ella said, "there's this lovely sense of equality to all of our interactions."

They were sitting outside on the terrace in the dark, the lights of town twinkling below them, a riot of stars twinkling above. Jaden had already gone to bed and was sleeping soundly.

"But then they find out," Ella added. She glanced at Amelia's phone, which was sitting on a small, low wicker table between them in the dark, its screen glowing. "Are you recording this?"

"I am. Is that okay?"

"Well, yes. Of course. I want you to get this right. So, to continue. I'm anonymous, and enjoying a simple exchange. This is back in the eighties when I was in the US, of course. Because since I've been here nobody has found out who I am. Not until you came along, anyway. The balance is a sweet thing. The person says something about him- or herself and then I say something about me. Repeat as necessary. Just two people. Very comfortable. Very fitting."

"Couldn't you just not tell them?"

"Well, I learned not to eventually. But for a time it tripped me up, because almost always the first question a person will ask is 'What do you do?' It's an odd question, isn't it? Well, anyway, it seems so to me. Because they don't say straight out that they mean professionally. 'What do you do for a living?' But that's what they mean, and if you don't believe me, try answering the question exactly as posed. 'What do I do? Well, let's see. I get up in the morning and wash my face. I take a walk. I eat three meals.' No, that will not fly. They want to know how you earn the money for those three meals, and I'm not sure how that became our defining quality.

"In any case, I would tell them. Because I was still naive. And in that moment, everything turns on a dime. Everything. The conversation is utterly transformed. Now their energy is excited and their voice too loud, and now there's no back-and-forth at all. Now I'm required to tell them all the things they've always wanted to know about a famous author. Now I'm a trained bear, performing for treats, but there are no treats. Not for me. It's now me giving and them taking, entirely. Now I am to put on a show by answering their questions.

"And a big part of the problem is that they're always the same two questions.

"Question number one: 'Where do your ideas come from?' Well, darling, if I knew *that* I would bottle the knowledge and sell it, and I'd be a very rich woman indeed. If I knew *that* there would be no such animal as writer's block. The ideas come from pure imagination. And, now: 'Where does pure imagination come from?' Of course I don't know. Nobody does. Really what they're asking, I think, is: From where do I copy these ideas? But I don't copy them at all. I think them up. Have you ever noticed that when a novelist is portrayed fictionally, in a movie or on television, they're never actually writing fiction? They are thinly disguising their own story or stealing the stories of the unwilling-to-be-stolen-from people around them. And while I can understand the housewife or the plumber thinking it must be this way, I'm not sure why the fiction writers who created the movie or the TV show don't know better. But I suppose I'm digressing.

"'Where do your ideas come from?' is the quintessential question one asks an author, and it's as old as time. It never goes away because we never answer it to anyone's satisfaction, and the reason we never answer it to anyone's satisfaction is because we don't know. They come from the ether. Once I got so frustrated with a woman interrogator that I asked her, 'What was the last idea you had and where was it before you had it?' 'Where was it before I had it?' she asked. 'Why, I don't understand that question at all.' 'Good,' I said. 'Now you have some idea how I feel.'"

She paused a moment and breathed deeply, as if she had been trudging up a steep hill instead of sitting still and speaking.

"Make sure that's really recording," she said. "This is important and I don't want any of it to be lost."

Amelia leaned over the phone and confirmed that she had almost five minutes in memory.

"It is."

"Good. Now where was I?"

"That was question number one. You said there were two."

"Right. Question number two. 'Do you base your characters on people you know?' Well, this is a silly question, because any fool can see that the people all around me—all around just about any of us—are not nearly interesting enough to carry a novel. No, back to question number one. *I'm making every bit of this up.* It's called being a writer of fiction.

"Now, I don't entirely blame people. I do realize that there are no purely fictional characters running around in their heads, so of course they lack the imagination to accept that they might be running around in mine. And I do realize that each of these individuals means no harm, and does not realize I've been asked these questions hundreds of times before. But the fact remains that I've been asked these questions hundreds of times before. And there's a special sinking feeling one gets when asked a question they've already answered countless times. It's like a huge, internal sigh. A sinking feeling in the gut. Pure psychic exhaustion. I simply get tired of saying the same thing again and again and again. I want to shout at them and tell them I only came to this place to choose a head of lettuce or drink a coffee or eat my lunch, and that everyone around me is enjoying this privilege in peace, and I'm the only one who seems to have no right to it. I want to shrink back into anonymity, but no. I'm a public figure, and I'm not entitled. I don't belong to myself anymore. I belong to the world. If someone says I must put on a show by giving a lecture on the life of an author, they fully expect me to obey.

"But after a time I stopped obeying. After a time I simply told people that I wanted to do what I wanted to do, not what they felt entitled to insist of me. And this of course is how I got a reputation for being a rude and abrasive person. Because I wanted to choose my head of lettuce or drink my coffee or eat my lunch in peace. I wanted simply to be a person like everyone else. I wanted my anonymity.

"And now, knowing all that, do you really question why I would make a move into permanent anonymity?"

Amelia breathed deeply for a moment.

"No, I really don't," she said. "I get it." She breathed a few more times, then added, "I apologize for barging into your life and breaking your anonymity and asking you questions."

"Thank you," Ella said. "I appreciate that acknowledgment. If not for your delightful young son I expect I would find it unforgivable. But he's been a real light in my life since you two arrived. I've been happier than I've been in as long as I can remember. So I suppose there's a give-and-take to the whole thing. And it does feel good to get these complaints off my chest. But enough for tonight. I feel quite wrung out now."

"Fair enough," Amelia said.

She reached for her phone, stopped the recording, and slipped it into the pocket of her slacks.

She leaned back on the lounge chair and they watched the brilliant night sky for a few moments in silence.

"At least I didn't ask you where your ideas come from and whether you base your characters on the people around you."

"And don't think I didn't give you points for that," Ella said.

—

The author disappeared into her room before ten p.m.

Amelia couldn't go to sleep that early, and she had no idea what else to do.

She tried lying down next to Jaden and engaging in something vaguely related to meditation, but she couldn't keep her mind—or, ultimately, her body—still for very long.

She got up and decided she would find a book from Ella's library and a small lamp by which to read in the massive living room.

As she walked down the dim hallway past her host's bedroom, she heard a distinctive sound. It was the rhythmic metallic tap of a person typing. But not on a keyboard, from the sound of it. It sounded like a typewriter.

Amelia hadn't heard that sound since her childhood, and she briefly wondered if it might be some kind of app made to imitate the old-fashioned typewriter experience. But just then she heard the bright ding that signaled the end of a line, and the zip of the carriage return. Did the apps do that? She didn't know.

She reminded herself that this was Ella of the flip phone. Ella who rode a donkey into town rather than use the four-wheel-drive utility vehicle. It made much more sense to imagine she was using a typewriter.

But to do what? To write what?

Amelia had no idea, nor did she think she had a right to ask. Really it wasn't any of her business.

E. L. Swann had opened up and allowed Amelia's investigation to probe far more deeply than either had likely expected. There was no point pushing the issue across some invisible line.

She continued walking to the living room in search of something to read. Anything that would help pass the time until she could sleep.

Chapter Ten

He Is Good Boy

When she woke in the morning, Jaden was staring into her face at very close range.

She blinked several times, trying to clear sleep from her eyes and achieve a sharper focus.

"Hey," she said.

"I'm bored," Jaden said. "I'm really, really, really, *really* bored."

"We go through this every time you're sick. Sometimes you have to stay in bed and rest even when you don't like it."

"I've been laying here for days."

"*Lying* here. And it's been less than forty-eight hours. And you haven't held still nearly as much as you think you have. You rode a donkey, for heaven's sake. You sat out on the terrace with Señora Steinbach and talked about space."

"Also I'm hungry," he said.

"That I'll try to solve for you."

Just as she finished the sentence, her phone let out a series of chimes from its spot on the bedside table. She reached over and turned off the alarm.

"Why did it say that?" Jaden asked her.

"It's time for your antibiotic."

"I don't need it. I feel fine."

"The doctor was very clear that you need to take them all." She swung her legs over the side of the bed and reached for her robe, which was draped over a nearby chair. "The reason you feel good is because you're taking them. If you stop taking them you'll stop feeling good."

"No, I'm fine. Really. Look."

He jumped out of bed, ran around to her side, and began doing jumping jacks in his Batman pajamas. He managed two without incident. On the third he wavered, lost his balance, and almost fell over backward.

"Oops," he said as she reached out to catch him. "I guess . . . maybe I only feel medium good. Maybe I should take them for just a little bit more."

They found Marta in the kitchen.

"Good morning, señora. You sit. I'm making pancakes."

"I want pancakes," Jaden said. Then, after Amelia gave him a stern look, he added, "Please."

"Sit down," Marta said. "I will fix them."

They sat at the kitchen table—a massive round wooden thing that looked very old—which had already been set for two.

"Where's Señora Steinbach?" Amelia asked.

"Working. She says she has work to do and she is not to be disturbed. She says you can take the gator today. I can show you how. It's easy. Maybe you take a boat ride or fly on one of those . . . what do you call that?"

"Parachute?"

"Sí. That."

"I don't really think Jaden is well enough to do something that energetic."

"Then you can take a drive down the coast. Very beautiful. Get lunch in town."

"You don't think she'll be done by lunch?"

"She says she will try to see you at dinner. But no promise."

"Dinner," Amelia repeated, unable to hide her shock.

She watched in silence for a few moments as Marta poured pancake batter onto a griddle. Apparently the batter had been made in advance of their getting up.

She turned to Jaden, who returned her gaze immediately.

"What?" he said.

"You're going to be spending Thanksgiving with your dad."

"Will you be there?"

"I'm afraid not."

"Why can't you be there?"

"Your dad wants to have you for the holidays. Possibly Christmas too."

"*Christmas too?* Why can't I spend them with you?"

"*Possibly* Christmas. Because we missed one of your weekends with him, and we might be about to miss another one. And he wants those holidays in return."

"That doesn't seem fair."

"No, it really doesn't. But he insists."

"What's 'insists'?"

"It means he won't have it any other way."

"He's like that a lot," Jaden said.

Amelia felt relieved, because she wanted that flaw in Mark acknowledged, but she hadn't wanted to be the one to say it. She had never wanted to be one of those parents who used her child as a sounding board for complaints about the ex.

"And anyway," she said, "if it happens that way, you'll have two Christmases. One on Christmas Eve with me and one on Christmas Day with him."

He said nothing for a time, but his eyes widened.

"Two is good," he said.

Marta set a stack of three pancakes in front of her and two small ones in front of Jaden. She delivered them at exactly the same time, one plate in each hand. She spun away, came back with a saucer of butter, which she set in the middle of the table, and held a glass bottle high.

"Syrup?"

"Yes, please," Jaden said.

"That's real maple syrup," Amelia said, eyeing the bottle.

"Sí," Marta said. "The good stuff."

"Where do you get real maple syrup around here?"

"Canada."

Amelia laughed, then slowly gathered that it had not been a joke.

"Canada is not exactly 'around here.' It's two countries away."

"She has them send it. Some things she is very, very picky about."

It left Amelia wondering if there was anything the author was *not* very, very picky about.

Then Marta turned away and began washing dishes.

Amelia poured syrup on her pancakes and wondered if she would really get another crack at continuing the E. L. Swann interview. Granted this was the first long, unexplained delay. But it was going slowly. And it was hard not to imagine that the author could change her mind without warning at any time.

She wondered if she could get by on what she had.

On the one hand, even ten words from the author would be ten words more than anyone had managed in forty years. But a good interview required more. Not just: "Why did you hate fame?" Also: "Why no second book?" And: "What made you so resistant to people before you were ever published?" And: "What do you see for your future?"

But Amelia's own future very much remained to be seen.

They rumbled down the rutted dirt road, Amelia pressing one foot on the brake and one on the gas, the way Marta had shown her. So the gator didn't take on a mind of its own on the steep downhill slope.

With one hand she held her hat in place.

"We need to get you a sombrero in town," she said. "Before we do anything else."

She had to raise her voice to be heard over the wind and the noisy engine.

"I don't know what that is."

"A hat," she said, steering around a deep rut.

She wasn't nearly as good as Marta at avoiding the worst parts of the road, and she bounced them around unmercifully.

"Then why didn't you just say we have to buy me a hat?"

"Because in Mexico they're called sombreros."

"Everything is called something else in Mexico, but you usually say it in English."

"But a sombrero is a whole different kind of . . . oh, never mind."

They rode in silence to the bottom of the hill, where Amelia was relieved to drive onto a flat, graded road.

"How do we know where to find a store that sells hats?" Jaden asked.

"A lot of the stores sell hats. Every souvenir store sells them. And every third store is a souvenir store."

"I don't know that word."

"It's something you buy that you can't get at home. Something that's special to the place where you took the vacation. And because it's special like that, it helps you remember that nice time."

She slowed and turned the corner onto the main drag, and immediately saw souvenir stores with racks of sombreros sitting outside their open front doors.

She pulled over and shifted the gator into park. Shut off the noisy engine.

"See?" she said. "Sombreros."

"Hats," Jaden said.

"Suit yourself. Just so long as you wear one."

They cruised slowly down the coast together, Jaden holding his new sombrero down with both hands, despite its having a cord that secured it under his chin.

It had taken only a couple of miles for almost all signs of civilization to disappear. Suddenly they were in a different world. The dark side of the moon, except beautiful, and adorned with water as far as the eye could see.

Rock mountains rose everywhere, often right at the edge of the gulf, creating tiny inlets that looked greenish-turquoise and were so clear that Amelia could see the mottled sand on the bottom, even from the road. Flocks of seagulls and some other seabird she did not recognize flew in shifting free-form groupings up and down the shore.

"Where are we going?" Jaden asked, raising his voice to be heard.

"I don't know," she said. "We're just taking a little tour of Baja, so we can see more of the place we're visiting. And really just to give us something to do with the day."

"We could have gone snorkeling or parachute sailing."

"I wanted to wait until you were feeling better for that."

"Oh. So we just keep driving?"

"Marta said there's a nice little spot south of Santa Rosarita that's really quiet and serene and not touristy, but where you can take a tour in a small boat and really see the gulf the way it should be seen. Not so many people and lots of natural wildlife, like birds and fish."

"Maybe that's it," he said, and pointed.

Down a long hill in front of them was a sandy beach with a rustic dirt parking area. No cars were parked there except the trucks that towed now-empty boat trailers—though a few hundred yards away there seemed to be a patch of RVs parked near the water. But there were at least twenty small boats on the sand, each with a person standing nearby or sitting inside.

She pulled in and parked the gator, and was immediately surrounded by boat operators. Each seemed to be offering them a tour, some in English and some in Spanish, but as they were all talking at once it was impossible to understand or respond.

Amelia unbuckled her seat belt, then her net door, and stepped out of the vehicle. She walked around to the passenger side, unbuckled Jaden, and lifted him out. And, without thinking much about it, she carried him over to the only boat operator who seemed inclined to let them come to him.

His boat was white and sleek, very long and narrow, with a pointed bow that seemed designed to cut wind resistance.

The man was extremely old. At least ninety, she thought, with a thin head of white hair and a long, wispy beard. He wore shorts and a tank top in the cool morning, and his skin was sunbaked and dark. His gnarled feet were bare.

He smiled as they approached.

"You pick just the right boat," he said. "You are very smart about that. My boat is better than all these other boats, and as soon as we get out on the water you will see exactly why."

"How much?" she asked, setting Jaden inside and settling him onto a bench seat.

"Thirty dollars US an hour. We will go maybe two hours. Longer if you like. I will show you the most beautiful spot on Earth. A bahía. You will think you are in Heaven. And if you like, we can fish. I have all the gear. Many fish. Best fishing anywhere."

She stepped in and sat.

"Okay," she said. "Deal."

The old man climbed out and pushed the boat off the beach and into the shallow water. For a moment it almost seemed as though he planned to send them out alone. But a moment later he came splashing up to the side of the boat, the water up to his thighs, and climbed aboard, tipping the edge of the boat frighteningly close to the water until he sat down behind them.

He pulled a cord and the motor roared to life. Though, once it had settled and shifted into gear, it was much quieter than Amelia had anticipated.

They slid across the water, away from the shore.

"Now you see why my boat is the best," he said. "Look down below your feet."

She and Jaden did as he had suggested, at exactly the same time. They found themselves looking down at the gulf floor. It was sandy, mottled with sunlight. A smallish striped fish with long spikes along its back swam by underneath them.

"It has no bottom?" Jaden—whose feet did not reach the bottom—asked, his voice full of alarm. "Then how does it not sink?"

"It has a glass bottom," Amelia told him.

"Not glass," the man said. "Very strong. I don't know how you say it in English, though."

"Plexiglas?"

"Maybe. Like plastic. But strong. I take you to the Bahía de Santa Rosarita. The most beautiful place on the Earth."

"I'm not sure what a bahía is," she said.

"I'm sorry. I don't remember how to say in English. But you will see."

Amelia slipped her phone out of her pocket, hoping to look up a translation. But she had no signal.

The boat slid over the water, and as they came around a bend in the shore, they saw hundreds of seabirds sitting on a forty- or fifty-foot rock stained white with their droppings.

Jaden pointed but did not speak.

They motored on.

Amelia took a tube of sunscreen out of her pocket and began to slather it on Jaden's face. He pulled his head away.

"I have a hat."

"But the sun reflects off the water."

"Then why did we even buy me a hat?"

"Because we won't be on the water all day."

Jaden sighed, but held still for the slathering.

"Mira," the old man said after a time. "Look."

They turned around to see where he was pointing.

A pod of dolphins was swimming through the water about twenty feet from the boat. As they swam, they arced up above the surface in a curved motion and then dove below again. It was nearly impossible to count them, as they were never all visible at the same time, but Amelia counted enough to guess there were well over a hundred. And they were moving at an impressive rate.

The man turned off the engine, and they drifted for several minutes in near absolute silence. The only sound was the lapping of the water as the dolphins broke its surface, and the wind across Amelia's ears.

Then, without warning, one of the dolphins leaped a good three to four feet into the air. It seemed to freeze there for a split second. Then it turned its nose down to knife back into the water, but it still made a powerful splash with its tail as it smacked the surface. The whole thing happened so close to the boat that Amelia felt two drops of gulf water hit her cheeks.

Jaden shrieked with surprise and delight.

They sat for several more minutes until the pod was nearly out of sight.

Then the old man started up the motor and they moved on.

"Maybe this is a thing you don't see at home," he said.

"This is definitely something we don't see at home."

"We go to the bahía now."

"What's a bahía?" Jaden asked her quietly.

"I have no idea," she whispered back.

Long before they reached their destination, Jaden fell asleep face down on the transparent bottom of the boat. He had stretched out down there to watch for fish, his face propped on his crossed arms, but the gathering morning sun and the rocking motion of the boat was too much for him, depleted as his poor little body had been.

Amelia watched the land and the small islands slide by, and enjoyed the way the sun glinted on the water. And she thought, *I get to have a vacation. I'm on a vacation.*

She tried to remember the last time she'd been able to get away. It was before Jaden had been born. Mark had made it a nightmare by finding every aspect of the trip lacking, and commenting loudly and petulantly about each disappointment.

But this. This was silent and calm. And, in that moment, it felt more perfect than she could remember any moment feeling. And it had sneaked up on her, because this was actually a tension-filled work trip. She had only pretended it was a vacation for Jaden's benefit.

But in that moment she remembered why people make the time to get away.

The engine cut out suddenly, jarring her back into the moment.

"Wake the boy," the old man said. "He must not miss this. He might never get another chance again in his life."

"What is it? I don't see anything."

"There," he said, and pointed. "Just below the surface, but you can see. A tiburón ballena."

"A what?"

"I don't know how you say in English."

Just then, Amelia saw.

It was swimming just beneath the surface, as he had said. Lazily. Slowly. She had no idea what it was, but she could see the full outline of the beast, and it was humongous. Startlingly huge. Longer and wider than the boat. Possibly over thirty feet long.

"Jaden," she said, and reached down and shook him by the shoulders.

"What?" he asked, sounding half drunk.

He opened his eyes, but didn't get up immediately. He just lay there, face down on the bottom of the boat.

And, just in that moment, the tiburón ballena swam underneath them.

"Holy cow!" Jaden shrieked and jumped into her arms in what seemed to be one smooth motion. "What *is* that?"

"A kind of shark," the old man said.

For a moment they just stared.

Its motions were laconic and smooth, as if it were drifting weightless in air. It had a strangely wide mouth at the very front of its strangely wide head, and patterns of white spots all up and down its body. It swam so effortlessly that Amelia was struck with a wave of envy.

"Why is it so big?" Jaden asked.

"I have seen them bigger," the man said.

"It's the size of a whale," Amelia said.

"Sí, that's what you call in English. I remember now. Whale shark."

As they talked, the behemoth made a lazy turn and moved toward the boat again, diving slightly to slide underneath.

Jaden grasped her more tightly.

"He's going to tip over the boat," he shrieked. "He's going to eat us."

The man laughed lightly.

"No, niño. The tiburón ballena, he is very . . . how do you say it? Placido. Pacifico."

"Peaceful," Amelia said.

"Sí. He is very peaceful."

"But he has to eat things," Jaden said.

"He is very big fish," the man said. "But he eat very little things. Tiny fishes."

Jaden turned his wide eyes up to hers.

"How can that be enough for him, Mom?"

"I guess he just eats an awful lot of them," she said.

And for the next several minutes they just watched the massive outline of his bus-sized body as he made lazy turns and circles and slipped beside and beneath them. He seemed almost to be drawn to the boat, the way its occupants were drawn to him. Jaden's grasp on her softened gradually.

Then the tiburón ballena swam away. And Amelia felt an unexpected but palpable sense of loss, watching him go.

"This is the Bahía de Santa Rosarita. The most beautiful bahía in the Sea of Cortez."

As he spoke, he turned the boat into a narrow inlet, with greenish-turquoise water so shallow and so clear she could see every detail of the tiny sea plants on its floor. And then it dawned on her what a "bahía" was.

"A bay," she said.

"Sí. Yes. That is it in English. I forget until you say. The Bay of Santa Rosarita."

"Wait," Jaden said. "The Sea of Cortez? I thought this was the Gulf of California."

"Sí," the man said. "Same gulf. Same sea. It is called by both names. You want to fish? I have everything you need."

"It's up to Jaden," she said.

They drifted along, watching dozens of dark birds with wide wingspans wheel and float on air currents above a mountain of loose-looking stones. They watched a striped eel and a silvery fish like a small tuna slide underneath them. Watched a massive sea turtle paddle by.

"No," Jaden said. "I don't want to fish. They're pretty. And they're peaceful. And they don't hurt us. I don't want to hurt them. I want them to keep swimming. I don't want them to have to die."

On the way back to the parking area, Jaden fell asleep face down again, watching the sea bottom and its inhabitants until he could no longer keep his eyes open.

"He is tired," the man said.

"He's been sick."

"Belly sick?"

"Yes."

"He will be better soon."

"I hope so," Amelia said.

"He is good boy."

And, just for a moment, when the old man said that, she stepped outside herself and saw her son as a stranger would. Saw him with new eyes, as if for the first time.

"Thank you," she said. "He really is."

Chapter Eleven

Even Literary Legends Get the Yips

"I remember the first time I saw a whale shark," Ella said. "I was out fishing in the gulf. This thing's finned back rose up out of the water, and I swear it was twenty-five feet long. The boat operator, he said, 'That's just a little one.' Turns out the biggest one on record was over sixty feet."

They were sitting together on the terrace in the dark, drinking wine. Jaden was off brushing his teeth and changing into his pajamas.

"I'm sorry if he talked your ear off about it during dinner."

"Oh, nonsense. It was nice to see him so excited."

Amelia had been expecting the author to offer an apology for leaving her guests to their own devices all day, no matter how perfunctory and insincere. She was just beginning to accept that none was forthcoming, and she was wondering why she had been foolish enough to anticipate any such thing.

Jaden popped out of the living room and onto the terrace.

"I'm ready to go to bed now," he said.

"I'll come tuck you in in a minute."

"You don't have to. I'm big. Good night, Señora Steinbach."

"Good night, honey," Ella said. "I'm glad you had such a good day."

"Oh, it was so great. It's the nicest place I've ever been to in my whole life. And I've been to *Big Sur*."

He fell silent suddenly. Amelia looked to his face for a sense of what he was feeling, but the only light was coming from the living room behind him.

"Oops," he added. "I think I wasn't supposed to talk about that."

He disappeared quickly into the house.

Amelia shook her head slightly and tried to let it go. To let things from home remain at home.

"May I begin recording?" she asked her host.

"Fine with me. And before you even ask a question, there's one other thing I want to say. There's one more question you should never ask an author. 'What is your book about?' Talk about demanding someone perform like a trained seal. Four hundred pages of sweat and blood, but just boil it down into two or three sentences for me. You know. Without making it sound any less deep or meaningful or exciting. Hard to imagine an author's heart not falling down into her shoes every one of the three or four hundred times that gem was thrown at her. After a while I started copying that author who would say 'It's about four hundred pages.' I don't remember who first said that, though."

Amelia felt a mild impatience, because this felt like complaining, and it was surfacy and without much substance. She wanted to get down to something real.

"Why no second book?" she asked her host.

Ella sat back against the wooden slats of her propped-up lounge chair. She took a long gulp of wine.

"No beating around the bush, I see."

"You know it's on everyone's mind."

"I guess I just didn't have a second one in me."

She's blowing me off, Amelia thought. *She dug down a little at first and now she's just giving me quick platitudes.*

Now the only question was what Amelia was going to do about it.

She could finesse the situation. Feed Ella more wine and more comfort and hope she would go deeper of her own accord. But a feeling in her gut told her it wasn't the way to go. E. L. Swann was tough and direct, and if Amelia did not show a similar degree of fortitude she risked losing the author's respect. And then it was over.

"That answer doesn't track," she said.

"Excuse me?"

"That's not the genuine answer."

"Well, if you know the answer, why did you ask the question?"

Ella was clearly on her guard now, and jabbing back. And Amelia was not at all sure she hadn't made a mistake.

"I'm not saying I know the answer. I'm saying I know that wasn't it."

"Enlighten me. Since you know more about the inside of me than I do. Tell me what part of my answer doesn't track."

"You said you don't copy your ideas from real life. You said it's called being a writer of fiction. Everything comes from the ether. From pure imagination."

She paused, just to test the ground on which she stood.

"And?"

"Pure imagination is not limited. And it's not *in* you. If you're pulling a book down from the ether it's coming from outside of you in some way. So you can't really say you don't have a second book in you, because in some very real ways you never had a *first* book in you. You pulled it in from pure imagination. It's not something one runs out of."

"Maybe I ran out of whatever it takes to pull it in."

"Okay, never mind," Amelia said. "We can talk about something else. Or I can just turn off the recording and we can try this another time. It doesn't seem like you're wanting to dig all that deeply tonight."

The tactic was brave and quite risky, and Amelia knew it. But she was doing it all the same, because it felt preferable to taking a helpless role in front of a woman who didn't seem to respect helplessness in those around her.

"You seem to have an idea of this place I'm not willing to go," Ella said. Her voice sounded detached and cool. The way it had before she had even admitted her identity. "Go ahead and tell me why you think I never wrote another book."

"I think you got the yips."

"The whats?"

"It's a kind of performance anxiety. Professional athletes get it sometimes. It's like you get too much 'in your head' about something and it ends up being this loop that you can't quite fight your way out of. It happens to a lot to authors who have overwhelming success with their debut novel. They can't stop second-guessing themselves. They can't seem to let go of trying to figure out how they captured lightning in a bottle the first time. And it becomes paralyzing. The writer's version of the yips."

"After everything I've told you already, that's what you think?" Ella's voice was full and deep and angry. "You think it had nothing to do with all the experiences I laid bare for you? How can you think that?"

"Because you could have written a second book from isolation. And avoided it all. You wouldn't have had to come back to the world to publish it. You could have just sent it to your agent and your editor and continued to live an anonymous life."

They sat for a long time in silence.

Amelia couldn't see much detail of the author's expression, but she seemed to be genuinely thinking. She definitely had no flippant answer for that. Which was not entirely surprising. It had been a bit of a checkmate move on Amelia's part.

"I'm going to have to sleep on that and get back to you," Ella said at last.

"Fine. I think that's probably a good plan."

"Now let me ask *you* a question."

"Okay."

"You're obsessed with this author and this book. You built a career in academia around it. You came all the way to Mexico because somebody showed you a picture of an old woman who might be me."

"Why?"

"Yes. Why?"

Amelia sighed deeply, and took a few more sips of wine before answering. Just as a way of gathering her thoughts.

Ella apparently got tired of waiting.

"Were you one of the readers I said bothered me the most? The ones who thought I had exactly what their life needed and were willing to tear me apart to get to it?"

"No," Amelia said. "It wasn't that. At least, not the way you mean it. I didn't have a hole in myself when I read that book. I might now, after a failed marriage, but I didn't then. It wasn't that I was in search of something outside myself. It was . . . okay, I avoided saying this the last time it came up, but . . ."

Then she paused, and wondered if she should really let this next part go. Especially to someone who could almost be described as an enemy combatant.

"I've never told anybody this before," she said as a preface.

"It's up to you how much you say."

"I really did have dreams of becoming a novelist."

"I knew it."

"Your book was . . . it wasn't what I needed in my own life exactly. It was like this perfectly formed example of what I wanted to be able to do. To give others. What I wanted to put out into the world. I guess I felt like if I could create something that beautiful I would never have to doubt the purpose of my own existence. It was just this perfect thing, and I wanted to be capable of something like it. I didn't want to drag something out of you. I wanted to *be* you."

Ella said nothing for a strangely long time.

When she finally spoke she said, "That's a good answer."

"Thank you."

"I'm going to have to give you better answers."

"I'm happy to hear you say that," Amelia said. "Maybe we'll both do a better interview after a good night's sleep."

In the morning, she and Jaden walked out of their room together, dressed and scrubbed. They found Ella in the kitchen with Marta.

Rays of light from the freshly risen eastern sun poured through a big wall of windows and lit up their host's face, and Amelia had the odd sensation that she might be seeing—really seeing—E. L. Swann for the first time. Every flaw and wrinkle, but also the window into the more important interior of the woman through her rich brown eyes.

Ella turned her gaze onto Amelia, and she did not seem to be exactly the person she had been the previous night. She was not distant or detached, or guarded. She seemed almost vulnerable. And she did not turn her gaze to Jaden, which struck Amelia as surprising.

"Marta," she said. "Take the boy out back with you to feed Francisco. And show him how to curry his coat. I need to have a talk with his mother."

Marta took Jaden by the hand and they walked out of the kitchen together. Ella turned her head to watch them go.

Then she turned back to Amelia, took three steps in her direction, and clutched her by the forearm. Hard, and with some kind of reaching or yearning. It felt almost alarming, but Amelia knew it meant something real was headed her way.

"Fine," Ella said, her voice intense. "I froze. You were right. I froze up and I couldn't do it again. Are you happy now?"

"No," Amelia said. "I'm not happy to be right. I didn't wish any of that on you. I just was hoping to hear a truthful account of it."

"Turn on the recording," Ella said. "I'll pour us each a cup of coffee. And I'll tell you what you want to know."

"You're sure you want this part recorded?" Amelia asked.

They sat out on the terrace together, the slant of morning sun in their eyes, blowing into their coffees. Yes, Ella had already told her to turn on the recording. But in an abundance of fairness, Amelia wanted to confirm.

"Of course I do. I want people to know this."

Amelia pulled out her phone and began to record.

"Go on. You were saying you wanted people to know that you froze up and couldn't write a second book."

"Yes. I want them to know. Because it goes to my being a person just the same as everybody. Like I told you before. I'm not better or worse than anybody else. People freeze up. We get scared. I'm people. Whether you think someone else is below being a person or whether you think they're above it, the effect is the same. You're not giving them space to have a normal amount of human foibles. But we all have them. So the sense that they're disallowed is restrictive to say the least. It takes you apart from your true self.

"I had no idea why people loved *Labyrinth* so much, so I had no idea how to do it again. I didn't know if I would hit that sweet spot a second time or miss it by a mile, though the odds seemed to favor the latter. And the praise I got for that first book . . . I don't even know how to describe it. I was treated like I laid golden eggs. Like I could do no wrong. That was my legacy. The woman who could do no wrong. But if I wrote a second, and it flopped, it was all over. Suddenly I'd be a flash in the pan. Someone who had hit and then missed. All the success I'd had would be seen as a fluke. So, yes. You were right. I got the yips. I didn't want to admit it at first. But then I couldn't sleep last night, and I was thinking about it, and I realized that by keeping that information to myself I was doing to myself what I always complain about other people doing to me. Holding myself to a higher-than-human standard. So I'm spilling my guts in the light of morning.

"Maybe I would have knocked it out of the park on my second go. Maybe I would have fallen on my ass. I chose not to find out."

Amelia opened her mouth to speak, but Ella was not done.

"But no, it wasn't even a decision. I got too scared of finding out, and I froze. And that's the honest answer."

Amelia picked up her coffee and took a sip. It was dark and strong, and it hit a spot inside her and hit it just right. And it perfectly underscored the moment, in which everything about her interview was just right, after a couple of distressing detours during which she had not been sure they'd ever find their way back.

"I got to *brush* him!" Jaden's excited voice said.

They looked up to see him standing with Marta at the edge of the terrace.

Marta looked at their faces and seemed to quickly size up the situation.

"You talk," she said. "I will go make breakfast. The boy, he can come with me and help."

"Okay," Jaden said, sounding cheerful.

They disappeared into the house.

"And I know it will sound strange to say it," Ella continued, "but even if I somehow could have known it would be great, I wasn't really clear on what you said last night. That I could have published a second book without leaving my complete isolation, and so avoided all the issues. I guess I must have known it on a purely mental level, but I suppose my gut didn't know it. My gut still saw it as leaving myself just as vulnerable as the first release did. And, in my defense, people would still have said everything they were inclined to say. They just wouldn't have been able to say it to my face. Now I suppose you'll say I could simply have avoided reading the reviews and comments, but could I really? Is it possible to look away from a thing like that?"

"I doubt I could do it," Amelia said.

"Thank you." Ella reached over and clutched at her arm in that intense and almost desperate way. "Go ahead and tell me what you think of everything I just told you."

"I think it all sounds very human," Amelia said. "It sounds like the kind of thing that could happen to anybody."

Ella didn't come out of her room until Marta was almost ready to serve their evening meal.

"What did you do all day?" she asked as they sat down at the dinner table on the terrace. It was clear that she was talking to Jaden. "Did you go into town?"

"No," he said, sounding disappointed. "I sort of wanted to but also I was sort of still tired from everything we did yesterday. I keep thinking I'm okay but then I'm not really all the way okay. Not as okay as I thought. Anyway, I was so, so, so bored. But then Marta went into town to buy fish for dinner and she brought me two coloring books and some crayons. So that helped. That was nice of her."

"That *was* nice of her," Ella said. "Very thoughtful." Then she turned her attention to Amelia. "Will he eat fish?" she asked quietly.

"Normally," Amelia said.

"But after that story he told at dinner yesterday about why he didn't want to fish . . ."

"I thought of that too," Amelia said. "I guess we'll see."

They sat quietly for a minute or two, watching the sun disappear behind the hills to their west.

Then Marta appeared with a steaming porcelain serving bowl, which she set in the middle of the table.

"Caldo de pescado," she said.

"Thank you, Marta," Ella said. "But be prepared to make a peanut butter sandwich. We're not sure if the boy will want to eat it when he knows it's fish."

"He knows," Marta said. "He helped me make it."

She ladled a serving into Jaden's bowl and he pitched in immediately.

"It's good," he said.

Marta ladled out a bowl for Ella, and one for Amelia, and hurried back into the kitchen.

Amelia took a sip of the stew—or soup, she wasn't sure—and it was heavenly. Fluffy white chunks of fish and small shrimp in a light tomato broth, with thinly sliced green chilis adding just the right amount of spice.

"So it's okay with you that it's fish?" Amelia asked her son.

"Yeah. I like fish."

"Okay. Good."

"I know what you're thinking," he said.

"Do you?"

"You were thinking I wouldn't want to eat them because I didn't want to catch any yesterday. I wanted them to keep swimming and I didn't want them to die. But I think it's different when you meet them first. Do you know what I mean?"

"I think so," Amelia said, and took another spoonful.

"Maybe it shouldn't be different. But it sort of is. I know they died. I'm old enough to know that. Do you think it's okay that I feel different because I didn't meet them first?"

"I think whatever you feel is okay," Amelia said.

"Okay, good."

They ate in silence for a long time, the light of evening taking on a dusky quality.

Jaden was the one to break the silence.

"What do you two keep talking about that you don't want me to hear?"

Amelia exchanged a glance with her host.

"It's not that we don't want you to hear it," Ella said. "It's just that it's extremely boring grown-up stuff."

"Like what?"

Another look was exchanged, and the job of fielding this one was wordlessly handed to Amelia.

"I might write a feature story about Señora Steinbach," she said. "A human-interest sort of thing. I think her life history is interesting. She lived in Germany as a very young girl," she said, slipping into the story Ella had created for the locals to go with her German pseudonym, "and then in the US for a long time, and she retired here in Mexico. She's led an interesting life."

"Is she the story you thought you wanted to do when we came down here?"

"No," Amelia said. "I was looking for somebody else. But Señora Steinbach is interesting enough."

Jaden looked up from his soup and into his mom's face, his expression open and utterly without guile or subtext.

"You thought that writer you like lived here. That swan lady."

Amelia felt it as a little electric jolt to her stomach.

"Why would you say that?"

"Because when she came to the gate you just kept talking about that writer lady."

"Oh," Amelia said. "That's right. I guess I did, didn't I?" Once again a glance flowed between the adults, conveying a nervous sort of "What else are we forgetting about?" message. "But it turned out that author doesn't live here after all," Amelia said. "I knew she might not, but I had to give it a try."

Jaden turned his attention to their host.

"You don't know anything about the swan lady?" he asked her.

Amelia waited to hear what lie Ella would tell, and to get a sense of whether and how much it bothered her to lie to a child for whom she held such affection.

But what the author said was "Not as much as one might hope, no."

It wasn't exactly a lie. More of a quiet inside joke for Amelia's benefit, especially relevant after their interview segments of the previous night and that morning.

She followed with a knowing glance in Amelia's direction.

"But it really worked out fine," Amelia said, "because we got to meet Señora Steinbach."

"And Francisco," he said.

"Yes, and Francisco. And I think she's interesting enough to write about."

"Are you going to write about Francisco?"

"I wasn't going to. No."

"Why not? I think you should."

"But he's a donkey. So even if he has an interesting life story, he can't tell it to me."

"Oh," Jaden said. "Right. That's true." He took another sip of his fish soup. "I agree with you. Señora Steinbach is an interesting person to write about."

"We were lucky to meet her."

"I think so too," he said.

Then he finished his bowl of soup in silence and asked for a second helping.

Chapter Twelve

This

They sat out on the terrace after dark, after Jaden had gone to bed, each drinking a small glass of cognac.

Marta came out with a dark wooden box, opened the lid, and extended it in Amelia's direction. She was surprised to see that it was filled with thick cellophane-wrapped, banded cigars.

"No, thank you," she said, and waved it away.

Also surprisingly, Ella accepted one, along with a couple of small tools, and a lighter that appeared to be sterling silver.

Marta disappeared into the house, turning off the living room lights on her way through. As Amelia's eyes adjusted to the darkness she watched her host trim the base end of the cigar in preparation for lighting it.

Ella glanced over at Amelia as though she'd forgotten she had guests.

"Turn on the recording," she said.

Amelia set the phone to record and watched the author puff on the cigar until it was fully lit and drawing.

Once again Ella glanced over at her guest as though her presence was unexpected.

"Don't just sit there," she said. "Ask me a question."

"Tell me what you see for your future," Amelia said.

Ella puffed. Leaned back in her lounge. Sighed.

"I think when I tell you, you won't understand. That's not to suggest that I think you're stupid. You're obviously an intelligent woman. But you're young."

"I'm not that young," Amelia said.

"You're in your thirties, yes?"

"Late thirties. I won't be in them much longer."

"Then you're about forty-five years younger than I am, and I'm not sure that's old enough to understand the answer you're about to hear from an eighty-four-year-old woman."

"Try me," Amelia said.

Ella smoked without speaking for a moment. Amelia could just barely see the milky darkness of the curls of smoke in the starlight and the faint glow of lights from town. She watched the bright-red heater at the end of the cigar glow as Ella puffed. She wondered if it was only happenstance that they mostly conducted their interview sessions in the dark. Of course they had to wait until Jaden was asleep, but a few lights on in the living room would have lit up the area where they sat. Maybe Ella chose darkness for a reason. Or maybe she simply liked darkness.

The orange cat jumped up onto Amelia's lap and arched her back when Amelia stroked along the length of it, tail trembling.

"You know how these websites you go out to these days . . . ," Ella began, "you have to remember your username and password, but then they have a group of security questions. If you need to reset your password they'll ask you one of the questions to verify your identity."

"I'm familiar," Amelia said.

"Mostly they're silly little things like the name of your first pet or the street you grew up on. But I had one a month or two ago that was more interesting. It asked, 'If money were no object, what would you do all day?'"

"That *is* more interesting," Amelia said, wondering where they were going with this.

"Can you guess my answer?"

"Not a clue."

"I'll give you a hint. It's only four letters long."

"I haven't the faintest idea," Amelia said.

"'This.' My answer was 'This.' The future looks different when you're eighty-four years old. That's not to suggest that I think I don't have one, or much of one. I'm healthy enough and I could live to be a hundred and four for all we know, but the whole idea of these big plans for your future, that's for younger people. And I don't say it enviously. I'm not suggesting it's great to have big plans and ambitions and sad to be an old person and not have them. As you grow older you start to realize that ambitions are nothing more than schemes to fill the holes in yourself. You feel as though you're missing something, but you have this bright idea of how you can get hold of it and fill the void. But it never works, so you have to keep conjuring up new ambitions. I'm not missing anything. I have nothing I need to achieve. I've found peace here, and I'm happy. And that's what I plan to do with the rest of my life. This."

They sat in silence in the dark for a time, Amelia feeling strangely aware of the fragrance of the tobacco and the sound of the cat's purring.

"What about *you*?" Ella asked after a time.

"What *about* me?"

"You're young. What do you see for *your* future? Are you ever really going to write that novel you said you wanted to write?"

"How did this get to be about me?"

"You're asking *me* questions. Why can't I ask *you* one?"

"But you're the—"

She stopped herself suddenly.

"I'm the what?" Ella asked, clearly with her back up now. "What were you about to say?"

"Nothing. I don't know what I was going to say. Just that you're the subject of the interview, I guess."

"You were going to say that I'm the public figure. You're a private person and you have a right to keep your hopes and dreams private, but I'm famous and I have no such right."

Amelia did not answer straightaway.

"Admit it," Ella added.

"I'd love to say you're wrong," Amelia said. "But it did have a similar feeling to that. I'm sorry."

"What did I tell you?"

"You're right. I'm sorry."

"You can't help it. It's human nature. It's what people do to each other. I don't like it one bit, though. Now answer the question."

"Oh. I still need to answer the question?"

"You do."

"Okay. I guess . . ." She shifted in her lounge chair for a few beats. "I guess the honest answer is . . . I don't know. The plan was for me to begin by writing during the day when Jaden started school. And then I was going to write full time when he went away to college. But then my marriage fell apart and I had to go back to journalism. Which I like, but it leaves no extra time. And it's looking more and more like he'll end up living at home and attending community college, money being what it is. So I honestly don't know. I don't even know if I can do it. I don't know if I'd be any good."

"As opposed to everybody else," Ella said. "All the other people, everybody in the world except you, who go into a new endeavor with a full guarantee of exactly how it will work out for them."

"Okay," Amelia said. "Point taken. But the answer is still that I don't know."

"That's honest enough."

"I have to think if I even have more questions for you," Amelia said. "I might have enough to work with."

That seemed to upset her host.

"Nonsense," Ella said. "Why, we've barely scratched the surface. Sleep on it. I'm sure you'll think of a million more things we can talk about on the record. I'll think about it too."

It surprised Amelia, to phrase it mildly. After all, E. L. Swann had been clear that she was participating in the interview only under duress. And now she seemed unwilling for it to end. And Amelia had no idea why.

"I guess I do have one more question," she said.

"Shoot."

"Do you have any kind of work you do besides writing fiction?"

A long pause fell.

"I'm not even sure I understand the question."

"It's pretty straightforward. What other work do you do besides writing?"

"Nothing," Ella said in a cloud of cigar smoke. "I have no other work. I thought that was clear."

"So if you hole up and say you're working all day . . ."

Amelia felt an imaginary gate slam shut. She wasn't sure *how* she could feel it. There was no light by which to gauge her host's expression, and Ella hadn't responded yet.

"No," Ella said after a time. Her voice sounded the way it had at the gate when Amelia and Jaden had first arrived. "Not that. I've made very little off-limits to you, out of the goodness of my heart, but *that* is a bridge too far."

"Fine," Amelia said. "Sorry. Just pretend I never brought it up."

Another long silence fell, and this one felt decidedly uneasy.

"There must be something else," Ella said.

"I did mean to ask you more about your low opinion of people. You told me everything they did to offend you after your book was published, but then you said you already hated people by then. So tell me what that's all about."

"What do you mean, what it's all about?"

"I mean why? Did you have some horrible experience?"

"See," Ella said, sounding perturbed, "now that's a lazy way to go at a thing like that. Just assuming I'm painting everybody with the same brush because some big awful thing happened to me. It's also a little bit offensive, because it assumes that the fault is mine. You're telling me you figure people are fine, and I'm letting some bad experience color my opinion of everyone, even those not responsible for the trauma. So it's me that's the problem, not them. I beg to differ. I didn't have one big, bad experience. I had thousands of little ones. I have a low opinion of people because they earned it. People are self-serving and totally ruled by their fears. They'll claw you to pieces to feel a tiny bit safer and they don't even have the self-awareness to see what they're doing. And it's only getting worse. Societies are falling back into unenlightened tribalism. Everybody judges everybody else, and tries to change everything they don't like about the people around them to make themselves more comfortable, and nobody takes a closer look at him- or herself, because their self-image depends on defending to the death the notion that they're fine and everybody else is the problem. We're a mess."

"Hmm," Amelia said. "Very dark."

"I didn't make us dark. I'm just reporting it. What about you? You don't see what I'm saying? You think people are swell?"

"I see what you're saying, but it's not all I see. I also see people having a capacity to be kind and good. They're both true, and probably in equal measure, and I think our job is not only to decide which way we'll fall, but to decide which aspect in others is going to get most of our attention."

"Rose-colored glasses," Ella said.

"That's oversimplifying my answer. But I want to back up a minute. You say everybody judges everybody else. But didn't you just judge everyone quite harshly in that last tirade?"

"You're missing the point," Ella said. She puffed furiously on her cigar for a moment, causing it to glow red in the dark. "I said people judge others and then try to change what they don't like about them to make themselves more comfortable. And no, I don't do that. I judge people, but I leave them alone. I judge them on the one area in which I truly have a right to render judgment: Is this a person I want in my life? And with nearly all of them the answer is a resounding 'No.' But I don't burden them with my judgments. Are you following me now?"

"I'm not sure," Amelia said. "Maybe."

"I'll give you a good example. More than once after the publication of *Labyrinth* I received letters from readers who said they were enjoying the book, but they wouldn't finish it, or read anything else by me, because I used 'bad language.' Swear words. And that offended them, and they actually went to the trouble of writing to me to tell me I was wrong to do such a thing."

"Wait," Amelia said. "I'm surprised. That book was so clean. I can't even remember any swearing."

"That's what *I* said!" Ella nearly shouted, obviously unable to control her emotions. "Four rather mild expletives in the whole book, and here they are making sure I know that they're boycotting me for it. But boycotting me is fine. They have every right to. What was not fine was when they crossed the line into telling me I shouldn't use those words. That there are other, better words, and I should stick with those. As if I'm going to let each of my readers dictate what words I may not use. How soon would I run out of acceptable words? Seriously?

"But I'm skirting around the problem. The problem is trying to change those around you so you don't have to be uncomfortable. You want clean language only? Fine. Close the book and set it down. I will defend to the death your right to do so. Live a life free of swear words if it pleases you. But don't tell me it bothers you so I don't get to do it.

That's the kind of judgment I'm talking about. That's what I can't abide. And no, I don't do that. I don't try to change people. I only close their covers and set them down, as I have every right to do."

"This is good," Amelia said. "This is good stuff. And for some reason you seem not to want me to say this, but . . . I think it's enough."

"I'll think of some stories," Ella said, her voice breathy. Just at the edge of fear. "Just let me sleep on it."

"I have no problem with that. I'm happy to hear whatever you have to say. I just have to be home by the end of next week."

Amelia woke in the morning and discovered that she was in bed alone.

She rose and dressed quickly, and found Jaden in the kitchen eating scrambled eggs and toast with Marta and Ella.

"Hi, Mom," he said.

"Hi, honey. Sorry I slept so late."

"It's fine. I'm just going to finish really fast and then Marta is going to go saddle up Francisco and I get to ride him while you and Señora Steinbach talk."

Amelia sat at the table and tried to meet her host's eyes. She failed. Ella would not return her gaze.

"You thought of some stories?" she asked the author.

"No."

Jaden shoved what should have been the last three bites of his eggs into his mouth all at once and dragged Marta out the door before he had even finished chewing.

When they were alone in the kitchen, Amelia tried again to catch Ella's gaze. This time it worked. Their eyes locked.

"I'm begging you to stay," Ella said.

"But why?"

"I have my reasons. Can't you just trust me on that?"

"I can't stay beyond late next week. I'm sorry. I wish I could. Nothing would make me happier than to spend the whole summer with my literary hero. But I have to be back by next Friday."

"Fine," Ella said. "Go. But leave the boy."

Amelia laughed nervously.

"That's a joke, right?"

"Well, I didn't really mean it to amuse, but I wasn't seriously proposing it. I'm not detached from reality. I know you never would."

"I'm not the one who needs to get back. It's Jaden. I have an informal custody arrangement with my ex. His dad. I already missed one of his weekends, and it looks like I'm about to miss a second. If I do I'll be trading off not only Thanksgiving but also Christmas. That's what he wants in return."

"Why do you let him strong-arm you like that?"

"I don't really have a lot of choices here. This is a friendly arrangement. It's not court ordered. But nothing is really friendly between us. It's an acrimonious divorce. I'm violating our casual agreement, and we both know it. And if I violate it too many times he can haul me to court, and I could end up in a position where I couldn't take my own son on a Mexican vacation without my ex's written approval."

Ella stared out the big bank of eastern windows for a minute or two without answering.

Then she seemed to shake off some invisible fog, as if waking herself from a dream. She turned her attention to Amelia again.

"Get some coffee," she said. "Get some eggs. There are still some in the pan. There's a plate on the counter for you."

Amelia rose and crossed to the stove, and began to serve herself.

"Can't you tell him how very important it is?" Ella asked from behind her.

"Funny you should mention it. No. I can't. That's the whole problem. If I could tell him I had a chance to spend time with none other than the legendary E. L. Swann, well . . . honestly, I don't know what he would do. He might force me back just to prove he's in control. But at least I'd have a fighting chance of making him understand. But I can't tell him that. I can only say I found someone else interesting to interview, but how long can that possibly take? I can say Jaden is enjoying the vacation and I promised him a bunch of fun activities, but we all know that everything a boy can do here will fit into the coming week. So, no. I can't tell him how important it is. And that's not helping my case."

She brought the plate of eggs and a cobalt-blue mug of coffee back to the kitchen table and sat. She looked directly at her host, who avoided her eyes.

"How about you tell me why it's so important to you," Amelia said. "You've made no secret of the fact that you never wanted me here, and this is a big, wide U-turn on your part, to say the least."

"I want *him* here," Ella said immediately.

"I know you like him, but come on. We can always come visit you again."

"No, that's not good enough."

"Tell me why."

"Okay," Ella said. "All right. You leave me no choice."

Then, for a long time, she said nothing. Amelia only took bites of her eggs and waited.

"I'm working on something," Ella said at last.

"A new book."

"Yes."

Amelia's hands and feet tingled, and something inside her jumped with excitement, even as she said to herself, *But you already knew that.* The reaction came all the same.

"As you so rudely pointed out," Ella continued, "it's the only work I do. For the first time in forty years I'm actually working on a new book. And it's because of him."

"Are you writing about him?"

"No! Of course not! Don't you listen?"

"Right. Sorry. I did hear you. You don't base your characters on the people around you. You write from the ether. So what do you need Jaden for?"

"I don't know, but I do. I think he makes me believe there can honestly be a human being on the planet worth writing about."

Amelia said nothing, because her head was beginning to spin with the realization that there could be a second book by the author, and that she could have some part in making it possible.

But she couldn't. That was the plain truth. That was the problem. She had to get Jaden home.

"I have almost thirty-five pages," Ella said.

"It's only been two or three days."

"I know."

"Is that unusually fast for you?"

"Not really. *Labyrinth* just flowed out of me like that. I think it's a good sign. The only thing is . . . I don't know if it's any good. How do I know if it's any good?"

"I guess . . . the same way you knew *Labyrinth* was good?"

"But I didn't! That's what I'm trying to tell you. Am I not making myself clear, or are you not listening? I had no idea *Labyrinth* was good until other people told me it was. I was just lost in it. And now I'm lost in this. I have no idea how to judge."

Marta walked into the kitchen, stopped short, and assessed their faces with a nervous expression.

"You want I should go?" she asked.

"No, it's fine," Ella said. "Our guest just needs some time to think."

"Who's watching Jaden?" Amelia asked.

"Francisco will take care of him. I told him not to go outside the gate."

"I'm not comfortable with this," Amelia said.

She rose, leaving her coffee and eggs, and walked through the living room and out onto the terrace.

She found the path that led around behind the house, and made a complete loop of the property without seeing a donkey or her boy. With each turn and each hurried step she grew a little more panicky.

When she arrived back at the terrace, Jaden was there. He was standing on the ground, holding the donkey's reins and talking to Ella.

"Honey," she said, running to him. "Did you fall off?"

"No. I didn't fall. But I wasn't good."

"What do mean you weren't good? What did you do?"

"Marta told me not to go out the gate, but I wanted to ride him into town like Señora Steinbach does."

"All by yourself?" Amelia practically shrieked.

"It doesn't matter," Jaden said. "Francisco wouldn't let me do it. I tried to ride him right up to the gate so I could open it, but he kept backing away. So I got down and opened the gate, but he wouldn't let me get back up again. He kept moving. I was holding his reins and then he pulled me all the way back here."

Amelia exchanged a look with her host.

"Told you," Ella said. "That donkey is like a male nanny."

"A manny," Amelia said again.

"You keep saying that, but I don't know what it means."

"It's so completely self-explanatory!" Amelia bellowed. Then she realized she had yelled at her lifelong hero. "Sorry," she said. "I'm just upset. Good donkey," she said in Francisco's direction.

The donkey looked back at her and blinked lazily.

She turned her attention down to her son.

"And you get a time-out in your room," she said.

"My room is in San Francisco."

"You know what I mean."

He sighed, handed the reins to Ella, and shuffled off into the house, shoulders slumped.

Amelia and Ella looked directly at each other for what felt like a long time.

"Just think about it," Ella said.

"There's nothing to think about. You can talk to him on the phone every day. We can do video calls. But I have to get him home. I'm not going to risk losing him to my ex. He's the only thing in the world that's more important to me than the work of E. L. Swann. I'm sorry, but I have to take him home."

Chapter Thirteen

Watch Out for Sudden U-Turns

"What are you going to say to Señora Steinbach?" Amelia said.

She was standing in the kitchen behind Jaden, a hand on each of his shoulders.

It was the following morning, but it was the first they had seen of her since Jaden's time-out in his room for donkey-riding infractions. She had not come out for dinner the previous evening. She had typed straight through.

"I'm sorry, Señora Steinbach," he said.

Ella looked up from her coffee, but the look in her eyes said her mind was still far away.

"For what, dear?"

"For trying to ride Francisco where I wasn't allowed to."

"Apologize to your mother for that. She's the one who was worried for your safety. I knew the donkey would look after you."

"I did apologize to her," Jaden said. "But then she told me all about how he's your donkey, not mine, and if you say I can ride him, I have to ride him just exactly how you say I should, because he's not mine."

"Well then," Ella said, "I accept your apology. What are you two planning on doing all day?"

"My mom decided I was okay enough to do the fun things she promised me."

"We're going to go parasailing," Amelia said. "And maybe snorkeling, or maybe we'll save that for another day, depending on how tired he gets, and how fast. This is all assuming I can borrow your utility vehicle again."

"Of course, dear," Ella said, still seeming far away. "My gator is your gator. Get some fresh fish just as the boats come in. I'll try to get free to join you for dinner."

They bounced down the hill together in the gator, the cool wind of early morning sailing by their ears and threatening to take their hats away.

"After we go home," Amelia said, her voice raised to be heard over the wind and the engine, "Señora Steinbach will want to call and talk to you. Maybe she'll call a lot. Maybe we'll do video chats. Is that okay?"

"You think she'll take the phone out back and let me talk to Francisco?" he asked, holding down his sombrero with both hands.

"She has a flip phone, honey. But also . . . you have to promise me you'll talk to her too. I don't want you hurting her feelings by making her think you like Francisco better than you like her."

"I like Francisco better than I like just about anybody. But I like Señora Steinbach."

"You do?"

"Yeah. A lot."

They reached the end of the dreaded dirt road and pulled out onto the flat and graded road into town.

"What do you like about her?"

"I guess the way she talks to me and the way she listens to me. She asks me what I think about things. And then I tell her, and she listens. Grown-ups don't usually do that. They talk to me, and I'm supposed to listen, but when I talk to them they just act like I'll know something when I grow up and why bother listening till then?"

Amelia felt her face twist into a frown. She slowed quickly to avoid a pickup truck approaching an intersection unmarked with anything like a stop sign.

"I hope *I* don't do that to you," she said.

She accelerated again, headed for the beach.

"Less than most grown-ups," he said. "And then also she talks to me like I'm a whole person. You know. Not just a kid. Sometimes she goes too fast or uses big words and I don't get it. But then she stops and asks me if I get it, and if I don't she'll say it some other way. But she never says it like I'm stupid."

"Nobody thinks you're stupid. You're obviously a bright boy."

"But I'm a kid. And grown-ups think kids are stupid. But not Señora Steinbach. She thinks most kids are nasty little rug rats. But not me. She says I'm different. And she talks to me like I'm different."

"That must feel good."

"It does."

"What does she ask you about?"

"Different things. She just wants to know what I think about things. People. Life. Animals. The stars. She just wants to hear what I think. It's nice."

"I guess that *would* be nice," Amelia said.

"I don't know how many times she'll call. I might run out of things to tell her. I only have just so many things I think. But I'll try."

"I think we should let them go first," Jaden said, and he sounded more frightened than polite.

They were on the speedboat, and there was only one other party waiting to parasail, a young couple who spoke to each other in German and mostly smiled and waved rather than speaking.

"Is this making you nervous?" she asked Jaden.

"Sort of. But I want to do it. I just want to see *them* do it first. Is that okay?"

"Of course. They're probably happy to go first."

They watched in silence as one of the boat operators helped the other two passengers secure their side-by-side harnesses. The couple sat on a flat, nonskid platform on the back of the boat, and then eased onto sturdy nylon seats, like flexible swings. Their torsos were then surrounded by a number of straps that kept a person from falling.

Next a kind of pantomime took place—charades between two sets of people who both spoke languages Amelia and her son did not. But the boat operator seemed to be asking them if they wanted to be dipped down into the water. He used his hand to indicate the sweep of downward motion.

The couple smiled, nodded, and flashed two perfectly timed thumbs-up.

The boat took off; the brightly colored, striped parachute opened and rose; and the couple soared high above the water over the wake of the boat.

"Whoa," Jaden said.

He had to shout to be heard over the roar of the boat's motor.

"Does it look like fun, or does it look scary?"

"Kind of both," he said.

"Do you still want to do it?"

"I think so."

"You don't have to."

"I know. But I think I'll do it."

He sounded nervous, though.

The boat eased around in a wide but rapid circle, causing the parachute to turn in an arc behind it.

"They look like little ants," Jaden said. "They're really, really high up."

"We could tell them we don't want to go so high."

"No. I want to go high. I think." After a small silence he added, "Do you think the harnesses are really good and strong?"

"I do," Amelia said. "I think they do this all the time and they know how to do it safely."

"Okay then."

Before he could even finish agreeing, the parachute and its dangling occupants lost altitude rapidly until the lower halves of their body dipped into the water, creating a wake of their own. Throwing walls of water out behind them, and causing them to let out sharp squeals.

"It's not working!" Jaden shouted. "He's dropping them! It's not safe!"

"No, honey, he's dipping them in the water. He asked if they wanted that and they did."

"Are you sure? Who would want that?"

"A lot of people think it's fun."

"I don't want that," Jaden said. "Tell them I don't want that."

"Okay, I will."

"Don't forget."

"I won't. I promise."

"No dipping."

"Got it," Amelia said. "Definitely no dipping."

As the boat started up again and lifted them off its deck, Jaden reached out for her hand.

They held hands tightly as they rose.

"We're going so high," Jaden said.

"Is it okay?"

"I don't know."

From their current altitude the boat looked about the size of a cigar floating on the water, and Amelia could see the town spread out below them. She watched him swing his bare, dangling legs nervously.

"You're not afraid of heights," she asked him. "Are you?"

"I think I might be," he said.

"Why did I not know that?"

"Because I've never really been at any heights before, I guess."

"Do you want me to signal them to bring us down?"

"No, I want to do this. But don't let go of my hand."

They sailed around in an arc, holding hands. Each looking down and around at the hills and beaches, the sprawling home where they'd been staying, and the fishing boats and Jet Skis on the water.

"Do you want to go snorkeling when we're done here?" she asked him after a time, still at high altitude. "Or would you rather do that tomorrow? It's okay if you're tired. I know you're still not all the way back from being sick."

For a moment, he didn't answer.

Then he said, "Can I say what I really think about that?"

"Of course."

"I don't want to go at all. I don't want to go in the water."

"Okay. It's up to you. Do you know why?"

"It was that big whale shark we saw, that was, like, the size of a bus. I mean, I liked him. I'm glad we got to see him. But it was scary when he went under the boat, even though I knew there was a boat bottom. But if it was just me and no boat bottom . . . I know the man said he only eats little fishes. But he's not the only kind of shark out here. Right? Now that I know what could be under there, I just don't want to be in the water at all."

"Okay. I understand. I was just trying to think of fun things for you to do."

"I know that," he said. "But it's nice up at Señora Steinbach's house. And really . . . I just want to ride Francisco again. That's really all I want. That's definitely the best, best thing you could let me do."

"I'll tell you what we'll do," Ella said over dinner.

They were sitting out on the deck in the last of the evening sun, eating the fish Amelia and her son had brought back from town. Marta had grilled it with local vegetables, and Jaden was wolfing it all down.

"Tomorrow is the fresh market in town," Ella continued. "When the farmers bring fruit and various produce. We'll go down there tomorrow, the three of us. You and I will go in the gator," she said, turning her attention to Amelia. "And Jaden will ride Francisco into town."

"Yes!" Jaden shouted, and pumped his fist in the air.

Amelia felt her eyes grow wider.

It was not the sort of offer one should make in front of the child in question, because if the mother was concerned, it tended to create a conundrum. Her child had already been offered something wonderful, and no parent wanted to be the mean monster who ripped it away again.

Ella seemed to be gauging her reaction.

"Oh, stop worrying, darling," she said in Amelia's direction. "We'll be right behind him."

"I just keep thinking about all those intersections in town with no stop signs."

"I've been doing it for years and never had a problem."

"But he's a novice rider."

"Trust the donkey," Ella said. "Not the rider. He knows how to protect the boy and himself. He's not going to step out in front of a speeding car. He's not stupid. He's stayed alive all this time, and he has his heart set on continuing the streak."

Amelia sat in silence for a moment, then took another bite of her fish.

"And then the following morning," Ella said, "I think you two should head home."

Amelia's head snapped up. She stared at her host, who refused to return her gaze.

"I don't understand," she said.

"I know you want to spend Christmas with your son, and I feel guilty for begging you to stay."

Amelia mulled that over for a moment, then shook her head several times.

"You really are the queen of those sudden U-turns," she said, "aren't you? And no signal to warn the cars around you, either."

"I believe it was Gandhi who said, 'I serve truth, not consistency.' Though I probably slaughtered the quote. In any case you'll give me your address and your phone number and your email and all that. And I'll have conversations with the boy. It will all work out."

Still the author would not meet her gaze, and Amelia was left with the impression that there was some kind of subtext. Something she was not being told.

Chapter Fourteen

The World Will Right Itself Tomorrow

They followed Jaden and Francisco down the hill at, literally, two miles per hour. Amelia was driving, because Ella had insisted.

I hate that thing, she'd told Amelia. *You drive.*

"I feel like there's something you're not telling me," Amelia said, staring at the donkey's round behind.

"Even if that were the case," Ella said, "it's not something you can do anything about."

"Oh, that's cryptic. And kind of annoying."

"What can I tell you, darling? We never entirely know what another person is thinking, do we? Do I strike you as being a woman who lays all her cards out on the table? I'm trying to respect your desire to get back on time. I should think that's something you'd appreciate."

Amelia thought it was interesting that Ella had understood her reference exactly. Especially since it was the following afternoon, and no additional mention had been made of their leaving.

Jaden turned around in the saddle and waved enthusiastically, a big grin on his face. They both waved back.

"I've been rethinking our cover story," Ella said. "I don't think you should say you got another tip. I don't think you should go off on another trip. Or pretend to, anyway. No sightings for forty years and then two tips in a few months? Seems a bit coincidental. I think we should leave it that *I* found *you*."

Amelia felt her brow furrow.

"That makes no sense."

"It makes perfect sense. I'm eighty-four years old. I realized I had quite a few things I wanted to say to my public before it was too late. So I sought you out."

"But how would you even know I was the person to find? How would you even know I existed?"

"Because I read your thesis."

Amelia stomped on the brake without really meaning to. They sat, unmoving, for a moment. The donkey and the boy got several steps too far ahead.

"You mean you'll pretend to read it? Which still doesn't explain how you even knew it existed, and that it was about you."

"No, I mean I read it."

"When? Since I got here?"

"No, I read it when it was first published."

Amelia sat a moment longer, trying to sort out the threads of information in her head. Then she realized Jaden and Francisco were leaving them too far behind, and she accelerated down the bumpy hill again.

"So when I came to your gate," she began, "and told you who I was, you knew my name. You knew my work. You had read everything I'd written about you."

"Yes."

"So you kept up with everything people were writing about you, long after claiming to want to leave it all behind."

"I'm only human, darling."

"And you didn't tell me this because . . ."

"When would you have had me say it? Right before or right after I claimed never to have heard of this E. L. Swann person?"

"Got it," Amelia said.

But there was still quite a lot she did not "get."

As they rolled through town at a ridiculously slow rate, Amelia pulled level with the donkey and the boy, and kept pace for a few painfully slow beats.

"What are you doing?" Jaden called over.

"Yes," Ella said. "What are you doing?"

"I thought I could be sort of a . . . shield," she shouted. "Going through intersections."

"Francisco is not going to walk in front of a car," Jaden said. "He's not stupid."

"Told you," Ella said quietly.

"But a car might be coming fast," she said, quietly, more to Ella than her son.

"If he sees or hears one, he'll stop immediately," Ella said. "And he hears a lot better than you or I do. Have you checked out the ears on that beast?"

Amelia sighed. Braked. Dropped in behind them again.

When she saw the market at the end of the street, its back up against the beach, she was surprised to see it was held in the unpaved extension of the parking lot of their hotel. Or what had so recently been their hotel. She could see her rental car a few dozen feet away from a table full of plantains.

She parked the gator, and she and Ella stepped out.

"You coming down?" she asked Jaden, reaching up for him.

"No way," he said. "I want to ride him as long as I can. Just hand me up the fruit and I'll put it in the saddlebags."

"We can bring the produce back up in the gator."

"No," Jaden said, and shook his head firmly. "That's not the right way to do it. Francisco wants to do it the way it always gets done."

Amelia sighed. Shook her head. Followed Ella over to a stack of crates filled with huge ripe red-orange mangoes.

"You'll take some on the drive with you," Ella said. "Trust me, you won't get fruit this good back in the States."

"Sounds messy," Amelia said. "But . . . yeah. Probably a good idea anyway."

She followed the author up and down rows of oranges, limes, papayas, dates, figs, guavas. Tomatoes, cucumbers. Cilantro. A few bits of produce Amelia didn't even recognize.

"Do you call everybody darling?" she asked suddenly.

She honestly had not realized she was about to bring it up.

"Well, I'm not sure," Ella said, gently squeezing an avocado. "I guess it's something I do without thinking. Why? Does it trouble you?"

"Not really. I suppose I wondered if it was only a figure of speech, because you don't really act as though you find me all that darling."

For an awkward several seconds Ella looked her up and down as though Amelia were a piece of fruit that might be too bruised to buy.

"I like you more than I like the average person," she said at last. "Let's get some papayas for both of us. Very good for the digestion. Good for the boy as he's getting back on his feet."

"Fine," she said.

And they wandered again.

Amelia looked over her shoulder to check on Jaden. He sat proudly on his donkey at the edge of the parking lot, straight and tall. He waved enthusiastically.

"Did you like my thesis?" she asked as Ella gathered handfuls of plump limes.

Ella's hands paused briefly, but she never turned to look at Amelia.

"The truth? I read it so damned long ago that I don't remember all that much about it. And when I read anything about myself I read it with one judgment and one only: whether or not it pisses me off. So I really couldn't go back and tell you if I thought it was well written or not, because my memory is not that good and I wasn't reading for that anyway. Here. I can't carry all this. Take the mangoes and the papayas over to Jaden and help him put them in the saddlebags."

Amelia accepted the armload of fruit, but did not initially move.

"Did it piss you off?"

"It did not," Ella said.

"I guess that's something."

"That's everything, darling. That's all I ever asked for."

Amelia walked over to Jaden and the donkey.

A few feet behind him she saw Guillermo standing outside the hotel with two women in maid uniforms. All three were staring at her.

She waved over the donkey's behind and Guillermo waved back.

"I feel like people are staring at us a lot," she called to him.

"We are just wondering how you are doing this thing."

"Yeah," Amelia said. "I'm not sure how I'm doing this thing either. But anyway, tomorrow she's throwing us out."

"Ah," Guillermo said. "Then tomorrow the world goes back to being a place that all of us can understand."

"Good night, Señora Steinbach," Jaden said.

He had stepped out in his pajamas, teeth freshly brushed and feet bare, onto the cool terrace in the dusk.

"Sleep well, darling," Ella said.

"Thank you for letting me ride Francisco into town. I had a really nice trip, but the best, best part of it was that ride. Will we get to say goodbye to you before we go in the morning?"

"Well, I'm not sure, darling. We'll have to see."

"After we go home can we do video calls and you take the phone out back so I can talk to Francisco?"

"Jaden," Amelia said. "I told you. She has a flip phone."

"Yeah, but I don't know what that is."

"It doesn't do video calls. She'd have to do them on her computer."

"Is it a laptop?" he asked Ella. "Can you take it out back?"

"No, I'm afraid not," Ella said. "It's a big old-fashioned thing that lives under the desk. It's attached to the monitor by cables, and I couldn't even lift it if I tried. But maybe I can bring Francisco to my office window. We'll see. Get a good night's sleep now, and we'll let the future be the future."

"Okay," Jaden said. But he sounded disappointed.

"Want me to tuck you in?" Amelia asked him.

"No, I'm too big for that."

He turned and walked back into the house, his shoulders slumped in a way that nobody but Amelia would likely notice.

"Do you have a calling card?" Ella asked, pulling her attention back.

"A what?"

"A card. You know. With your contact information. I suppose I'm dating myself by using the phrase 'calling card.' Used to be you'd call on somebody by dropping by their house, and if they weren't home you'd leave your calling card. You seem to be a fan of dropping by people's houses unannounced, so I thought you might have one."

"Most people don't these days," Amelia said, ignoring the dig. "But actually . . . I do. They come in handy when I'm trying to get someone on record for a story. It's in my purse, though. Which is in the house. I'll be right back."

She went after her purse quickly and rejoined Ella on the terrace. She sat, rustled around inside it, and pulled out the leather case that held her business cards. Leon had given it to her, on her first week at the newspaper. Mark had pitched a fit, calling it inappropriate for him to give her a gift. It made no sense on the face of the thing, so he must have picked up on something.

She handed one of the cards to her host.

Ella squinted at it in the fading light.

"This doesn't have your address on it."

"Sure it does. Right under my name."

"No, I don't mean your *email* address, darling. I mean your *actual* address. Where you *live*."

"Well, no," Amelia said. "Of course it doesn't have that. I hand these out to total strangers."

"But I'm not a total stranger," Ella said, holding the card out in Amelia's direction. "Write it on the back."

Amelia took the card and rummaged in her purse for a pen. Meanwhile she was wondering why Ella needed her street address, and whether it paid to ask.

As if reading her thoughts, Ella said, "In case I want to write him a letter or send him a birthday card or some such."

But there was something insincere-sounding about it. Then again, the author only bounced into sincerity quite occasionally.

"Do you even know when his birthday is?"

"Well . . . no. I don't. But we'll talk on the phone. And when his birthday is coming up he'll be excited, and he'll tell me."

Amelia wrote their address on the back in neat block letters and handed it over again.

"Good," Ella said. "Thank you. Now back to work for me."

And with that she rose and bustled away, leaving Amelia to watch the last of the sunset in perfect solitude.

In the morning, Marta was in the kitchen preparing their breakfast, but their host was nowhere to be seen.

"She's not up yet?" Amelia asked.

"No, she's sleeping late today. And you never, never wake her up when she's sleeping."

"We might have to leave without saying goodbye, then. I got us a flight, but we have to be back at the airport in San Diego by two o'clock."

"But I get to say goodbye to Francisco," Jaden said. "Right? He's not still sleeping, right?"

"No, he's eating his breakfast," Marta said. "But even if he was sleeping, the donkey it's safe to wake up. It's the señora you have to watch out for."

She stepped out into the morning sun, Jaden at her side, holding both of their suitcases. Marta was waiting in the noisily idling gator to take them back to town. Back to their rental car.

Before she got in, Amelia set down their bags and glanced over her shoulder at the house. She felt suddenly bowled over, not only by the enormity of leaving E. L. Swann's home, but by the enormity of ever having stayed there. She wanted to believe that Jaden would be her ticket to come back sometime, but she knew by then that the author ran hot and cold, and made a lot of sudden turns. And she knew enough to accept that it might never happen.

But it happened this once, she thought to herself. *And nobody can ever take that away.*

Then she loaded their bags and her son into the gator and they headed down the dreaded road.

She looked back once, but it was so overwhelming that she kept her eyes forward for the rest of the drive.

As they spun up the coast together, the sun gleaming on the water to their right, Jaden fell back asleep, as tended to happen in moving cars.

Amelia picked up her phone and held down the right-side button.

"Siri," she said, "text Leon."

"What do you want to say to Leon?" Siri asked in that familiar voice.

"Coming home late today. Dinner sounds good. Maybe Friday?"

Siri read the text back to her, then asked if she wanted to change it or send it.

"Send it," Amelia said.

"Done," Siri replied.

Of all the times the virtual assistant had said "Done" to Amelia, this time seemed the most significant and weighty.

She had just accepted a date with Leon.

It was done.

Chapter Fifteen

You Are Now Leaving the Friend Zone

She sat across the table from Leon in an Italian restaurant. The kind with red checkered tablecloths and glass-bowl candles in the middle of the table.

"Never knew you to be big on Italian food," he said. "I was surprised you didn't suggest seafood."

"I totally got my fill of seafood in Baja."

"Right," he said, and clapped himself on the forehead with the heel of his hand. Not hard. More symbolically, from the look of it. "I completely forgot about that."

"Yeah, we ate fresh fish that came into town on boats at the end of the day, and lots of local produce. Which was great. Best fish ever. But after a while something starchy and fatty starts sounding really good."

The waiter came by to take their order. She ordered the fettuccine carbonara and a glass of red wine. Leon ordered eggplant parmesan and sparkling water.

Meanwhile she stared at him and realized he was dressed quite a bit nicer and more thoughtfully than usual. Not formally, but obviously with attention to detail. A black V-neck tee with a tweed jacket, and even a contrasting pocket square. She couldn't help picturing him in front of the mirror in his room, trying on outfit after outfit. She had no idea if it had happened that way, but it seemed quite real in her head.

Also he wasn't wearing his glasses. Whether he sometimes wore contacts or could just manage without them she didn't know.

The waiter left, and Leon turned his attention back to her. She quickly looked away, as though she'd been caught doing something wrong.

"Tell me all about your trip," he said.

Bizarrely, it was the first time it had occurred to her that she could not.

It would have made a lot more sense for her to have anticipated the problem, and she wasn't sure why it hadn't happened that way. Maybe because she was tired from the traveling. Maybe because she was a little nervous about the date, and had tended to turn her attention away from it during the waiting.

In any case, that was the moment things got awkward between them, and the fact that she hadn't seen it coming didn't help.

"I think Jaden had a good time," she said after a long and embarrassing pause. "Even though right off the bat he got sick from the water."

"Oh, poor guy. Where is he tonight? Did you have to get a sitter?"

"No, he's with Mark."

"Right," he said. "Friday night. Duh."

"We took this boat trip, and the old man who took us out had a glass-bottom boat. Jaden was still a little bit sick, even though he was on a course of antibiotics, and he fell asleep face down on the glass bottom. And then we saw this whale shark. Do you know what they are? Have you ever seen pictures of one?"

"I don't think so," Leon said, seeming happy that she was filling the air with words.

"They're so enormous, I swear you'll never believe me when I tell you how huge this thing was. You'll think I'm exaggerating. I think it was about thirty feet long, which is by no means unusually big for a whale shark. Anyway, I woke Jaden up to see it, and when he opened his eyes the whale shark was swimming right under the boat. I'm telling you, he just about levitated into my arms. Jaden, not the shark. It would have been funny if he hadn't been so scared. Now I'm thinking, why didn't I take out my phone and get a photo or some video? And I honestly don't know the answer to that. I think I was kind of stunned by what I was seeing. Anyway, later in the trip we went parasailing, but he didn't want to be dipped down into the water, and we were supposed to go snorkeling but he didn't want to go, and after a while he admitted that he didn't want to go anywhere near that water after seeing the size of the things that can be alive under there."

It was one of the longer sentences of her life, and as she listened to the words spooling out of her, she realized she was chattering nervously.

She responded by clamming up for far too long.

For a time Leon, who was clearly also nervous, could not seem to find it in himself to break the logjam.

Finally he pulled a deep breath and dove in.

"Tell me about this woman," he said. "You said you're going to do a story on her?"

"I'm thinking about it."

"You said she's led an interesting life."

"Very."

"Tell me one of her stories."

And, in that moment, it became clear to Amelia that she'd allowed herself to be herded into a box canyon. Again, she might well have seen it coming. But for some reason she had not.

"I . . ." she began. And stumbled. And did not continue for an awkward length of time. "I'd have to go through my notes," she said finally.

"You must have heard something that stuck with you."

Another painful silence.

The waiter arrived with their food, giving her a good excuse to say nothing as he hovered. While he was grinding a massive amount of black pepper onto her pasta, it came very clearly into her mind that she had two choices: Take Leon into her confidence or risk losing him.

The waiter left.

She took a big bite of pasta. Too big. It bought her another minute to think, though.

"How's your pasta?" he asked.

She nodded approvingly.

Then she finished chewing. Swallowed. Looked directly into his eyes.

"I have this thing about confidences," she said.

"Confidences? Like, when someone takes you into their confidence?"

"Yes, exactly. When I tell someone I'll keep a secret for them and not tell a single soul, that's something I take very seriously."

"Good," he said, though it was clear he was unsure where she was going with this. "That's a good trait."

"Most people are more lax about it."

"True," he said, nodding too vigorously. "Most people tell their significant other and a few people from work and figure that's close enough."

"Exactly!" she shouted.

She honestly hadn't meant it to come out so loud. The couple at the next table stopped talking abruptly and glanced over.

She waited for them to return to their own conversation, then leaned closer to Leon.

"If I say what I'm about to say, it's going to be a very rare exception to that rule. And if I do, you can't make any exceptions at all. Not even one. I know it's an unreasonable thing to demand, but I'm asking you to do a better job with a secret than I did, and it's not optional."

"I'm not sure who I'd tell," he said. "We have no mutual friends. Except for you I don't see anyone from the paper anymore. Nobody asks me how you're doing or anything like that, because no one even knows we're still friends. But even if everything I just said weren't true, I can still do that. I can definitely do what you just asked. I've been doing something similar all my life. I try to say the very least I can get away with on any important matters. To say my lips are not loose would be wildly understating the case."

"Then I guess . . ." she began.

But she felt mildly lightheaded from the gravity of what she was about to do, and she had to pause to try to steady herself.

"Let me save you some guilt here," he said, lowering his voice to a near whisper. "Don't tell me. Say nothing and be satisfied knowing you really never did tell a soul. Instead, let me tell you. The old woman in Mexico really was E. L. Swann."

Amelia opened her mouth to answer, but she was too flustered, and no words emerged.

When she had finally gathered herself she said, simply, "How do you do that?"

"You seemed so full of stories until I mentioned the woman you met there. But more importantly, you looked like you were dying over there. And I just felt like there was only one secret that could be such a big deal to you."

"You're good. I'll give you that."

"I just listen and pay attention is all. I suppose I developed it as a defense, but it comes in handy for all kinds of different things. Did you get anywhere with her at all?"

"We stayed at her house for days. I really am doing a story about her. I have interviews recorded. I wasn't making that part up."

"Amelia," he said, and the emotion in his eyes seemed to catch up to the moment. "That's amazing. That's just so wonderful. What an opportunity!"

"Tell me about it! You know, I didn't realize until this exact second how badly I needed to share this with somebody before I exploded. It's just such a big deal."

"Huge deal," he said. "Gigantic deal. Not only will it put your career on the map and turn you into a household name, but it means I was wrong to think this was about to be the most awkward dinner ever and that you didn't even want to be here. So there's a lot to be happy about right now. I hope you realize I want details."

She gave him details.

She spewed out so many details for so long that her pasta got cold. But it was worth it. She had really needed to let it all out.

After a breathless dinner that seemed to flash by in a couple of minutes, Amelia hit another awkward spot when he walked her to her door.

They stood without speaking for a moment while she tried to put the right words together.

"Here's the thing," she said.

"Okay. Tell me the thing."

"I'm thinking we should go slow."

"I'm fine with that."

"Good, but that's not exactly the thing."

"Okay. What's the thing?"

"I've just known you for so long. And any other time, before this, if you had walked me to my door I would have told you to come in. And we'd have tea, or decaf coffee, or a glass of wine, and just keep talking."

"Actually, you wouldn't have," he said. "Because Mark would have been inside."

"Right. True. But you know what I mean. At least, I think you do. Here we are on a first date and suddenly I feel like I can't do that, and that feels wrong. It feels like it doesn't make any sense. But after a first date, if you ask a man if he wants to come in . . . that moment seems a bit loaded with connotations, if you know what I mean. A guy could get the wrong idea."

She searched his face for reactions as she spoke, but there wasn't enough light by which to judge. But his energy felt smooth and calm across the approximately two-foot gap between the spots where they stood. Maybe because now he understood the thing, and knew it didn't hurt.

"I would like nothing better," he said, "than to come in and drink a cup of tea and not get the wrong idea."

—

"I'm actually surprised you're so open to company," he said, after taking his first sip of tea. "I would think you'd want to hole up and start writing immediately."

He was sitting on her couch with his legs crossed underneath him, shoes on the floor, sock feet just barely showing under a very new-looking pair of black jeans.

"I have a lot of time," she said. "I promised I'd hold off until next year."

"You can't write it for a year? Won't that make you crazy?"

"No, I don't have to wait a whole year. Just till after the end of this year. Not quite six months. Then we have this plan that we're going to say she wanted to be heard on some issues, and she looked me up. Because she read my thesis. Oh, hell, did I remember to tell you she read my thesis? I was trying to say so many things at once."

"She read it while you were there?"

"No, she found it online. Back when it was first available."

"So she keeps up with what's being said about her. That seems counter to the vibe she puts out."

"Yes, I brought that up. To which she replied, 'I'm only human, darling.' She's a very complex character. She makes a lot of sudden turns. She's kind of like a bad weather report. The wind keeps changing, and she starts raining while the sun is still out. Half the time I felt like she was going in two opposing directions at once. Like, for example, she begged me to stay because Jaden was helping her write somehow. Then a day or so later she's like, 'Tomorrow you'll go home.' I still don't know what that was all about."

"So the six months is to keep people from thinking you found her on your trip to Mexico?"

"Exactly. We don't want it to seem too coincidental. I mean, for all the years I was studying her I never got one sighting. Not one tip on her whereabouts. And then suddenly she looks me up right after the first tip ever."

He didn't answer for a time. He sipped his tea and seemed lost in thought.

"But they don't know that," he said at last.

"Who doesn't know what?"

"The only person who knows you never hear about sightings is you. Can't you just give the impression that it happens two or three times a year?"

She sat very still for a moment, letting that sink in.

"Why are you so smart?" she asked him. "Or . . . an even more important question. Why am I so dumb?"

"You're not dumb. You're a very intelligent woman. You just don't have the luxury of perspective the way I do. So, listen. Here's a weird question, and I'm not sure if you've considered it or not. You said she's working on a second book after all this time. You think she'll follow through and finish it? That's not the weird part, though. I just had to ask that first."

"It's a good question," she said. She settled back against the couch cushions, as if it would help her think. She slipped out of her shoes and pulled her feet up underneath her, not realizing until after she'd done so that she was mirroring Leon's body language. "If I were a betting woman I'd say no. I even wonder if that's why she suddenly told us to go home. There was definitely some kind of subtext in there that I never managed to crack open. She says she needs Jaden to write, and so if I take him away she has an excuse not to. But I could be wrong. I hope I'm wrong. Just think. A second E. L. Swann book. Wouldn't that be amazing?"

They mulled that over in silence for a few seconds.

Then she added, "What's the weird part?"

"You'd be the only person who knows she's writing it."

"True."

"What if she asks you to read it and tell you if it's any good?"

"That would be such an honor."

"If it's good. But what if it's not any good? What if she can't do it again?"

"Oh. Wow. I hadn't thought of that. Now I'm not sure what I hope."

"I guess you'll cross that bridge when you come to it," he said.

"*If* I come to it."

"Right. If you come to it."

"She might just send it straight to her agent," Amelia said. "Oh, no. Wait. Her agent died year before last."

"Maybe she'll just submit it directly to the publisher," he said. "She might not even welcome opinions. She's probably got all the confidence in the world."

"Oh, no. She does not."

"Well. Cross that bridge when you come to it. We don't even know if she'll finish the thing."

"Yeah, I've definitely lost track of what to hope for," Amelia said.

By the time she walked him to the door it was nearly one a.m.

They stepped outside and stood on the stoop in the city night.

"I just have to tell you," she said, "it's been such a huge relief to talk to someone who's not a temperamental author. And also who's not . . . you know . . . seven."

He let out a small laugh, but she thought it sounded uncomfortable.

"But I didn't mean to make it sound like I have you in the friend zone," she added.

She was facing the streetlight on the corner, and he had his back to it, so she could see very little about his expression. She knew her face was well lit, though, and it made her feel vulnerable.

"I accepted being in your friend zone a long time ago," he said. "I just figured you didn't think about me that way."

"I was married to an angry, jealous guy. I thought about you the way I had to think about you. I was going for survival—figurative survival, I mean—for both of us. I have no idea how I think about you now, if I'm being honest. I just barely stepped out of that constant stress, and being cautious about things like that is a hard habit to break."

"I guess we'll see, then."

"Yeah," she said. "I guess we will."

She took a step in toward him.

"Let me just see something," she added.

She stood up on her tiptoes—he was well over six feet tall—and kissed him fairly briefly on the lips.

At first he seemed surprised, and not very open. By the time he seemed ready to relax into the idea she had pulled away again.

"I think we missed our timing," she said. "Let's try that one again."

They kissed for a longer moment, and more earnestly. His lips felt soft and dry and so wonderfully different from Mark's. So much . . . safer. Everything about Mark was thin and harsh. Nothing about Leon was. It all felt very welcome.

"Huh," she said when they pulled apart.

"Was that a good 'huh' or a bad 'huh'?"

"Good 'huh.'"

"Glad to hear it. So a second date might not be too much to ask?"

"There better be a second."

"Good," he said. "Good night, then."

He trotted down the stairs and moved along the street toward his car.

She watched him go for a moment, then closed herself back inside.

She spent a couple of hours staring at the ceiling when she should have been sleeping.

Chapter Sixteen

Life Is Ultimately Futile 1A

Amelia was blasted out of sleep by a knock on the door.

She sat up and blinked at the alarm clock. It was after eleven a.m.

She got up, pulled on a robe, and walked through the living room to answer it.

She peered out through the peephole first, but it didn't tell her much. The person on her stoop seemed to be a short woman wearing a big, broad, dark hat.

But, seeing as it was a woman, and someone much smaller than she was, Amelia threw open the door.

"May I help you?" she asked.

The woman wore sunglasses under the huge hat brim, and a wildly colored silk scarf thrown around her neck in such a way as to cover a lot of the bottom of her face. She reminded Amelia of a person preparing to rob a bank.

Two big leather suitcases sat on the stoop by her side, as though she thought she were moving in for a time.

"Yes, you can help me," a deep and overpoweringly familiar voice said. "You can let me in before I'm recognized."

"Ella?"

"Yes, it's me."

"Ella, what are you doing here?"

"Trying to get you to let me in."

Amelia stepped back out of the doorway.

"Finally," Ella said as she barged past her into the living room. "Grab my bags, will you please? They're too heavy for me to carry. The Uber driver brought them up the stairs for me."

Amelia carried her bags into the living room.

When she had closed the door and turned around, Ella stood before her, revealing herself to be Ella. The hat, scarf, and sunglasses had all landed on the couch.

"What are you doing here?" Amelia asked again.

"Well, you know what they say, darling. If you want something done right you have to do it yourself."

"Try that again," Amelia said. "This time the way people normally speak."

"I'm here to finish my second book."

"Wait. You're staying here with me until it's finished?"

"With you and Jaden. Yes. Where *is* Jaden?"

"At his father's until tomorrow night."

"Oh. Well. I can live with that, I suppose. Now, will you please show me to where I'll be sleeping? And offering me a cup of coffee couldn't hurt. I *am* your guest, after all, and last time I looked we were both civilized people."

Amelia only stood a moment, trying to absorb what was happening. When the full perspective arrived, it came like the dawn. Clear, bright. Steady.

"You knew you were coming here all along," she said. "That was the part you weren't telling me. You told me to leave your house so you could come to mine and be with Jaden for as long as you needed."

"Like I said about doing things yourself . . ."

"You could at least have told me you were coming."

The author placed both hands on her hips and assumed a stubborn, nearly belligerent stance.

"You can*not* mean to tell me you're honestly going to complain because I showed up at your door uninvited, and when you weren't expecting anyone. Because that would be a laugh."

"Right," Amelia said. "Point taken."

—

"I'm going to put you in my room," Amelia said as she lugged the heavy suitcases down the hall. "I'll just have to bunk with Jaden for the foreseeable future."

Ella stepped into the bedroom, looking all around as though she found the accommodations wanting.

"Do you always sleep this late?"

"No, I never do. I have a child. I'm usually up before six. But it was a late night last night."

"Stayed up because you had a night off from motherhood?"

"I stayed up because I had a date," Amelia said.

"Boring," Ella replied without pause.

Amelia found it off-putting, to say the least.

"Not for me it wasn't."

"I have no interest in all that romantic nonsense. It's for chumps. Now, what about that cup of coffee we were discussing?"

"*You* were discussing it."

"Fine. What about that cup of coffee I was discussing? No, you know what? Never mind. It was a long trip, and I'd like to take a nap."

She waved Amelia out into the hall and closed the bedroom door behind her.

She didn't come out until nearly four o'clock.

Amelia had to stay in her pajamas that whole time, because all of her clothing was in the bedroom with her sudden guest and she hadn't been given time to retrieve it.

—

Amelia was at a Thai restaurant, waiting to pick up a takeout dinner for two, when she got a text from Leon.

"Am I supposed to play it cool?" it read. "Or do I get to just go ahead and ask when I can see you again? I would have given it another day or two, but I know Jaden is back tomorrow night, and I thought it might be nice if you didn't have to pay for a sitter."

She typed back, "I might have a built-in sitter for a while."

"Your mother is coming to visit?"

"Nope. Guess again."

No text came back for a time, and she decided it was a purely impossible guess.

She typed, "You'll never believe who showed up at my door."

"Please don't say Mark."

"Not Mark."

A pause between texts. No bubble to suggest he was typing, either. Not for several seconds.

Finally: "I give up. Who?"

"I have a sudden artist-in-residence."

"Not . . ."

She waited, in case he typed more. He didn't.

"The one and only."

"She showed up at your door?"

"I couldn't make a thing like that up. Even E. L. Swann couldn't make a thing like that up. Or wouldn't, in any case."

A waitress appeared with two bags of food and handed them off to Amelia. She walked them to her car, set them on the passenger seat, and then typed another text before starting the engine.

"I promise to tell you all about it, but right now I have to bring this Thai food to Her Majesty. She says you can't get decent Thai in Mexico. It's a good thing I told you about all this, because holding it in would be killing me right about now."

She started the engine and headed for home.

Her phone rang, and she answered it hands-free.

"I'm sorry," Leon said. "I just had to know more. But . . . are you trying to order food or something?"

"No, I'm driving it home. But I can talk to you over the car's sound system without killing myself or anybody else. You want to have dinner tomorrow and I'll fill you in?"

"You're really okay leaving Jaden with her?"

"Oh, sure. He likes her."

"You're not worried she'll teach him that people are evil and the world is a cesspool and life is ultimately futile?"

"Honestly? You can't believe how good she is with him. It's like he brings out a completely different side of her. I don't know any other way to explain it. Okay, does tomorrow at seven work? Where should I meet you?"

"I could cook if you want to come over."

"Perfect. I'll see you tomorrow. I'm sure I'll have more stories to tell you by then."

"You got me the pad thai?" Ella asked as she settled at the kitchen table.

"I got you the pad thai."

"With shrimp?"

"Exactly how you asked me to get it. With shrimp." Amelia took two forks out of the drawer and two real china plates down from the cupboard. "It's a little more casual here than at your house."

Ella looked around as if expecting more accommodations to suddenly reveal themselves.

"You don't have a dining room?"

"Of course I don't have a dining room. This is a small San Francisco apartment. Rents are expensive here. I'm trying to get by on my own with a child . . ."

"All right, all right. You don't have to get persnickety about it."

Amelia settled at the table as Ella took her first bite of pad thai. She watched her guest chew and swallow before speaking.

"How I've missed good Thai!" Ella said.

"Oh. I was waiting for a complaint."

"About what? It's good."

They ate in silence for several minutes.

Then Ella said, "I noticed you can see a bit of the Golden Gate Bridge from here."

"You can."

"Not much, though."

"No. Not much."

"I want to see the Golden Gate Bridge. I've seen pictures of it, of course. It looks quite majestic."

"You've never been to San Francisco?"

"No, never."

"How do you feel about going out?"

"It would have to be dark. I'd probably stay in the car. I'd put my big hat and scarf on. Nobody would see much of me that way."

"I suppose not," Amelia said.

"All right, then. It's settled. After dinner you'll take me to see the bridge."

It was not a question.

"Oh, my," Ella said when the lighted bridge came into view. "That really is quite impressive, isn't it? I love the way they light it up, and the way the lights reflect on the bay. It's kind of rugged for such a big city. The area all around it, I mean. So many hilly areas that aren't developed at all. It looks wooded and almost wild."

"Most of what you're seeing is a national recreation area."

"Well, it's a nice surprise. Wait, why aren't you stopping?"

"Why would I stop?"

"So I can get my fill of the view."

"You can't stop here. You'll get your fill while we're driving over it."

"We can't drive over it," Ella said, sounding panicky now. "There's a toll taker. The tollbooth person could look into the car and spot me."

"There are no tollbooth people," Amelia said. "That's a relic of the past. It's all done with FasTrak or toll invoices. And even that's only on the way back."

"I'll be damned," Ella said.

"About what? The fact that things change over time?"

"I suppose so."

They pulled out onto the bridge, Amelia careful to stay in the right-hand lane. Ella stared out the passenger window over the bay.

"Oh, my," she said. "There are big ships coming through here, aren't there? What's that rock?"

"What rock?" Amelia asked, keeping her eyes on her lane.

"That sort of flat, rocky island with some kind of building on it."

"Oh, that's Alcatraz."

"The infamous Alcatraz? They don't still have prisoners there, do they?"

"Oh, no. It's open for tours, though."

"I should think that would be quite depressing."

"I think so too."

"You've never gone?"

"No, and for that exact reason."

Ella stared in silence for the second half of the crossing.

When they reached the end of the bridge Amelia stayed in the right lane and turned into the vista point parking area.

"Wait, where are you taking us now?" Ella asked.

"Just a place with a nice view of the bridge and the city."

But it was crowded, being a Saturday night, and Amelia realized they'd likely never find a place to park.

Just as she was about to give up and circle the parking lot only to head to the exit, she saw brake lights on one of the parked cars.

She stopped and put on her turn signal. The car pulled out and she pulled in.

She turned off the engine and they sat looking back over the bay at the city skyline.

"I truly hate cities," Ella said.

Amelia sighed quietly and wondered why she had even bothered to try.

"So it's quite a compliment to yours," Ella continued, "when I say I find it beautiful. Normally to me beauty only resides in those places where one experiences nothing man-made as far as the eye can see. And this is certainly not that. But it's breathtaking."

They sat in silence for a few minutes.

Then Ella added, "Thank you for taking me here."

"You're welcome."

Another silent minute or two ticked by.

Then Amelia decided she needed to get a few things straight.

"I have a longtime friend," she said. "His name is Leon. I know him well and he's a very dependable person. I was married for most of the time I've known him, but I'm not married now. And it looks as though we'll be dating. And I definitely don't say that to hear any more commentary from you on dating. This is my life, not anybody else's."

"What does any of this have to do with me?" Ella asked without taking her eyes off the city skyline.

"If you're going to be at my house for weeks or months, he's going to have to know about you."

Meanwhile her gut ached and burned with guilt because she wasn't admitting that he already knew.

"Well, I don't like that idea much."

"I have a life here."

"And I have a life in my home, too, but I guess I'd forgotten that yours might have people coming and going. That's such a foreign concept to me. I don't like the idea of him knowing."

"I don't see much way around it," Amelia said. "And of course we could have settled our differences on a lot of these details if I had known you were coming."

"Don't get me started on that again."

For a time, nothing more was said.

Ella broke the silence.

"It's just that I've never been more vulnerable. Being here in the city with you as I am now."

"I think it's just the opposite," Amelia said. "I think you're vulnerable at home, because if anyone finds you, they find where you live. If someone does find out you're at my house, that gives them no clue as to where you were before you arrived or where you'll go when you leave again. Besides, Leon can be trusted."

"I certainly hope so. I don't like it. I don't like it one bit. But I suppose now it's your house, your rules. But swear him to secrecy."

"I will."

"Couldn't you just tell him that you have a houseguest but not who I am?"

"But then it would make no sense to swear him to secrecy. Then he'd feel free to tell people that I have someone staying with me, and that opens a can of worms."

"I suppose."

"I would think the one you should be worried about is Jaden."

"You let me handle Jaden," Ella said.

"Except I'm his mother and I demand a say in how you 'handle' him."

"I'm going to tell him the truth. He's a smart boy. I believe I can make him understand the essential nature of his discretion."

"You'd better figure out how to simplify the wording."

Amelia reached for the ignition button. As she did, Ella grasped her arm in that way she tended to do when feeling frightened and intense.

"I think it's good," she said in a hushed whisper.

"You think what's good?"

"What I'm working on. I think it's good. I could be wrong, of course. It's easy to get one's head turned around with a thing like that. Or is that only me?"

"I think it's safe to say it's not only you."

"When it's done, you'll read it," Ella said. "And you'll tell me the truth."

Again, it was not a question.

So there it was. In all its terrifying glory.

"Wouldn't it be better to let the publisher decide?"

"I can't send it to the publisher until I know I'm right about it. That could be utterly humiliating. You have a background in literature. And, more importantly, you loved my first novel. If you love it, I can bring myself to submit it. If not, then it falls short of *Labyrinth*, and you will have spared me the humiliation."

Amelia only sat a minute with her finger on the ignition. She did not answer.

"Don't you *want* to read it?" Ella asked, sounding uncharacteristically vulnerable.

"Of course I do. It just feels like a huge responsibility."

"Oh, buck up, darling," Ella said, the vulnerability having completely vanished. "Life is like that sometimes. Now take me home. It's late, and I'm tired."

Chapter Seventeen

How Dare You Not Be Rude

When Amelia woke in the morning her mind was muddy, and for several seconds she couldn't quite shake herself awake. She couldn't absorb why she was sleeping in Jaden's little bed and Jaden was not.

She sat up, blinked too much, and slowly focused on the fact that she could hear the sound of a typewriter through the wall between bedrooms.

That clarified a lot.

She picked up her phone from the bedside table and checked the time. It was almost nine a.m., a decent time to contact someone. Even on a weekend.

She texted Leon.

"Possible issue with tonight," she wrote. "I realized as I was going to sleep last night that I can't leave until Mark has brought Jaden back. I mean, I can't very well have Ella answer the door, now, can I?"

A pause. A typing bubble.

Then: "What time does he drop off?"

"That's exactly the problem. I never know. He texts when he's double-parked on the street out front and he wants me to come out to get Jaden. I try and try to get him to text me when he leaves the house. He says he will and then he ignores the request. It can vary by hours."

For a minute or two, no bubble. No reply.

Just as Amelia had allowed herself to get lost in her email, his reply came in.

"So tonight is off."

He sounded disappointed, which she knew was ridiculous. How can words on a screen sound disappointed? Still, she couldn't shake the feeling.

"Not necessarily. I had a different thought about it. Did you already buy the groceries for dinner?"

"I did, yes."

"Would you be willing to bring them over here and cook? It wouldn't be exactly like a date, because there would be a reclusive and temperamental author here, and Jaden would show up at some point. But better than bagging our plans, right?"

"Wait. You're inviting me to meet E. L. Swann?"

"I seem to be, yes."

"How does she feel about that?"

"No idea. She's working, and I just woke up, and I haven't run it by her yet. But last night I laid down some ground rules and told her you and I were dating and you would have to know about her, and that's just the way it was going to be. Of course you'll need to reassure her that you've been sworn to secrecy."

"Wow," he typed back.

"Can you elaborate on 'wow'?"

"That takes some stones, to lay down ground rules with the legendary E. L. Swann."

"Maybe," Amelia typed. "But she's in my house for months. Right in the middle of my life. And she's not the easiest person to have as a guest. She tends to expect everything to revolve around her. So it just felt necessary."

"I couldn't agree more. Still, congratulations. Dinner at 7:00?"

"Yeah, 7:00 is good."

"What if Mark finds a parking space and comes to the door?"

"She'll have to hide."

"Will I have to hide?"

"Oh hell no. Mark and I are divorcing. I can see anybody I want."

"Glad to hear you say that. Should be an interesting night."

"I'd bet some money on that. See you at whatever time you need to get here for dinner at 7:00."

She sat still for a moment and realized the typing in the next room had stopped.

She rose, pulled on a robe, and found Ella sitting at the table in her very bright kitchen, drinking what Amelia's nose told her was fresh coffee. She blinked at the author until her eyes adjusted.

"I hope it's okay," Ella said. "I figured out your coffee maker on my own."

"Fine. Make yourself at home. I hope you made enough for two."

"I made enough for an army, darling."

Amelia poured herself a mugful and sat down at the table.

"You look like you had a rough night," Ella said. "Didn't you sleep?"

She was wearing what appeared to be men's dark-green plaid pajamas. Her hair was disheveled and did not appear to have been combed.

"I think I slept *too much*," Amelia said.

"When does Jaden get back? I need his inspiration."

"It was nice to hear you getting some work done without him."

"Oh, it was dreck, darling. It was nothing at all. I was mostly just writing about how I couldn't write. Sometimes that helps to break the logjam, but it did me no good today. Now, again, when is he coming back?"

"Hard to know with Mark, but late in the day. Dinnertime or after. Whenever he deigns to get in the car and drive him over."

"You shouldn't put up with that from him."

"And what other choices do you think I have?"

"Lay down the law."

"I lay down the law all the time. He flagrantly breaks it."

"Tell him he can see his son only if and when he gets on the ball."

"I can't do that. He could drag me into court and get a custody arrangement that's court ordered. I told you."

"Oh," Ella said. "Right. I guess you did tell me, didn't you? Well, I for one would never keep someone in my life who can't keep his word and cooperate."

"Spoken like someone who has no children. Once you have a child with someone you're never really free of them. Look. Not to change the subject, but . . . well, in all honesty, definitely to change the subject . . . Leon is coming over for dinner tonight."

"Who's Leon?"

"The man I told you about last night. The old friend I've started dating."

"Well, where am I supposed to be?"

"At the dinner table. I told you last night. He needs to know about you."

"I didn't know that meant I had to *meet* him," she said, sounding almost comically horrified.

"He's a perfectly nice person."

"Ah," Ella said, and took a long sip of her coffee. "You've hit on the problem right there. He's a person. And you know my opinion of *them*. No, I don't like this one bit."

"Have dinner with us, please, and if you're uncomfortable you can retire to your room afterward."

"Won't he think me rude?"

"I'm sure he expects nothing less," Amelia said.

Leon arrived at six to begin dinner, hauling two huge cloth tote bags of groceries into her kitchen.

Ella was in Amelia's bedroom, typing away. Whether she was typing a novel or typing complaints about her inability to type a novel was impossible to say.

"I almost forgot to tell you," Amelia said quietly as she helped him unload the bags. "Please under no circumstances ask her questions. I mean . . . you can ask her questions like 'How was your trip? Did you come by plane?' Which, amazingly, I haven't yet thought to ask her. Or 'What do you think of San Francisco?' But no author questions."

"Author questions?"

"'Where do your ideas come from? Do you base your characters on people you know in real life?' She hates that."

"Got it," he said.

"Am I making you nervous?"

"Well. I was already nervous. But . . . yeah. Little bit."

"Sorry."

Just as she said the word "sorry," the typing stopped.

They both stared at the kitchen doorway for a minute or more, and then Ella appeared. She had changed out of the dark-green pajamas for the first time that day, and her hair was neatly combed and pulled back into a loose ponytail. She wore a roomy, flowing white linen overshirt and pants.

"Don't just stand there, darling," she said. "Introduce me to the company."

"Ella, this is Leon. Leon, this is the author E. L. Swann."

Ella moved quickly across the kitchen and took his hand. She didn't shake it, exactly. Just held it and looked into his face.

"It's an honor," Leon said.

"Yes, I can imagine it would be, darling. Oh, I'm sorry if that sounded arrogant. Even for me. What I mean is, no one except this person standing beside you has knowingly been in my company for forty years, so you've just become a member of a remarkably small and exclusive club."

Leon opened his mouth as if to speak, but no sound came out. So Amelia jumped in and rescued him.

"We heard the typing," she said. "We hoped it meant you were getting work done."

"Oh goodness no. Just more exercises in futility. When does the boy come again?"

Just as she finished the question, Amelia's phone announced a text with a sharp bing.

She pulled it out of her pants pocket and checked it. It was Mark, and he was double-parked at the curb.

"Exactly now," she said.

She hurried out onto the street and opened the passenger-side door. Jaden unbuckled his seat belt and climbed out.

Mark leaned over and said, "Wait," before she could close the door.

"What?"

She held Jaden tightly by the hand because that's what you do with a child on a city street, especially if your attention is being drawn away.

"Why are you in such a hurry?" he asked.

"As opposed to what? The imaginary nice friendly chats we normally have when you drop him off? I have company."

"So I see. I saw a man go in."

"How long have you been sitting out here?"

"Doesn't matter. Jaden and I were talking."

"You had all weekend to talk."

"It looked like Leon."

She bent down a little farther to look in at him. Despite their having been married for eight years, he seemed less than familiar to her now. Somehow she was already more used to Leon, and now Mark looked small and thin and a little mean. He was wearing a suit and tie. Maybe on his way somewhere. But he didn't look nice in it. Not to Amelia, anyway. He just looked like danger, and a cloud of bad feelings.

"It's none of your business," she said. "We're as good as divorced, and you're already seeing someone."

"Oh, so you *are* seeing him."

"None of your business," she repeated. "Don't bring it up again."

She slammed the door hard.

Still holding tightly to Jaden's hand, she walked up the stairs with him. She glanced quickly over her shoulder to be sure Mark was driving away. Thankfully, he was.

"I have a surprise for you," she said.

"Leon's here."

"I have two surprises for you."

She opened the front door and they stepped inside.

From just inside the door they had a clear view of Ella leaning on the kitchen island, talking to Leon.

"Señora Steinbach?" Jaden said, amazed, and loudly enough for her to hear.

She came hurrying to him, her face morphing into a smile more genuine than Amelia had seen her manage before. Bigger and brighter than she had thought of as a possibility for the author's face.

"My tiny companion!" she shouted, and wrapped Jaden in her arms. "How I've missed you!"

"But it's only been, like . . . a few days," he said, still half smothered by her.

"Oh, I know, darling, but you're my muse."

"Did you bring Francisco?"

"Well, no, honey. I couldn't very well have brought him, now, could I? He wouldn't be allowed on the plane, and he wouldn't be a good fit for your apartment. He needs space in the outdoors."

"Jaden's going to say a quick hi to Leon and go wash up for dinner," Amelia said. "And then he'll come talk to you more."

"Fine. I'll just be in the kitchen entertaining our guest."

And with that she hurried away again.

"What's a muse?" Jaden asked quietly.

"Tell you later when we have more time."

"But is it a good thing?"

"Oh, yes. Very good."

"It looks like dinner isn't even cooked yet. Why do I have to wash up now?"

"I just need a minute to talk to Señora Steinbach privately. And put on a nicer shirt, please. That one has mustard on it."

Jaden sighed and trudged down the hall.

"Ella?" she called. "May I see you for a moment?"

Ella emerged from the kitchen still beaming.

"Yes, dear?"

"If you have any thoughts at all on interracial relationships, please tell them to me right now and spare our guest over dinner."

Ella's face turned horrified and a bit hurt.

"I'm shocked you could think so," she said. "I'm not a troglodyte."

"I just thought possibly . . . being from a different era . . ."

"We weren't all like that, you know, even if it was the prevailing sentiment. My mother flew to DC for the March on Washington in '63. I was in college and she didn't tell me about it until afterward, because she knew I would have gone, and she was worried about violence. But I would have been there in a heartbeat. Give me a little credit, darling."

"I apologize."

"You shouldn't assume. You know what they say you do when you assume."

"I wasn't assuming," Amelia said. "I was worrying. There's a difference."

"I was born in the forties," Ella said over dinner. "Well before the civil rights movement had its sails unfolded."

Amelia was in the process of winding fettuccine around her fork, and she paused, wondering how this was about to go.

She glanced at Leon's face, but it looked smooth and open. He was not tensed or bracing as far as she could tell. Just listening.

"And when it came along it was quite welcome to me. Also to my family, and to more or less everyone we knew. You choose who you'll have around you, of course. Like attracts like." She reached over and placed a hand on Leon's arm, patting it firmly. "Please don't think me a clueless dolt," she said, and took her hand back. "I know you can have a perfectly nice conversation with a person of color without the topic having to be race. I'm only mentioning it because *she* brought it up."

She gestured broadly in Amelia's direction on the word "she."

"She did?" Leon said. "When was that?"

"Before dinner. Out of everyone else's earshot."

Amelia immediately regretted having started this. She felt her face burn slightly. She wondered why Ella had felt the need to rat her out. Or, anyway, it felt like that kind of betrayal.

She raised one hand meekly, a single finger pointing toward the ceiling.

"Mea culpa," she said quietly.

"Anyway," Ella continued. "After the sixties I think we felt real progress had been made. Oh, I knew it wasn't fully solved, but it seemed to have taken off in the appropriate direction, and I think we all simply assumed it would keep going, and more or less in a straight line at that. If you had asked me at the time, I'd have told you it would be at least close to a nonissue by now. Of course I was younger then, and I didn't know what I know now: that progress never proceeds in a straight line. But in any case, it seems like we're losing ground in this country. Though, honestly, I don't know why I say 'we,' being an expatriate as I am. But the point remains. And now I wonder if the progress I thought I saw was never genuine, or if it was quite real but we've begun to backtrack away from it again."

She paused. Waited. Took a big bite of her fettuccine.

"It's a thoughtful question," Leon said.

And Amelia thought, *They're getting along. Who would have guessed it?*

"Again," Ella said, "so you know I'm not a complete dolt, I realize a lot of us who consider ourselves allies make the mistake of talking when we should be listening. Case in point, here I am telling you my thoughts about societal progress on race when I could be inviting you to share yours."

A moment's silence. Leon seemed to want to be sure she was done.

"Which I'm doing now," she added.

Leon set down his fork and dabbed at his lips with one of Amelia's cloth napkins.

"I didn't see it as you trying to explain my own experience to me," Leon said. "If that's what you're thinking. I've had enough of that to know how it feels. I figured you were telling me your experience with the way things were before I was born. As far as the question you asked, I don't really think the two are mutually exclusive. I think the progress was genuine in a lot of ways, and I think we've lost ground. Both. I also think of the quote 'You haven't converted a man because you've silenced him.' I think the big advances were not so much everybody changing their mind. I mean, people feel the way they feel, but the prevailing attitude changed to 'It's no longer okay that you feel that way.' So people keep to themselves whatever thoughts don't conform. Then we'll have a backlash where somebody stands up and tells the people to be loud and proud about their opinions, no matter how ignoble. So I think a lot of times what we're seeing is more of a change in how loudly and openly these things are expressed."

"Well said," Ella replied. "I hope it's okay that I broached the topic."

"It is," Leon said. "Now tell me about your trip up here."

"Yes!" Jaden said, slapping himself on the forehead. "Finally! Something I can actually understand!"

And they small-talked in a surprisingly normal way for the rest of the dinner.

As Amelia got up to clear the table, Ella said, "I approve of your new beau, darling. He's quite intelligent and charming. You chose well. And he cooks! Hang on to this one."

It was a long journey away from "I have no interest in all that romantic nonsense. It's for chumps." Then again, Amelia was growing more accustomed to the sudden U-turns.

She sat on the couch with Leon after dinner, when Jaden had gone to bed. Ella was typing away in what had so recently been her bedroom.

"I found her surprisingly agreeable," Leon said.

"I *know*," Amelia said, her voice on a kind of blast mode. "What's *up* with that?"

Leon laughed.

"You didn't want her to be?"

"I guess I just feel like now you won't believe me when I tell you how hard a time she's giving me."

"I've read about the author," he said. "I'm the only person I know who claims to find her agreeable."

"But she likes Jaden and she likes you."

"Maybe she's bending over backwards to like us because we mean something to *you*. And she seems to need your cooperation to finish this book."

"Then couldn't she just cut out the middlemen and be nice to *me*?"

He laughed again.

"Good question. Hard to say."

"All I know is that she always seems to do exactly the opposite of what you expect her to do." Then she remembered a dangling issue, and it brought a little clutch to her stomach. "Hey. Is it okay that I talked to her privately before dinner? I just didn't want her to say anything to make you uncomfortable. But now I'm looking back and thinking you're a grown man and perfectly capable of taking care of yourself, and now I'm embarrassed that I said anything."

"If you'd asked me," he said, "I would have told you it probably wouldn't be an issue."

"Based on what?"

"I read her book."

"There was nothing about race in the book."

"There didn't need to be. You can generally tell where an author stands on social justice. It bleeds through."

"So I *did* make a mistake."

"The only mistake," he said, "would be if you start worrying about making a mistake every time you turn around. And then everything gets awkward. You're okay. We're okay. Everything is okay."

Amelia sighed.

She moved closer to him, lifted his arm, and tucked herself underneath it. She pulled the arm back down around her, lacing her fingers through his. She set her head down on his shoulder.

For a few minutes she said nothing. Just basked in the surprising comfort of the moment. Amelia was acutely aware of the warmth of him, and the places where their bodies rested together.

"You know," she said, "if I didn't have a legendary, reclusive author camped out in my bedroom, I'd invite you to stay."

He didn't answer straightaway.

After a few beats he said, "It's only our second date."

"True. But I think the whole idea of waiting a certain number of dates is for people who are only just getting to know each other."

"You said you wanted to take it slow."

"Oh. Right. I did, didn't I? I was feeling a little nervous that night."

"Well, I'm not going to argue with you," he said. "Next time we can get together at my place. Ella can stay home and babysit. It'll be her way of paying you back for all the stress."

Another comfortable silence fell.

Amelia broke it.

"She *did* ask me to read her second book when it's done."

"Oh. How do you feel about that?"

"Terrified."

"Maybe it will be good."

"You have no idea how much I hope so," Amelia said.

When Amelia woke in the morning, Jaden was watching cartoons in the living room with the volume up too loud. She crossed the room and picked up the remote, turning down the volume slightly.

She felt almost hungover, but she had not had anything to drink the night before. It was more of a hangover from stress. From holding everything too tightly.

"Hey!" he said. "I was watching that."

"You still are. You just don't need it that loud. You want breakfast?"

"I had cereal."

"Oh. Cereal. Fine."

She wandered into the kitchen.

Ella was standing at the counter, making a pot of coffee.

"Just a quick cup, darling," Ella said. "Then back to the old typewriter."

"Make plenty."

Amelia plunked herself down at the table. For a moment she just watched the author's movements.

Then she said, "Why do you like everybody except me?"

Ella turned suddenly, her face a mask of surprise and something akin to amusement.

"I don't like anybody, darling. You know that."

"You like Jaden. And now you like Leon."

"They're good people."

"And I'm not?"

Ella came to the table and sat across from Amelia, resting her chin on the heels of her hands. Amelia could hear the rumbly sound of water heating in the coffee maker.

"I already told you I like you more than most," Ella said.

"You did. But you don't really act like it. And, just so you know, yes, I'm hearing myself, and yes, I do realize this makes me sound pathetically needy. But it seems like it needed to come out, and it's too late to stop it, so there you go."

For a moment the kitchen was quiet except for the drip of coffee and the wild music of cartoons from the living room.

"I'd like to think you were paying attention when I answered your interview questions," Ella said.

"Of course I was. I hung on your every word."

"Then why don't you already know the answer to this?"

Amelia tried to force her brain into action. But she'd been forcing it into action too much, and for too long, and it felt like it wanted to buckle under the strain.

"I don't know," she said. "I just know I'm tired. Help me, please."

"I think you, Jaden, and Leon are all good people. But your son and your beau don't want anything from me. It's not that I don't like you. It's that I brace against you. I bar the door because you want to come in."

"Oh," Amelia said.

Then she, too, wondered why she hadn't arrived there on her own.

Ella rose, poured herself a mug of coffee, and headed out of the kitchen with it.

"Try not to trouble yourself, darling," she said at the doorway. "You look as though it's getting to you."

Chapter Eighteen

Swann's Host Apologizes in Advance for the Author's Untimely Murder

Amelia woke to a kiss on her forehead.

She opened her eyes to see Leon standing over her, holding a tray. The aromas nearly knocked her over.

"Don't tell me you made breakfast in bed," she said, sitting up as best she could on short notice.

"I did."

He set the tray down on her lap.

"*Eggs Benedict?* Holy crap, Leon. That's some pretty fancy stuff. I haven't had eggs Benedict for years. And I don't think I ever had it anywhere but in a restaurant."

As she spoke, he climbed back into bed beside her. She looked around his spare studio and took it all in, nursing the simple yet overwhelming fact of being there. It was the first time she had ever been to his new apartment. The old one had been bigger and fancier, but had also come with a roommate. This one was tiny but blessedly private.

She looked down at the tray again. It was an intimidating amount of breakfast. Two split English muffins with four poached eggs, swimming in the most lovely-looking hollandaise sauce.

"Eggs Florentine," he said. "Even better."

"What's the difference?"

"There's a bed of fresh wilted spinach hiding under the eggs."

Amelia only sat a minute, letting the gratitude of the moment wash over her. Home had been tense for weeks since Ella's arrival, and being a single parent had been leaning on her for much longer than that. She simply wasn't used to luxury, or being pampered. For a moment she thought it might make her cry.

"I have no idea what I did to deserve you," she said. "If you know, please tell me, so I can keep doing it. You don't honestly think I can eat all this, right?"

"It's for both of us. I just put it all on one plate in honor of the fact that we officially know each other well enough to lean in close while we eat. Also it's a small bed. I wasn't sure about two trays side by side. And, probably more to the point, I only have one tray."

"Works for me."

She picked up one of the two sets of forks and knives and cut herself off a little piece. As she chewed it, her eyes literally rolled back in her head.

"Amazing," she said, her mouth still full.

"I'm glad you think so. I'm ridiculously proud of my hollandaise sauce. It's the first time we ever woke up together, and I wanted to celebrate. I wanted everything to be extra nice. Oh wait. I made coffee. I forgot. I couldn't carry it all at once."

He jumped up again and crossed over to the tiny kitchen area. In mere seconds he returned with two steaming mugs.

She took one from him, and they raised and touched them together as if in a toast.

"To Ella," he said.

"Okay, now I just lost my appetite."

"But she babysat so you could stay over."

"Yeah, and it only took me three weeks to convince her."

"I'm surprised she wasn't happier to spend time with him. She likes him so much."

"Yeah, but she likes having me there to tend to his needs. She likes to enjoy him when she's in the mood to enjoy him and then walk away when she's done. That woman is used to having everything. It's counter to her nature to contemplate not having every little thing just the way she wants it, all the time."

"Then I'm glad you didn't let her bully you into staying home."

They ate in silence for a long time. Several minutes. Nearly half the breakfast. The word "bully" had kicked off a set of worries in her, but she didn't want to ruin the moment by talking about it.

"You got awfully quiet," he said after a time.

"I was just thinking about something that happened in Mexico. But I didn't want to spoil breakfast."

"If something is troubling you, I'd rather hear about it."

"Okay," she said. She set down her fork—a bit regretfully. "I overheard a conversation Jaden had with Ella. Pretty shortly after we ended up in her house. He basically confided in her that he was being teased and picked on at school. Which I sort of almost halfway knew, because he clearly doesn't want to go. But I kept asking him if someone was hurting him, and he kept saying no. But they *are* hurting him. Just . . . emotionally. And do you know what he said to her? I'll never forget this. He said, 'I didn't know I got to count that.'"

"Ow," Leon said. "I felt that one right in the gut." He sat a minute with his hand on his abdomen. Then he said, "I was bullied in school, too."

"Oh, I'm sorry. I didn't know. You never mentioned it."

"I told you before, I tend to say the least I can get away with. What brought this up just now?"

"Oh. Well. It was in there. I mean . . . I heard him say it, and I didn't forget it—how could I forget a thing like that? But I just kind of put it away because school was out for the summer and I guess I figured I had time to think about it. And there was so much going on, what with having a chance to get an interview and everything. But it's been hanging on me, because school is coming up. It's still a ways off but I'm watching it come roaring at us. And then you said the word 'bully' just now. But . . . you know what? I'm putting all this away again until after breakfast. There's no way I'm letting this amazing food go to waste."

They fell silent again, and ate.

At one point he leaned over to snag another bite and she kissed him on the cheek and he smiled. She was exploring what it meant to be close with a man and not feel slightly afraid. But she didn't say it, because that would only be one more intense and heavy topic to spoil things.

When they were all done eating, Leon lifted the tray off her lap and set it on the bedside table. They leaned back against their pillows and continued to say nothing for a time.

"I just wondered why he would tell Ella and not me," Amelia said, surprising herself.

"Because he knows it would hurt you to hear it. He knows it would make you hurt on his behalf. It's like sticking a knife in your mother's heart. What kid wants to stick a knife in his mother's heart?"

"Did *you* tell *your* mother?"

"No. The principal called her in to discuss it."

"Ouch."

"No kidding."

"Do you have thoughts on what I should do?"

Leon sighed.

"Definitely don't do the obvious thing. Don't go down there and insist that the kids who are picking on him be punished. That just sets off the whole 'snitches get stitches' cycle, and his life is guaranteed to get worse."

"What did your mom do?"

"She sent me to counseling. And it actually turned out to be a pretty good deal. The kids just kept tormenting me, but the counselor gave me all these tactics for how to react. And I'd go in there once a week and tell him what they were putting me through, and he'd keep me really laser-focused on the fact that it had nothing to do with me and my self-worth."

"Oh," Amelia said.

"You don't like the idea?"

"I was hoping the solution wouldn't be expensive."

"Your insurance might cover most of it."

"I never thought of that."

"Find out, at least. Ask the question. I have to jump in the shower now. I have work in less than half an hour. Take your time. Enjoy the silence. You can always let yourself out after I'm gone. I know you haven't had much alone time."

"So true," Amelia said. "It's not easy having two needy dependents constantly clamoring for your attention."

"Hey," he said as he was getting out of bed, "were you bullied in school?"

"Not really." She thought about it for a moment, then added, "I was bullied in my marriage."

"Maybe you should talk to somebody too."

"Maybe I should."

When she got home, Jaden and Ella were just clearing breakfast dishes off the table and into the sink.

"Ah," Amelia said. "Señora Steinbach made you breakfast."

It secretly made her happy that Ella had done something around the house. Anything, really.

"Oh no," Ella said. "Nothing of the sort. *He* made breakfast for *me*."

Amelia looked to her son, who looked back with an unjaded sense of pride.

"You did? What did you make?"

"Cereal," he said. "It's the only thing I know how to make. It's about time you got home. We need your phone."

For the moment, Amelia chose to ignore the part about the phone. Instead she turned her slightly irritated attention on her guest.

"You couldn't have poured cereal into a bowl and gotten the milk out of the fridge?"

"Well, you know me, darling. I'm used to being waited on hand and foot. I'm sure I could have figured it out, but he wanted to play the good host, and there's nothing wrong with that. Am I right?"

Amelia sighed.

"I suppose so."

"Just as I thought," Ella said. "I was actually doing him a good turn. I just know you want him to grow up to be a gentleman like your handsome beau."

And with that she set the last of the dishes in the sink and walked away from them, leaving them for Amelia to wash.

She and Jaden walked out of the kitchen together.

A moment later Jaden stuck his head back in.

"Phone, please," he said.

"Why do you need my phone?"

"We're going to FaceTime with Francisco."

"I'm not sure that's a fully baked plan, honey. You need a phone on both ends. And thumbs to answer the call."

"Marta has one of those smartphone thingies," Ella called in from the living room.

"Oh. Marta has one."

She rummaged around in her purse and handed him the phone.

"Keep it brief," she said. "I don't want to go over my minutes."

"What's brief?"

"The opposite of long."

"I thought it was underwear."

"That's briefs. Plural."

"But what if it's only one underwear?"

"Just go call Francisco," she said. "Please. I have dishes to do."

When she had finished the breakfast dishes, she got online on her computer and made a list of three child and family counselors within a five-mile radius.

She still didn't know where Ella and Jaden were, so she poked around the house, finding them in her bedroom—or, at least, what had been her bedroom before Ella utterly took it over.

They were still on the phone with the donkey.

"Come say hi," Jaden said.

"Honey."

"What?"

"We agreed you'd keep it brief. It's been . . ." She walked over to where he sat on the bed and took the phone out of his hand. She checked the numbers in the upper corner, above the image of the face of the donkey, blinking lazily in the sun. "Twenty-three minutes!"

"That's not brief?"

"Not at all."

"Sorry. But say hello to Francisco anyway."

"Hello, Francisco," she said. No reaction from the donkey. "Hi, Marta."

The young woman's face appeared on the screen, but far too close. Mostly just the area around her nose.

Marta adjusted the zoom to show her whole face.

"Hola!" she said brightly.

Then she turned the phone back to the donkey. This time Amelia could see everything but his tail. He had one of the cats sitting on his back. The big gray tabby.

"Look at that," Amelia said.

"Yeah," Jaden said. "Bella likes Francisco. I asked Marta if she put Bella up there but she said no. She said she does it all the time, all on her own."

"Okay, well, say goodbye to the donkey now, honey. This is getting to be too long a call."

"Bye, Francisco!" he called, waving wildly into the phone.

Amelia reached to take it back, but Ella swooped in and got to it first.

"I hope you're not forgetting to water the plants on the terrace," she said to Marta. "They need to be watered twice as often as the ones in the house, or they'll dry out. And don't forget Soolie has a vet appointment next week."

"Sí, señora. I remember. You wrote it all down."

"And one other thing—"

"Ella, please," Amelia said, her irritation flaring up out of her control. "I only pay for a limited number of minutes each month."

Ella glared at her for a moment. Then she turned her attention back to the phone.

"I have to go now, Marta. My host is being ungenerous."

She handed the phone to Amelia, who clicked off the call, her face burning.

"That was seriously unfair," she said to Ella.

"What was?"

"Calling me ungenerous."

"Well, I only know that when you were at my house I was a good host and provided whatever you wanted or needed."

"Jaden," Amelia said. "Go watch TV, please."

When he had left the room she turned her attention back to Ella, who sat on the bed looking slightly aggrieved.

"I was at your house for a few days. Not a few weeks with months left to go. And I might have showed up unexpectedly, but I didn't simply announce that I was going to stay and be your guest. You invited me. And you had an employee to do the cooking and cleaning, which, you might have noticed, I don't. But, more importantly, I don't have as much money as you do. I probably don't have ten percent of the money you do. I'm doing my best to get by here, and the system doesn't stretch much further than it's already stretched. I'd like nothing more than having the space and the budget to host you properly, but this is my reality. You have a phone, such as it is. Why not call Marta on your own phone?"

"I left it at home."

"Purposely?"

"I never carry it. I hardly ever use it."

"How did you call an Uber from the airport?"

"I used a pay phone, like I've been doing all my life. Granted they're harder to find than they used to be, but I managed, given time. Then later I found out that there's a whole line of Ubers idling in a nearby lot. I like my old ways. Sue me. Do we have a problem here? Do I need to think about packing my things?"

"Of course not," Amelia said, and sighed out a lot of her tension. "I would just appreciate it if you'd be mindful of the fact that I don't have your resources."

"I'll make a concerted effort," Ella said. "I'll pay my way where appropriate."

"Thank you."

Amelia carried the phone out of the apartment and onto the front steps, where she sat in the morning sun and called all three therapists to get a sense of her options.

It was two days later, and she was driving Jaden home from meeting one of the therapists.

Only one of the three had picked up his phone, and he had sounded warm and supportive, and had openings, so they had given it a try. It had been a sort of introductory session, which Amelia had not attended. She had sat in the waiting room and tried not to think about eavesdropping.

"Did you like Dr. Walker?" she asked him on the drive.

"Yeah. He's nice."

"Did he seem easy to talk to?"

"Sure. I guess."

"Would you like to start seeing him once a week?"

"No, thank you," Jaden said.

Amelia braked without meaning to, and the car behind her honked.

"We could try someone else," she said, accelerating again. "I left messages for two others."

"No. I like Dr. Walker. He's nice."

"But you don't want to talk to him once a week?"

"No, thank you."

"Can you tell me anything about why you feel that way?"

"Señora Steinbach said I don't need to go. She said seeing somebody like that is for people who aren't . . . what was that word she used? Like that place where you keep horses."

"A barn?"

"No, not a barn."

"Oh. Stable."

"Right. She said it's only for people who aren't stable. It's really weird when the same word means so many different things. Makes it hard to learn. Anyway, she said I've got a good head on my shoulders so it's not for me. It's for people who . . . I guess when their head is not so good."

"I see," Amelia said, doing her best to remain calm. "I guess we'll just have to go home and have a talk with Señora Steinbach."

"Okay. That's what I usually do in the afternoon anyway."

They drove for several blocks without speaking. Amelia was already deeply into the argument in her head.

"Mom?" Jaden ventured. "Are you mad?"

"Why do you ask that, honey?"

"I just wish you could see your face. You really look mad."

Amelia glanced at herself in the rearview mirror. She really looked mad.

When they arrived home, Ella was closed into her room, tapping away at her typewriter.

Amelia set Jaden down in front of the TV and texted Leon from the kitchen.

"Turns out there'll be no second book by the author after all," she typed.

She waited a minute or two for a response. She pictured him finding a private spot at work to reply.

"Oh, that's too bad," his message said. "Do you know why?"

"Yes. Because I'm going to kill her and it can't wait that long."

"Uh-oh. Let me take a break and go outside and I'll call you."

"I'm really surprised," Leon said when he had heard what Ella had done.

"That I'm going to kill her? You shouldn't be. I've been teetering at the edge of that cliff for a while now."

"No, that she would say that to him. She's usually so supportive."

Amelia sighed deeply and took the phone into Jaden's bedroom. Partly so the sound of the TV wouldn't bother her. Partly in case Ella stopped typing suddenly and stepped out into the common areas.

"In her defense," she said, "and this is the *only* thing you'll hear me saying in her defense, I think she might have thought she *was* being supportive. She told him he was stable and had a good head on his shoulders, and she probably thought of all that as a compliment. She just followed it with the wildly misinformed advice that therapy is only for unstable people."

"Is she there right now?"

"She's working."

"How about if I come over after work and we'll have dinner, and put Jaden to bed, and then we'll talk to her together? I'll just be the backup, of course. He's your son, and you're the injured party. I just thought it might help because she thinks I have a good head on my shoulders, and I can tell her how much it helped me as a kid."

Amelia didn't answer straightaway. It was a comforting idea to have him there, but it also involved waiting hours to speak her mind.

"Wouldn't it be quicker and easier to kill her?" she said.

Leon laughed slightly. But then he said, "Don't even joke about it."

"Who's joking?"

"I don't have to be there if you don't want."

"I would actually like it if you would be there," she said. "If for no other reason than it would be nice to have someone on my side for a change. I'm feeling outnumbered in my own home, and this would be a nice break. Thank you."

Chapter Nineteen

My Son the Lucky Bottle Cap

They sat at the kitchen table together, the four of them, eating dinner. Leon had brought Thai, and they were enjoying it mostly in silence. If Ella knew Amelia was mad, she was doing a good job keeping it to herself and not letting on. More likely she wasn't paying enough attention to Amelia to notice.

Jaden's head came up suddenly, and he had a wry smile on his face.

"Señora Steinbach told me a joke. It's a really good joke. Want to hear it?"

"Sure, honey," Amelia said.

But inside herself she was less than sure. Did Ella know what jokes were appropriate for a seven-year-old?

She made a mental note to ask Ella if she'd had that talk with Jaden about her identity. The fact that he still called her Señora Steinbach made it less than clear.

"A horse walks into a bar," Jaden said, his grin widening. "And the bartender says . . ." A few giggles rose up out of him and made it hard for him to go on. "Sorry. So the bartender says, 'Hey, buddy. Why the long face?'"

And with that he dissolved into fits of giggles.

And then, seconds later, Amelia was laughing too. Not so much at the joke, but laughing along with the giggling boy. Leon let out a few short laughs too, especially after Jaden's giggling caused him to snort inward through his nose.

Ella only smiled.

"See, it's funny because horses have long faces," Jaden said.

"It's a good joke," Amelia said.

But mostly she meant it was a good joke for a boy his age. One he could feel free to repeat to anyone. Which was a point in Ella's favor.

Jaden laughed another round to himself before he could quiet the reflex and go back to eating.

Amelia watched him, and smiled, and realized it was hard to be as angry as she had been all afternoon. Part of her wanted to hang on to the feeling until she had achieved the justice she sought, but at the same time she could not deny the relief she felt as it lifted away.

They ate in silence for a minute or two.

Then Ella said, "I have something I want to add to the interview."

"Oh?"

"Take out your phone and record it."

"I'll have to go get it," Amelia said.

"You don't have it with you?"

"Not at the dinner table. In this family we don't carry our phones at the dinner table."

"Well, go get it, then," Ella said. "This needs to be told."

Amelia wiped her mouth on her napkin, set it down by her plate, and got up and fetched her phone from her purse on the couch. She settled back at the table with the phone set to record.

"Are we on?" Ella asked.

"We are."

"All right. Here goes, then. Years ago I was in this coffeehouse in Malibu. This was maybe a year after the book came out. Maybe a little less. I had gone in because I had a serious hankering for a bear claw, but it was a little after seven in the morning and the place was just packed with people trying to get coffee before work. I didn't want to wait in that long line, so I just sat at a table and put my head in my hands and tried to decide if I should wait for the rush to subside or just get up and drive home.

"After a few minutes of this, I looked up, and there was a woman about my own age sitting alone at a table by the window. And she was reading my book. She was a good long way away, but an author knows her own book from across the widest room. When we used to go out on book tours in the old days, in every city a local guide called a media escort would come meet us at the gate—this was back before the big security measures—and you never knew what they would look like, so they'd stand there holding a copy of your book. Because we can always pick our own book out of a crowd. Your eye just goes right to it.

"But . . . sorry. I digress. The woman in the coffeehouse looked up and saw me. She stared at me for a long time. Then she flipped to the inside back cover of the book. That's where my author photo was. Oh, but you knew that. She looked at me again. Then she looked at the cover again. This went on for a while.

"After some time she closed the book and got up. And I thought, *Here we go. She's going to come over and gush on me and ask me all those questions.* You know, the ones I couldn't bear by that stage of the game. Well, she did come over. But all she said was 'What was it you wanted to order?'

"I said I would kill for an espresso and a bear claw, and she walked away. She actually walked around behind the counter. I'm not quite sure why the staff let her get away with it. I don't know why nobody called her out for cutting the line. Maybe they thought she worked there or something. Maybe she told them who I was. I really don't know. I only know that a minute or two later she came to my table with an espresso and a bear claw, and she set them down in front of me. And she said, 'This is on me.'

"Well, of course I told her that was very kind of her. And do you know what she said to me?"

Amelia braced for the complaint, though it was unclear how this story could end with one. Still, what E. L. Swann story about her readers did not ultimately add up to a complaint?

"I give up. What did she say?"

"She said, 'I wanted to do something to improve your day, even if it's only by ten percent as much as you improved mine.' And then she went back to her table and continued reading my book."

"I'm confused," Amelia said.

"By what, darling?"

"That seems to be a *positive* story about human beings."

"Well, I just thought it might balance things out a bit," Ella said.

"Don't run right off," Amelia said to her after dinner. "I know you want to get back to work, but let me just get Jaden to bed, and then Leon and I would like to talk to you for a few minutes."

"Oh dear," Ella said. "Sounds ominous."

"I'm sure we'll all survive."

Amelia walked Jaden down the hall to his room.

"I can change into pajamas on my own," he said.

"Of course you can."

"Did you really like my joke?"

"I really did."

"I guess it's really Señora Steinbach's joke. Usually grown-ups don't take time to teach me jokes. That was nice."

She walked to the spot where he stood unbuttoning his shirt. She bent down and gave him a tight bear hug.

"Whoa," he said. "What's that for?"

"I just love you is all."

"Love you too," he said. "Night."

She closed his bedroom door behind her and joined Ella and Leon in the living room. She sat on the couch beside Leon, took a big, deep breath, and addressed the author.

"First of all," she said. "I want to apologize for being short with you lately."

"Oh," Ella said on a long exhale of breath. "That's not where I thought this was going."

"That makes two of us," Amelia said.

In her peripheral vision she saw Leon raise his hand.

"Three," he said.

"I owe it, though. I owe that apology."

"I don't know as I'd say you do, darling," Ella said. "I realize I'm not the easiest person to live with."

"You're my guest, though. And it's been my lifelong dream to meet you. And I mean just to *meet* you. One time. A few sentences. The rest of this I never would have thought to imagine. And it's not like I didn't know there would be challenges if I ever did. I knew you had a strong personality, so I never thought a meeting would be without its ups and downs. And yet somehow I lost sight of all that and just focused on my own minor inconveniences. You were right. I was being ungenerous. And I'll try to do better."

"Well, thank you, dear. I suppose I could be an easier person to have around the house. I'll make an effort."

"I think part of my problem is that I'm just coming out of a marriage to someone with a strong personality. Someone who always seems to steamroll me and get his way. And I think I'm a bit oversensitive to that now. I seem to be set to battle mode, and I don't know how to tone down the self-defense yet."

"Understandable. We'll both do better."

"Thank you. Now. That having been said, under no circumstances may you ever do anything to interfere with the way I raise my son.

Some things are over the line, even considering everything I just said. And that's one of them."

"When did I do that?"

"When you told him counseling was only for unstable people. Now he doesn't want to go. He's having trouble being teased and bullied at school, as you well know. I'm trying to make him feel like he has some help with things. Someone to confide in. Someone who's on his side."

"But he has *you* for that, darling."

Amelia shook her head firmly.

"He won't confide in me about it, because he knows it would hurt me. And I realize you're from an older era, back when people really thought you had to be mentally ill to seek professional help. But you're wrong about that. You're just plain wrong, and you hurt him by being wrong. It's for people who are under some kind of stress and need help sorting out what they're facing. Leon is going to tell you more about that. Aren't you, Leon?"

"Yeah," Leon said. "Yeah. I wanted to weigh in on that, yes. When I was in school I got picked on by my peer group, too. All the time. Really unmercifully. I didn't want to tell my mom for exactly the reasons Amelia just said, but the school told her. And then, after she got over the fact that I wouldn't confide in her, she sent me to a counselor. I can't tell you how much it helped me. When that many different people seem to have a low opinion of you, it's hard not to take it on—for anybody, I think, but especially for an impressionable kid. But Ken, he was my advocate. He was on my side, always. I'd tell him everything that was said and done to me, and by the time we were done talking about it he had me seeing those bullies as pathetic, insecure people. I felt big compared to them, because I never tried to hurt anybody. I hate to think where I might have ended up if I'd gone through that without him. And you know me, Ella. You know I have a good head on my shoulders. You know I'm not unstable. I was under assault, and I needed help dealing with it."

He stopped talking, and no one else started for some time. Maybe even a minute or two.

"Well, that does give me something to think about," Ella said eventually. "Maybe I can even come around to seeing things a different way."

"But even if you can't," Amelia said, "he's *my* son, and I want you to commit to not undermining my parenting."

"Agreed," Ella said, quickly and with energy. "I was wrong and I apologize. What kind of mother would you be if you didn't take me to task? I'll have a talk with him tomorrow and tell him I'm an old fool, and I gave him bad information, and he should give the counselor a try."

"Thank you."

"Now, if you'll excuse me, my work calls."

And with that she rose and left the room.

Amelia leaned back against Leon's chest, and he threw one arm around her shoulders.

"Wow," he said quietly near her ear. "You were *good*."

"I *was*, wasn't I?"

She found herself unable to suppress a smile. But no one could see it anyway, so she didn't try.

"Did you know you were going to start with an apology?"

"I had no idea. The whole thing just sort of did itself."

"Well, I was impressed."

"Thank you."

"I guess I should go on home. Since you're sleeping in Jaden's room."

"No, stay a few minutes. Please. Stay and talk to me. I won't get to sleep now for hours. I wanted to ask you something. It's about this whole thing with Ella thinking she can only write when Jaden is around. I've had it on my mind a lot lately and I'm just not sure what to make of it. I wanted to hear you weigh in on it. Do you believe that's even possible?"

He breathed deeply, and her own body rose and fell with his breath.

"I believe it's possible based on the fact that Ella believes it's possible. Maybe it's like those athletes who have a lucky shirt or a lucky bottle cap. Do I think there's some magic in the bottle cap? No, of course not. I think there's some magic in the fact that the athlete thinks there's some magic in the bottle cap. I think the mind really latches on to that kind of self-fulfilling prophecy."

"You're so logical," she said. "I really like that about you. You're like Mr. Spock, except warm and cuddly."

"I think . . . ," he began, "I think I'm tempted to take that as a compliment."

"Oh, I definitely meant it as a compliment," she said.

After he left, she wandered back and forth in the apartment for a few minutes, feeling aimless.

She opened the door to Jaden's room. He was fast asleep, and sprawled right in the middle of the bed. Though, honestly, even if she could have brought herself to move him, the bed was too small for both of them. They had been proving it for weeks.

She decided to sleep on the couch, despite the fact that it was shorter than her fairly tall frame.

She pulled two pillows and a quilt out of the hall closet and tried to get comfortable.

She found herself wishing she had arranged for Ella to stay home with Jaden while she spent the night at Leon's. But Ella was typing furiously in her room, and it was too late to ask.

She felt like a foreigner in the country of her own apartment.

She picked up her phone and called Leon.

"Hey," he said when he answered the call on the fourth ring.

"Hey. You still driving home?"

"Yes and no," he said. "I don't have a hands-free system. So I pulled over."

"Oh. I'm sorry. I didn't know that. You can't talk through your entertainment system?"

"No, my car is too old for that."

"I'm sorry to bother you, then."

A silence fell. It was Amelia's job to talk, since she had called. But she honestly did not know what she had called to say, which was an unsettling feeling.

"What's up?" he asked eventually.

"You know . . . I'm honestly not sure. I wanted to call you and say . . . well, I don't know. That's the thing. That's the problem I'm trying to find my way out of. I wanted to say something but I don't know what it is. It's like . . . it's like I felt the need to tell you something but I can't put my finger on which something. Maybe I just wanted to connect with you. Which is weird, because you've only been gone for five or ten minutes. I mean . . . I think it's weird. Is it weird?"

"I think it's nice," he said, his voice soft.

Amelia realized her voice had been soft, too. That she had been reaching for something. And maybe that was why he hadn't tensed up when he'd heard she had something to say to him. Maybe it was obvious that the something would not injure him. Or maybe he was getting over that fear of falling and trusting her more.

"Nice-nice or weird but nice?" she asked.

"Either? Both?"

"I guess that's better than weird-weird," she said. "Honestly, I'm babbling, and I hear myself doing it, and I don't know how to stop. Oh! I think I know what it is. The thing. I think I've got it. I think I wanted to let you know how much it meant to me, what you did tonight."

"What did I do?"

"You backed me up. And I'm not used to having anybody back me up. I'm used to being out there in the world feeling totally exposed and alone, and the cavalry never comes. Or at least it never did."

"I couldn't have been happier to have your back," he said. "And next time you want to call me but you don't really know why, and you're worried it's weird? Next time you want to call me and say anything at all or nothing at all? Just do it. And don't apologize."

Chapter Twenty

One Month of E. L. Swann

It was a week plus two or three days later, a Friday afternoon, when Ella said, "Take me somewhere, darling. Anywhere. Please. I'm going positively stir-crazy."

Amelia had just walked Jaden out to the street and buckled him into Mark's car, and the minute she stepped back into the apartment Ella hit her with the request.

"I was going to have Leon over tonight," she said. "Because we actually have a whole bedroom all to ourselves."

"Oh," Ella said. "Okay." She had a look on her face like a puppy who's just been told she has to stay home alone while the rest of the family goes out. "I guess I could wait until tomorrow. It's just that I got myself looking forward to it, and it's just so awfully hard to postpone something I find myself needing so badly."

Amelia sighed, and already knew she had lost.

"Let me check with Leon," she said. "Maybe he can wait for tomorrow night without dying. Or, at least, it sounds like his chances of survival are better than yours."

"Maybe I can text you when I get Her Majesty home," she said to Leon on the phone. "We could make a sort of late date of it. Or you could come along."

"Where are you taking her?"

"I was thinking across the bridge and up Highway 1 until it lets out onto the cliffs over the ocean. She'll like that."

"I think you should go just the two of you," he said. "She knows you better, and she might open up more. Maybe she'll tell you something about how the new novel is coming along."

"Ooh," Amelia said. "I hadn't even thought of that. That would be delicious, wouldn't it?"

"Oh, my," Ella said. "This is a very twisty road."

"You haven't seen anything yet. Wait till you see the way it switches back when it starts climbing the cliff."

The last light of sunset was nearly gone, and all they could see of the forest around them lay within two cones of illumination from Amelia's car headlights.

"Maybe I should have told you I get carsick."

Yes, Amelia thought, trying her best not to sigh. *Maybe you should have.*

She didn't say it out loud, because she was making an effort to be more patient with her guest.

"You might need to pull over at some point," Ella said.

"I can't pull over. I have traffic behind me and there's no shoulder to speak of."

"Maybe slow down, then."

"I guarantee the people behind me are not going to like it. But I guess they can just hold on."

She drove for a couple more miles with a pickup truck dangerously close on her tail. Then she found a narrow but workable patch of shoulder against the cliff, and was able to pull over just enough to let its driver pass.

An SUV took its place at her bumper the minute she pulled out onto the road again.

"Oh dear," Ella said, sounding dangerously queasy.

"There's just no place to stop here. I'm sorry. Roll down the window if you have to. We can always drive through a car wash on the way back."

"What are all these people doing out here on a Friday night?"

"I don't know. What are *we* doing out here on a Friday night? It's summer, and people like to drive up the coast."

Then Amelia looked to her left and saw the ocean in the dark. It was marked by a long ribbon of moonlight, and lay at least a hundred feet below the road. Better yet, she saw a dirt pullout on the ocean side, currently unoccupied.

She put on her left-hand turn signal, one eye on the tailgater behind her, and quickly pulled in and parked.

They sat a moment in silence, watching moonlight shimmer on the water.

"Whew," Ella said. "Saved by the bell."

"You're going to be okay now?"

"I think so."

Ella opened the passenger door and stepped out, so Amelia got out of the car too. They leaned against her front bumper, nearly shoulder to shoulder, and looked out over the ocean in the dark.

"Now this is what feeds my soul," Ella said. "Nothing man-made as far as the eye can see. Well, there's a road. But anyway, it's behind us."

"It's just too bad you couldn't see it in the daylight."

That turned out to be exactly the wrong thing to say.

"Now why do people always *do* that?" Ella said, nearly shouting. "Why do you talk like that? Why does everybody insist on talking like that? What on earth is wrong with nighttime? I love the night, and I have no idea why people are always trying to obliterate it with their fancy electric lights and their daylight savings time."

"I just meant I thought you could see more in the day."

"I can see plenty," Ella said. "I had that good cataract surgery and my eyesight is nearly perfect. A person can see just fine in the dark if only they give their eyes a few minutes to adjust. We step out of our overly lit houses and think we see nothing but blackness and run back into the safety of our electric lights like little children afraid of the dark. Honestly, I'll never understand these night-haters. People who get so excited when the days get longer again. The day is just hot, and there are no stars. Give me a good dark night anytime."

Amelia said nothing for a minute or two, because there was nothing she dared to say.

Then she said, "Maybe we'll see more stars when our eyes adjust? You know, being outside the city and all?"

Ella snorted derisively.

"Not like Santa Rosarita we won't. If only you could drive twenty minutes outside the city and see a decent sky full of stars. Wouldn't that be convenient? But no. You'd have to get much farther away than that. It's just a semi-educated guess, but I'd say you'd have to drive probably a hundred miles in the direction of nothing and nowhere to escape the light bubble of the Bay Area. But I'm sorry. I don't mean to complain. It's a very nice place you've brought me to. It rivals my home for its beauty, and all I can do is get carsick and complain about light. Thank you for bringing me here. I've been too shut in for too long, and I can feel my soul relaxing already."

They leaned in silence for a time. Maybe five minutes. Amelia was surprised by how much she could see as her eyes adjusted. Ripples on the moonlit water. The white edges of waves as they broke near shore. The complex heads of weeds growing at the cliff edge, the breeze swaying them slightly.

Then Ella spoke.

"I'm going to tell you something I've never told anyone before."

Amelia only waited, thinking the moment too delicate to disturb.

"It's not just disliking people," Ella said. "Although, that too. It's thinking people will dislike me. I'm very sensitive to criticism of a personal nature."

"I sensed that," Amelia said. She waited, in case the author wanted to say more. Then she added, "Did you want me to say anything about that? Or did you just want me to listen?"

"Go ahead and say what you're thinking."

"If you're worried people won't like you, you could always be nicer to them."

"But that's just it. I can't, don't you see? Because I'm already afraid of them. So it just forms this perfect cycle. Well, this imperfect cycle. One might even call it vicious. In any case, I just can't seem to box my way out of it."

They leaned in silence for another minute or two. Amelia was aware of the faint roar of the tide below them.

"I don't know why I told you all that," Ella added. "No, that's not true. I do know, more or less. Because it feels good to let a secret like that out after holding it in forever. And because you're so far into my privacy anyway. You hold my whole life in your hands, so you know the old saying. 'In for a penny, in for a pound.'"

"How do I hold your whole life in my hands?"

"Darling, you're the only person on the entire face of the planet who knows where I can be found. Well. You and your exceptional son."

"So you told him who you are."

"Yes. We talked. And he'll hold my secret. He understands. And I believe you'll hold my secret too, and you'd better not let me down. And even if Leon were to let me down, which I doubt, I trust you haven't told him the specifics of where I live."

"I haven't, no. And he hasn't asked."

"Good."

"I can't be the only person who knows where you are," Amelia said.

"Oh, but you are, darling."

"Your publisher sends you royalty checks."

"My publisher sends checks to my agency, who subtracts their percentage and sends the rest to a personal mailbox in a business center in Los Angeles. The envelopes are addressed to 'E. Carmichael.' I'm sure they think I live close enough to go in and fetch them. You're the only one who knows that's not so. The owner of the business center forwards them to me at a mailbox in San Felipe for a small fee. But she has no idea who I am. Just another faceless, amorphous expatriate who can't afford to live in the US on her scant retirement funds. Marta picks them up."

Amelia sat with that information for a moment, and let it settle.

Then she said, "That's a pretty high price to pay for being left alone."

"There is no price too high for being left alone. It would be a bargain at ten times the cost. It's all I've ever wanted. It's all I've ever asked of the world. Look at the people around you, darling. It's a zoo you live in. A horde of brand-new and inexperienced dirt-level souls who haven't the foggiest idea how the game of living a human life is played. Armies of angry fools scratching each other's eyes out for the slightest sense of power, all the while not realizing that what they gain adds up to exactly nothing. I have never in my lifetime seen so many people so determined to lead an unexamined life, completely unconcerned as to whether they crush the tender souls only trying to survive all around them."

"But you don't feel that way about me. Or Jaden, or Leon. Or that woman who bought you a bear claw in that coffee place in the eighties."

"Well, of course there will be exceptions here and there, but it's not worth dog-paddling through the stink of humanity to find them. Take me home now, darling. I've gotten what I came here to get. And drive slowly, whatever you do. Wouldn't that just be perfect, if I threw up in your car? Talk about coming full circle. You came all the way to Baja to sully my terrace with vomit and then I come all the way back to the United States to return the favor."

"I'll drive slowly," Amelia said.

Amelia settled on top of the covers on Jaden's tiny bed. She left as much room for Leon as possible. He tried to lie next to her, but the effort was doomed from the start. There simply was not enough room.

The moment was punctuated by Ella's constant typing in the next bedroom.

"This is not going to work," Amelia said, "is it?"

"Not well."

"We could sleep on the floor."

"Yeah, or we could just go back to my place."

Amelia allowed the options to play through her head for a few beats.

"I could leave a note for Her Majesty. I can't tell her we're leaving. She's typing. I can't interrupt her when she's typing."

"Nor would you want to."

"True," Amelia said.

Then her mind veered off in a different direction.

"She didn't tell me anything more about the new novel," she said.

"So she's told you exactly nothing so far."

"When we were in Mexico she told me she had almost thirty-five pages. And when I drove her out to see the bridge when she first got here, she told me she thinks it's good. But she's also kind of desperate about it because she knows she could be wrong. She actually told me a few interesting things tonight. She was surprisingly forthcoming. But not about the new novel."

They lay together quietly for a minute or two, though Amelia was unsure how long poor Leon could maintain his awkward position. His feet extended well over the edge of the bed, and she suspected that most of his posterior was hanging out into sheer air on the other side of her.

She had expected him to ask her to betray Ella's confidences regarding the "interesting things," but he never did. Which was very Leon, when she stopped to think about it.

"Maybe I need to go out and buy a good cot," she said. "A nice roomy one."

"Is there any such thing?"

"Maybe an air mattress."

"That could work. I think you can get those in a lot of different sizes. And you can deflate it and put it on a closet shelf when she goes home again."

"It would make my weeknights a lot easier. I've been sharing this bed with Jaden for about a month, and it's no fun. For either one of us."

"Let's go to my apartment."

"Sure," Amelia said. "Just let me write Her Highness a note."

When Amelia got home in the morning, Ella was sitting at the kitchen table drinking coffee. Amelia took one look at her guest's face and stopped cold.

She looked furious. Positively boiling with rage.

She turned her searing stare onto Amelia, and it made her face burn.

"You left me *alone*!" she bellowed.

"I left you a note."

"Yes, you left me a note informing me you had left me alone. As if that makes up for leaving your guest in your apartment utterly on her own."

Amelia ventured a bit closer. When nothing terrible happened, she sat across the table from her furious guest.

"Help me out here," she said. "Just last night you told me that being left alone is worth anything. Any price. You said it's all you've ever wanted. All you've ever asked of the world."

"I was referring to throngs of humanity."

"You live alone."

"I have Marta."

"She goes home at night."

"And I'm in my own comfortable, familiar house. And besides, I told you. I'm not alone. I have Francisco and the cats. But listen. I feel the way I feel, darling. I told you before, I serve truth, not consistency—to probably badly misquote Gandhi. So if I tell you how I feel, just accept it. Don't tell me I felt differently a few hours ago, because you were probably misunderstanding me, and even if you weren't I reserve the right to be inconsistent. It's not a proper way to treat a guest and I stand by that, no matter what excuses you make."

Amelia breathed carefully a few times, a sort of variation on counting to ten.

"Okay, fine," she said. "My apologies. I had no idea you would feel this way. I'm going out today to buy an air mattress. In the future I'll only go to Leon's if Jaden is here with you. On the weekends we'll stay here."

"Thank you," Ella said. "There's coffee."

Amelia poured herself a cup and then carried it into Jaden's bedroom, where she closed herself in with her phone.

She texted Leon.

"You're not going to believe this," she typed, "but the reclusive author who wants nothing other than to be left perpetually alone does not wish to spend a night on her own in my apartment."

It took a few minutes to receive his reply.

"That's positively mystifying," he wrote.

"Welcome to E. L. Swann's wild world of sudden and unsignaled U-turns," she typed, "where you're only hurting yourself and inviting trouble by insisting that anything ever make sense."

Chapter Twenty-One

Three Months of E. L. Swann

On Jaden's first day back at school he stayed in bed too long, then requested that Amelia walk him there.

"I don't want to go in the carpool," he said, "and Larry says that's okay."

"Who's Larry?"

"Dr. Walker."

"Oh. Are you sure it's okay to call him by his first name?"

"He told me to."

"Oh. Okay."

Amelia checked her carpool schedule and then texted the mom who was driving that morning.

"Don't bother coming by for Jaden," she said. "He wants me to walk him today."

Just as they were leaving the house it struck her that she was leaving Ella home alone. But the author was typing furiously, and hopefully would never notice. Still, with Jaden back in school again she would have to schedule her time carefully. The days of getting errands done while he was gone all day were over. For how long, she didn't know. She still had been given no progress reports, nearly three months later.

As they walked down the steep hill together, she said, "Are you nervous about going back?"

"A little. But Larry told me a whole bunch of things I can do to make it not so scary."

"That's good."

"Will Señora Steinbach still be living with us on my birthday?"

His birthday was not until early January. Still, Amelia didn't know the answer.

"I'm not sure. Why? Do you want her to be?"

"Mostly. I guess. It would be nice to have her around when we have cake and all. But she's going to go home sometime, right?"

"That's what we're counting on," she said.

"It'd be nice to get my room back to myself."

"I hear you."

They walked quietly for half a steep block or so. Amelia was watching his shoulder blades above his droopy backpack. They still made him look vulnerable. But she couldn't help noticing that his posture was a little straighter.

"Remember you're not going to say anything to anybody about her staying with us."

"I know. I know. I know. She tells me, like, every day. The closer we got to the first day of school, the more she kept telling me. She says she trusts me, but then she can't stop telling me not to forget."

"It's important to her," Amelia said, "which is probably why she reminds you too much. I'm sure she trusts you, though. She cares about you very much."

Jaden stopped suddenly in the middle of the sidewalk. Amelia almost unbalanced forward, trying to stop as quickly as he had.

"What?" she said.

"You really think so?"

"Do I really think what? That she cares about you?"

"Right. That."

"I didn't know that was ever in doubt. Yes, I do think so. Why? Don't you?"

"Sometimes I think that," Jaden said. "But sometimes I'm not so sure. It would be nice if she spent more time with me. It seems like she comes and talks to me just till she thinks she can write and then she closes herself in your room and starts typing. And then it seems like she forgets all about me. I don't know if she really likes me, or if she just likes the way she can write after we talk."

He started to walk again. Slowly. Almost thoughtfully.

"Maybe it's both," Amelia said, walking with him. "But I know she likes you. She's told me so many times, in so many different ways."

"I hope so," Jaden said.

They stopped in front of his school. He looked in its direction once, quickly. Then he looked up into Amelia's face.

"No kiss," he added.

"I didn't forget."

"Good. And I won't forget to keep my mouth shut about Señora Steinbach. I don't really have anyone I talk to anyway. I don't have any friends."

Amelia felt his words like a cut from a blunt blade. It was a pretty sweeping assessment. He had kids he talked about, and kids he saw outside school very occasionally, and she had hoped for some real friendship there. Maybe more than she had seen with her own eyes.

She opened her mouth to speak, but he beat her to it.

"Well, one. Arnold is sort of my friend. We talk. Or at least we did last year. But we don't talk about stuff like that, like what's going on at home. We talk about . . . you know . . . science and stuff. And comic books."

"That's good," Amelia said.

She wanted to think of him surrounded by a healthy number of friends. But for the moment, Arnold would have to do.

She reached out to put a supportive hand on his shoulder, but he had already spun in the direction of school. She watched him walk up the stairs without looking back.

He stopped once and seemed to take a deep, bracing breath. Then he was gone from her sight.

—

On the walk home, she texted Leon at work.

"This is weird," she typed. "Jaden isn't sure Ella genuinely cares for him."

He texted back almost immediately, "And you are?"

That seemed like a curious answer. She found herself wishing she had called him instead, so she'd have his tone of voice to interpret.

"Well, I was. I figured I could count on death, taxes, and knowing she thinks Jaden is great. Why? Do you doubt her too?"

"I take her just as she is," he texted.

"I don't know what to make of that answer."

"She's a transactional person. I'm not sure genuine caring is her strong suit."

"So you think she's using us."

"You, definitely. Jaden, maybe."

"You never told me this."

"I thought you knew."

Amelia didn't type an answer for a time. She only puffed her way up the steep concrete hill.

She heard another text from him come in, and almost walked right into a brusque businessman as she tried to read it.

"Watch it," the man said.

She stopped, held still, and read what Leon had written.

"Then again, I think your relationship with her is transactional in both directions. You're kind of using her too, and I don't mean that as a criticism. You don't really like her. But she's an opportunity for you, and vice versa. Maybe that's all it's ever going to be."

"Maybe," she typed, still standing still at that sharp uphill angle. "I was hoping what she had with Jaden was genuine."

"It might be," he texted back. "I guess time will tell. I just think it's important that your expectations for her aren't unrealistically high. And by unrealistically high I mean normal expectations, like you'd have for pretty much anybody else. She's an odd character, and not all that affectionate. Take her for what she is. Don't set yourself up for a fall."

Amelia stared at the screen of her phone for a long time, feeling people stream around her but not looking at them.

Then she slid the phone into the pocket of her light jacket and walked home.

She was sitting on the couch with Leon, enjoying a glass of wine after dinner. Quite a while after dinner, actually. It was about ten thirty, and Jaden had long ago gone to bed.

The typewriter fell silent, and Ella stepped out into the living room.

"There you are," Amelia said. "How's it going?"

"As well as can be expected," Ella replied.

She didn't sound as though any deep meaning should be inferred from her comment. She was seemingly being cryptic, as usual, and answering with a nonanswer.

"Come have a glass of wine with us," Amelia said.

"Ah. Well, I suppose one won't set the work back any. And it might ultimately help me sleep. Some of the greatest writers of all time were sloppy drunks, so maybe they know something I don't."

She came and sat in the upholstered chair near the couch, and Leon got up and fetched another wineglass, and poured her a serving of the regional zinfandel they'd been drinking.

Ella raised her glass as if to toast them, but did not attempt to reach forward and actually touch glasses.

"Jaden isn't sure you have any genuine affection for him," Amelia said.

Ella rocked back in her chair and seemed to sit with that for a few beats.

"You never were one to hold back," she said. "Were you? Then again I guess it takes one to know one."

"I'm something of a mama bear when it comes to my son."

"As well you should be, darling. How long have you been sitting on this complaint, if I may ask?"

"He only told me this morning. I told him you cared a great deal about him and he was not at all convinced it's true."

"Oh, piffle," Ella said, and dismissed it with a dramatic wave of her hand.

"*Piffle?*"

She felt Leon tense up beside her, even though he was not close enough for her to literally feel it.

"It's an old expression."

"I know what it means. I'm not sure what it's doing in *this* conversation."

"I'm only saying that he knows how I feel about him. He knows where he stands with me. We all know where we stand with each other, even if we go on to talk ourselves out of it with petty doubts."

"It never hurts to make sure the other person knows."

Ella's face seemed to darken somehow. Something in her eyes changed, like a light being turned out.

"If there's one thing I have no time or place for in my life," she said, "it's anyone who requires the tedious act of constant reassurance."

"He's a seven-year-old boy," Amelia said, working hard to maintain her composure.

"Still . . ." Ella said.

She did not go on to finish the sentence. She only sipped her wine, seeming lost in thought. Or lost in something, in any case.

Amelia waited, in case she ever did choose to finish. When it was clear nothing more was forthcoming, she opened her mouth to speak. But Ella took the conversation in an entirely different direction.

"Here's something I've been meaning to ask *you*, darling. You never speak of that article about me. Have you written it?"

"No."

"Started it?"

"I've transcribed the interviews I recorded with you in Mexico. But I haven't put it all together into a cohesive form yet."

"What are you waiting for?"

"I can't submit it anywhere until the end of the year."

"But you could be working on it. What are you waiting for?" she asked again.

Amelia breathed deeply before answering. She felt put on the spot, and a little resentful of the fact that her conversation about Jaden had been so utterly derailed.

"I guess I just figured the real-life story I'd be writing isn't done yet."

"Meaning what?"

"Meaning things could change."

"Give me a good example of what you think will change."

"You've already added one more story since you got here. So there's that. More importantly, I might be able to end the piece with the bombshell announcement that your second novel has just dropped on your publisher's desk after all these years."

She paused, and waited for some feedback, but Ella only stared into her wineglass.

"I'm not sure, though," Amelia continued. "Because I do want to submit it around the first of the year, and I don't know if you'll be done by then. And if not, I have to decide if I want to hold the article back until I can make that announcement. Hard as it is to wait, it's probably worth it."

"I'll be done by then," Ella said.

Amelia exchanged a glance with Leon. Ella did not look up to notice.

"Great to hear that," she said. "It's the first clue I've gotten as to an ETA."

"A what?"

"It means estimated time of arrival."

"Oh. Go ahead and write that in, but don't weave it in so completely that it can't be lifted out again."

"In case you're not finished," Amelia said.

"I'll be finished. In case you decide it's not good enough to submit."

That sat for a moment with no one responding.

Then Leon cleared his throat.

"In case *Amelia* decides it's not good enough?"

Ella looked up into his eyes, her face set firmly.

"I said what I said, darling."

"Wouldn't that be *your* decision?"

"An author is the last person in the world who should try to judge her own work. One simply doesn't possess the necessary perspective. Amelia has a degree in literature and is probably the foremost expert on my work this country has. She's also one of only three people who are allowed to know the thing exists. Or . . . actually two people, if you subtract those not old enough to read at the level. So my options are limited, darling. The arrangement is that she will read it when it's finished and tell me if it's a worthy follow-up to *Labyrinth*. If so, it will go on to be published. If not, it will go into your fireplace and never be spoken of again. But one way or another it will be done by the end of the year."

Ella drained her wineglass in one long gulp and set it on the coffee table.

"Now if you'll excuse me, work calls. Try to keep the noise down."

And she closed herself into the bedroom again.

Amelia settled onto the air mattress with Leon, on top of the covers and fully dressed. They lay face to face, close enough that she could feel his breath on her cheek.

"I think we should just go to sleep," he said.

"Why do you think that?"

"Because she's right on the other side of that thin wall. And I'm worried by what she said about keeping the noise down. I wasn't sure what she meant by that."

"Right," Amelia said. "I wasn't sure what to make of that, either."

They lay silent for a few minutes, making no moves toward getting ready for sleep.

Amelia lowered her voice to a whisper.

"I wish you could have seen her with Jaden in Mexico," she said.

"E. L. Swann's wild world of U-turns," he said, also in a whisper.

"Right. I know. I should be used to it by now. But she was just enchanted with him."

"She wasn't working on anything. Or seeing many people. Maybe she needed something to be enchanted with. Maybe now she's enchanted with what she's working on, and maybe that's enough for her. Maybe that's all the enchantment she can maintain."

"I don't know," Amelia whispered. "I give up. I give up on trying to understand anything that woman does."

"I know you say that out of frustration, but I actually think it's a healthy statement. I think it's definitely better for your stress level if you don't try to sort her out."

Another quiet few minutes ticked by.

Then Leon said, "Hey. Can I ask you a question?"

"I guess."

"What *were* you waiting for? Before writing up that interview? I know you gave a couple of reasons. But I got the sense there might be more."

Amelia focused on pulling in a few breaths and letting them flow out again. She wasn't sure of the answer, and she had to wait and see if one would come to her in the stillness.

"I guess I was waiting to see where she landed on being a hermit. I figured after all this she might not go back into the same kind of seclusion. Once you come back to the world you might just end up staying. Maybe not the way someone else would stay, but maybe more than the former E. L. Swann. And that would change the way I approach the piece in a lot of different ways."

"That's an optimistic thought."

"I try to be an optimistic person."

As soon as she said it, she thought of something Leon had said earlier. About not setting herself up for a fall.

He didn't repeat it, or remind her. Then again, he didn't need to.

"That's a lot of pressure on you," he said instead. "Being the sole judge of the novel. I didn't know you were the one who was in charge of directing it to the publisher or the figurative fireplace."

"Right. I wasn't sure if I should tell her I don't have a fireplace. She might have just meant it as a metaphor."

"That's got to be weighing on you."

Amelia laughed, but it came out sounding slightly bitter.

Before she could answer, he said, "I'm sorry. That was a stupid thing to say."

"I wouldn't call it stupid."

"No, it was. It was stupid. It was completely the wrong thing to say. When people are under pressure, they know they're under pressure. The last thing they need is someone pointing it out."

"I still don't think it was stupid, exactly," she said. "But I'm definitely not going to argue with those last two sentences."

Chapter Twenty-Two

Five and a Half Months of E. L. Swann

Leon had spent all day working on Thanksgiving dinner. Amelia had done her share, but it wasn't the lion's share. Leon was simply the cook of the family. If you wanted to truly enjoy the meal when it was finished, he was your man.

He'd made a small turkey with stuffing, mashed potatoes, cranberry sauce from scratch, and a green bean casserole. Amelia had made the salad, along with take-and-bake rolls, and she had picked up a pie from a local bakery.

Now they were just minutes from serving it, and Ella was still in her room, typing away.

"I'm not sure how to handle this," she said quietly as she set the table.

"Maybe this is an exception to the rule of never interrupting her."

"I don't believe any exceptions exist."

"We'll give her a few more minutes," he said. "Everything can be kept warm to some degree. The potatoes might suffer a bit."

"No," Amelia said.

"You really should eat mashed potatoes while they're hot."

"Different kind of no. I told her Thanksgiving supper at five. You worked hard on this. We both did, though you did more. If she doesn't come out, I think we should start without her."

He only stood a moment, his hands invisible under enormous hunter-green oven mitts.

"That seems rude," he said at last.

"Oh, yeah. Sure. Rude. We can't be rude to Ella. It's not like Ella is ever rude to anyone else. All she had to do was set a timer or something. Or give me permission to come get her when dinner was served. The reason I have so much trouble keeping my temper with her is that I let her complicate my life. I let her ruin things by being inconsiderate. And then I get angry, because she ruined everything, but it's partly my fault for letting her. Well, this time I'm not going to let her. We'll sit down to eat at five and we'll get up and serve her whenever she deigns to come out."

He turned his wrist over, pulled the oven mitt back, and looked at his watch.

"That would be now," he said.

They both heard a little bing sound in the distance. The typing ceased. They heard the bedroom door open.

"I'll be damned," Amelia said quietly.

Ella showed up in the kitchen doorway with a surprisingly natural-looking smile on her face.

"Smells good!" she said.

"Your timing is great," Leon said. "I'm just about to serve."

Ella sat down and seemed to take in the decorated table. They'd put a linen cloth on it, and candles. Leon had brought an arrangement of pine cones in a basket to use as a centerpiece, and an ice bucket of champagne stood on its own near the only unoccupied place.

"Well, this is just lovely," Ella said. "I never would have thought you could make something this nice with nothing but an old kitchen table to work with."

Amelia was bent over at the oven, taking out a tray of rolls.

Leon placed one hand in the middle of her back, leaned down, and whispered close to her ear. "Breathe."

"Thank you," she whispered back.

No one spoke again until plates had been filled and everyone was just about ready to dig in.

"We had a tradition in my family," Leon said.

"It better not be a religious tradition," Ella said. "I have no affinity for religion. In fact, it gets on my nerves."

"It's not," Leon said. "I'm not sure anyone has a religious tradition for Thanksgiving. It's not a religious holiday. The thing you'll like about this tradition is that it doesn't keep anyone from eating. We can do it between bites."

"Super," Ella said. She picked up her knife and fork, cut a huge bite of turkey, and shoveled it into her mouth. "Mmm," she said while still chewing. "Good. Juicy. Very well prepared. You're right. It's not a religious holiday. It's about . . . well, I guess we've lost track of that as a society, haven't we? I suppose now it's about eating turkey."

"It's about gratitude," Leon said.

"Oh. Gratitude. Right. I hate that. Please don't tell me we have to go around the table and say what we're grateful for."

A brief silence fell. Because of course that was what Leon had had in mind, and they all three knew it.

"*I'm* going to do that," Leon said, doing an admirable job of keeping his composure. "You feel free to do what works for you."

"I'm in," Amelia said. "May I go first? I'm grateful that I got to meet my literary hero this year. And not just meet, as in shake hands in a coffee shop or a bookstore, but actually know. And I'm grateful for Leon moving into a bigger and more important place in my life, because he's supportive and kind and I didn't realize how miserable I had been without that."

She nodded to him to indicate that she was done.

"I'm grateful to be with Amelia," he said. "I've known her for five years, but only as a friend. It was a tough five years, but she was worth waiting for."

She reached over and gave his hand a squeeze.

They ate in silence for a time, assuming that Ella would not weigh in.

"Thing is," Ella said several minutes later, "I'm having trouble feeling grateful because I feel guilty. It's my fault you didn't get to have Thanksgiving with your son. I told you we'd knock out that interview in just a couple of days and then I dragged it out and dragged it out because I didn't want the two of you to go."

"I miss him today," Amelia said. "But it's only one day. And, honestly, it was worth the trade."

"Well, thanks for letting me off the hook," Ella said, "even if you're lying." Then, after a long pause, she added, "Here's a possible something. It was pleasant to come out of my room and have this nice Thanksgiving dinner cooked for me. I haven't celebrated this holiday for years, being in Mexico and what have you. And I didn't have to lift a finger. Does that count?"

"That definitely counts," Leon said.

Amelia was clearing away the dinner dishes in preparation for serving tea and pie.

"Darling," Ella said, her sights on Leon, "you've barely had a sip of champagne."

"I might be driving later," he said.

Amelia took that as her opening.

"You haven't asked me to take you anywhere for a really long time," she said to her guest. "Months. You must be going stir-crazy."

"You have no idea."

"Why not ask, then?"

"I thought it would help me finish the novel. The pressure, you know? The crazier I got to be outdoors and see home again, the more I just said to myself, 'Finish the damn novel and then you can do whatever you want.' I thought I needed that grindstone. I was scared that if I got at all distracted, or stopped even for part of a day, or let myself come up for air . . . I guess I felt like it might simply fly away. Maybe I'd reach to get it back again and it wouldn't be there. I know that's probably not true, but I get paranoid about things like that. I'm balancing all these threads in my brain . . . all these plotlines, and resolutions. Even lines of dialogue that I won't use until chapters down the road, and I feel like it will just run out on me. Desert me if I give myself even the slightest break. I guess that doesn't sound very healthy."

"It doesn't sound very fun," Amelia said.

"Why? Were you thinking we'd go someplace?"

"We had a thought," Leon said, "about a place we could go after dinner. It gets dark so early these days, which is good for you. But it's totally up to you. If it would add to your stress level, just say no."

"It *would* be nice to get out," Ella said. "And I'm so close to being done. Oh, hell. Let's take a chance. Let's do it."

"I haven't made carbon copies," Ella said on the drive. "I didn't have carbon paper and I didn't know where to get any."

"I'm not even sure they make it anymore," Amelia said.

Leon was driving, which allowed her to turn partway around and talk to Ella, who sat in the back seat.

"That means I have only one copy," Ella said. "Which is a funny feeling."

"I'll say."

"So you'll have to take it to one of those copy places before you submit it."

"Before *I* submit it?"

"Assuming it's good and we submit it."

"Wouldn't that be something you would do?"

"I can't very well go to a copy place or to the post office. You'll have to do all that for me. I can't be seen."

"But you took a plane here," Amelia said. She'd been meaning to say it for months.

"Well disguised, yes. And Marta drove me all the way to the airport in San Felipe. So if someone did recognize me, at least I'm not leading them close to my home. It's a tourist town and they'd probably think I'd gone there for a vacation. But I had to take that chance, darling, because no one could fly to San Francisco for me. But you can take a damned manuscript to the post office."

"Wait," Amelia said. "Are you picturing yourself mailing a big stack of papers to your publisher?"

"No, I'm picturing you doing it. I thought I made that clear."

"It's not done that way anymore. They want it electronically."

"How am I supposed to do that?"

"It has to be transcribed onto a computer."

"That sounds like a lot of work for you," Ella said.

Amelia pulled in a long, deep swell of air in preparation for blasting out her objections. Leon put a hand on her arm briefly.

"Keep breathing," he said.

She breathed a few times, more normally, before answering.

"I will not be transcribing your novel," she said. "We'll have to pay someone to do it."

"We couldn't possibly. Until it's safely at the publisher, no one else can read it. No one else can know it exists."

"Maybe the publisher would be willing to have it transcribed. In those sort of interim years, after most people had a computer, there was boilerplate language in literary contracts about it. Saying if it wasn't submitted electronically the publisher would have it done, but it would come out of the author's royalties. I suppose in your case they might even make an exception and pay for it themselves. They'll be so happy to have this. They'd probably take it if you'd written it in crayon on unnumbered cocktail napkins."

"Call my agency and find out, please. I don't know who my agent is there, now that Lila died, but someone there will represent me once they know there's something to represent."

"Then *you* should call them."

"Oh, I can't do that, darling. I hate phones, and besides, these days the people you call can always see the number you're calling from. No, I'm sorry, darling, but I need you for this. I'm doing the part that only I can do, but I need your support for the rest of it. But don't call them just yet, of course. We don't know if it's good enough. It might end up in the fireplace."

"Actually," Amelia said, "I don't have a fireplace."

"It doesn't really matter. If it isn't as good as *Labyrinth*, we'll destroy it. It doesn't matter how. We'll find a way to make it disappear. It will be as though it had never happened. Half a year of my life will be as though it had never happened."

Leon drove them slowly, on narrow roads, to one corner of the peninsula of land that was Point Reyes National Seashore. They stepped out of the car near the elephant seal overlook.

The surf was high and rough, though hard to see in the dark, and Amelia could both hear and slightly feel it pounding against the rocky land under their feet.

Amelia looked up and saw stars.

"Oh, it's dark here," Ella said. "That's nice for a change."

"There's an initiative to make this California's first dark sky preserve," Leon said. "I'm not sure if they've actually arrived at the designation yet or not."

"Leon did quite a bit of research to find a dark sky for you," Amelia added.

Ella looked up in silence for a minute or two.

Then she said, "Too bad it's not farther from the light bubble of San Francisco."

"But for this area," Leon said. "For the Bay Area overall this might be the best it has to offer."

"And Leon worked so hard to find it," Amelia said again, hinting hard that Ella might show him some appreciation.

Ella craned her neck back for a few moments more, considering the sky in silence.

"So what do you think?" Amelia asked straight out.

"Well, it's sure not home," Ella said. Then she glanced over at Amelia's face. Amelia didn't know if their eyes were adjusted enough to the darkness for Ella to read her expression. Probably not. But she must have read something, because she changed course fast. "Though I suppose I should be grateful to you for trying. I suppose you've caught on by now that gratitude is not a well-tuned muscle for me."

"I brought you a camping chair that reclines," Leon said. "I'll get it out of the trunk."

"Oh, I don't know, darling. I don't know if I can stay out here very long. It's so cold. I'm not used to this kind of cold."

"I also brought a big stack of blankets," Leon said.

When he had Ella all bundled up to stargaze, Amelia leaned against the rear bumper of Leon's car, close to his side, their hips nearly touching.

"Tell Leon what you told Jaden about your spirituality. About space as seen from Earth, and how we look at the stars all wrong."

That request was met with a long silence that felt stony, though Amelia had no idea why, or by what method she was able to judge.

"I most certainly will not," Ella said. "That was not even for *your* ears."

"But you knew I was there. Right on the other side of the door."

"I found out you were there when I came back into the house. I had no idea you'd been sitting there eavesdropping the whole time."

Amelia breathed a few times before answering. As though Leon had reminded her, but this time she was reminding herself.

"At the beginning," she said evenly, "I wanted to hear how you spoke to him. He's my son, and I'm cautious about the influences in his life."

"You thought I'd be a bad influence on him."

"Based on the fact that you despise people, yes. It crossed my mind. The good news is, I was wrong. I'm still not sure why that little speech about how we look at the stars was so personal."

"It's my spirituality!" Ella said, close to the border of yelling. "A person's spirituality is deeply personal. And besides, if I say it's personal, it's personal. You don't get to second-guess me on such things. Now, if you don't mind, I'd like to look at the stars in peace. What stars can be seen, anyway."

Amelia exchanged a glance with Leon in the dark. They stood up straight and walked down to the end of the narrow road together, holding hands.

When the road ran out, they stopped at the cliff edge, still holding hands and looking out into the night.

"I think," Leon said, "that I don't give you enough credit for how hard you have to work to get along with her. I give you advice about being patient with her, but now I think I should also commiserate with you more, because she sure doesn't make it easy. She's like this hurricane of negativity trained on whoever dares to be around her. And you've been living with this for . . . well, I'm not sure. But a long time now."

"We'll be coming up on six months before too long here."

"She's taken over your bedroom. You're having to cook and clean for her. Has she ever offered anything to offset all the extra expense of feeding her?"

"At the beginning I'm not sure she could even have imagined such a thing," she said. Then she broke into a fair imitation of Ella's affected, overly formal speaking style. "One does not ask a guest to contribute to her own keep. Why, that completely undermines the very idea that she is your guest."

"Did she say that to you?"

"She didn't have to. I know how her mind works by now. But I told her pretty straight out that I'm on a tight budget, so she started to contribute. But the problem is, she doesn't understand what things cost. Especially here in the US. I try to get through to her about it, but she already called me ungenerous once. I'm never really sure how hard to press the issue."

"You're doing a great job under the circumstances."

She gave his hand a squeeze.

"I'm not sure I could have done it without you. In fact, I'm pretty sure I couldn't have. You've been my rock through all this. So steady and helpful. And I just . . . I . . ." She paused, floundered. Berated herself for not simply spitting it out. "I'm . . . trying very hard to say I love you."

"And you just succeeded," he said, his voice soft.

She glanced over to see him looking into her face in the dark. Ella had been right. Give your eyes time to adjust and you can see a lot. His eyes looked deep, his face open. Or maybe she knew those things more by feel than by sight.

"That's wonderful," he said. "Thank you for saying it. And of course I love you, too. But only since the day we met."

"Did I never say it before?"

"Oh, no. You never did. I would have remembered."

"I thought maybe I did way back when. But . . . you know. Meaning it a little differently."

"I would have remembered," Leon said. "And, anyway, I wanted to hear it like this. The way you said it just now."

When they got back to their guest, she showed no signs of wanting to go home. She lay bundled under blankets in Leon's camp chair, its nylon back reclined as far as it would go, gazing up in silence.

"Are we in a hurry?" Amelia whispered to Leon.

"Not at all," he whispered back.

Ella spoke then, surprising her. Apparently surprising them both. Amelia had no idea she even knew they'd come back.

"I'm sorry for what I said before. Or, more accurately, for what I wouldn't say. I'd gotten my back up and started feeling defensive. It was ungenerous of me. Especially after you cooked that lovely meal and planned this thoughtful outing. And the last thing a person wants to be is ungenerous."

She paused, as if for effect, and looked around behind her, presumably to locate Amelia. But her neck would not crane that far.

"It's like this, Leon," she continued. "We're on this ball of a planet, spinning in space. And when we look out, we're looking out into the rest of the universe. In three dimensions. Some of the stars we see are a couple of hundred light-years away. Others are a couple of thousand, or a couple of million. But we foolishly think this little ball we're standing on is the world. We think our minuscule life here is what really matters. And when we do deign to look up, we think the stars are some kind of two-dimensional mural hung up there for our amusement. We don't realize we're looking out into the vastness of space. We don't realize how small we are. Even our Earth is so small as to be insignificant. So then how small are *we*? And if that's how small we are, then how small are our silly little problems and ambitions? When you look up as though you're looking out into the universe, which you are, you see what the world really is, and your own right size in it. And that's my spirituality. So thank you for bringing me out here to visit God. Now. I'm ready to go home anytime you are."

"Give me just a minute to try this," Leon said.

"Yes," Ella said. "I thought you might want that. When your brain comes back into functionality and your toes are done tingling, we'll go."

Chapter Twenty-Three

Six and a Half Months of E. L. Swann

It was Christmas night, and Jaden was overtired from the long day of excitement. Amelia was putting him to bed, which he normally did not allow. But in this rare instance they agreed that he needed some help staying put and not bouncing right back up and out with the company again.

She sat on the edge of his bed and brushed the wavy hair away from his forehead. His eyes looked too wide open.

"How did Señora Steinbach get me a present?" he asked. "She never goes outside."

"She ordered the train set online. I let her use my computer."

"Oh."

"It was very expensive. It might not even hurt to thank her again in the morning."

"Okay, I will."

"Do you like it?"

He looked up and to his left, as if searching for the answer in some quadrant of his room, or his brain.

"I think so. I never really thought much about trains before. But it looks like a nice thing. Maybe when I play with it a little more I'll get a better idea why people like trains so much. I know she didn't get the picture of me riding Francisco online. That's impossible."

"No, Marta took that with her phone when we were at the señora's house in Mexico. She sent it to my phone and we got it printed, and I got it a frame."

"I like that present best."

"I thought you might."

He lay still a moment, as if deep in thought.

"Here's what I don't get," he said. "Why didn't she get *you* something?"

"Oh, I don't know, honey. I gave up trying to figure her out a long time ago."

"I can see if she got something for me and not anybody else, because I'm a kid. But she got Leon that . . . what do you call that?"

"I'm not sure what you call it, but I know what it does. It's like a miniature projector, and when you turn it on it projects the stars onto the ceiling. The way they really are, like with the constellations all in the right place and so forth."

"But then it's flat," Jaden said. "And we're not supposed to look at it that way."

"True. But not everybody has a dark sky."

"She should have gotten you something."

"She's going to go home and give me my room back soon. That's good enough for me. She swears she can finish her book by the end of the year."

"That's only a week away."

"I know. Now, seriously, Jade. Jaden, sorry. I know you're still a little keyed up. But you need to go to sleep."

"Okay. Where's Leon?"

"He's in the kitchen washing the dinner dishes, and I need to get out there and help him."

"Tell him I said 'Merry Christmas' one more time, okay? And that I like what he gave me."

"Will do."

She kissed him on the forehead and stood, letting herself out of his room. Closing the door quietly behind her.

Ella was sitting in the big chair in the living room, leaning forward intensely. Nervously, from the look of it. She was staring at the coffee table. But Amelia had no idea what was so interesting about the coffee table, because the couch was blocking her view.

She walked around into the seating area.

Sitting on her coffee table was a thick stack of paper. Very thick. She roughly estimated it to be about four hundred pages high.

She sat down hard on the couch and stared at it, too.

"You thought I didn't get you anything," Ella said. "But I got you this. A second E. L. Swann novel, and a go-ahead to submit the only interview anyone has done with me in forty years. I'm giving you a career. One where you'll probably never have to worry about money again. You'll be a household name."

"That's what Leon said." Amelia heard her voice shaking slightly. "And that was back before we knew there would be a novel."

"Well, he was right, and it's a good thing he was. Because the interview might be all you get. The book might be trash. But the thing is, darling, I don't think it *is* trash. I think it's good. It's hard for me to say that to you, because that will only make it ten times more humiliating if I'm wrong. But I'm sticking my neck out."

Leon walked into the room and stood very still and very quietly, a dish towel in his hands. And then all three of them stared at the stack of paper together.

"I'm sorry," Amelia said. "I was coming out to help you with the dishes. But I got waylaid."

"So I see," he said, his voice reverent. "They're done, anyway. I think I should go home now. I think for the rest of the night you've got your hands full, and your attention is spoken for."

Amelia looked up at the author, who seemed ready to implode.

"You want me to read it now, right?"

"No, I want you to read it months ago, darling. But now will have to do. Time and space being what they are."

"Let me just walk Leon to the door," she said.

She met him there, and they stood a moment, Amelia listening to Leon's car keys jingling in his hand.

"I have never seen you look so scared," he said.

"And not because there were other, scarier times and you missed them."

He leaned in and kissed her briefly on the lips.

"Good luck," he whispered. "Call me."

Then he let himself out.

Amelia walked back to the couch, feeling lightheaded. She sat, and they both stared at the manuscript for several minutes more.

Then Amelia leaned over and pulled it closer to herself.

The title page read:

MORATORIUM OF THE SUN

A NOVEL

BY

E. L. SWANN

Amelia flipped to the first page and began to read.

It started off strong, if only because it was so obviously the work of none other than the author of *The Third Labyrinth*. There was something riveting about sentences from the same author, in the same style, but utterly new to Amelia. She had never imagined such a thing until a few months earlier, and even then it hadn't felt real.

After six or seven pages she looked up at Ella, who was staring at her face intently.

"You're kidding me," she said. "You're just going to sit there and stare at me the whole time I'm reading it?"

"Yes," Ella said.

"This is going to take me *at least* six or seven hours. Minimum."

"Yes," Ella said.

So Amelia went back to reading, and Ella continued to stare.

About two and a half hours later Amelia stood up and said, "I'm sorry. I have to go to the bathroom. I'll be right back. But so far—"

"No!" Ella bellowed, holding up one threatening stop sign of a hand. "You will say nothing to me until you've read every word. Not to give you any spoilers, but the last words of the manuscript are 'The End.' Until you've read them, you will say absolutely nothing. Not one word. The ending is everything. The whole thing comes together at the end. Or it doesn't, if I'm a fool. No partial thoughts."

"Have it your way," Amelia said.

And she took a very quick bathroom break.

What she would have said, if she'd been allowed, would have been highly encouraging. She would have said that unless it fell down at the end it would be a masterpiece. But one does not judge the work of the legendary E. L. Swann, not even to encourage her, until the exact moment one is told her judgment is welcome.

With E. L. Swann the houseguest, there had been some give-and-take, Amelia realized. Some arguments and misunderstandings about the power structure. But this was not E. L. Swann the houseguest. This was E. L. Swann the author. And in that arena she reigned supreme, and Amelia knew she could do nothing besides read and follow directions.

And consider herself lucky.

At what she would later learn was about two thirty in the morning, Amelia looked up into the author's face.

"The End," she read out loud.

Ella's brow furrowed.

"It's not sad, is it? I didn't think it was sad."

"No. It's not sad. It's just . . ."

Before Amelia could find the word of praise, which probably did not exist anyway, Ella said, "Then why are you crying?"

"Am I crying?"

"You didn't know you were crying?"

Amelia reached up and touched her face. She was crying.

"I don't know," she said. "It's just . . ."

Amelia was nursing a physical feeling—and had been for hours, she now realized. It was as though a balloon had expanded in her chest, displacing important organs and making it hard to breathe. She felt as though the breath had been knocked out of her, a few molecules at a time, as she read.

"Skip the platitudes," Ella said. "Tell me one thing and one thing only. Is it as good as *Labyrinth*?"

"I think it might be better," Amelia said. "Which feels like a very weird thing to say, since I didn't know such a thing existed."

"Well, there you go," Ella said. She flopped back against the chair for the first time in many hours, and sighed. "Merry Christmas, though I think it probably isn't anymore. I've given you the position of the most enviable journalist in the country right now. You get to call *The New York Times*, and *The Washington Post*, and *The Atlantic Monthly*, and tell them not only that you have the sole interview with the author in forty years, but that you are in personal possession of her second novel, which no one else has seen. You can ask them what it's worth to them to break that news, rather than letting it go to their competitors. And then you just sit back and relax while they wine you and dine you and try to be your best option. You are in the catbird seat, my friend.

"Now, if you'll excuse me, I'm exhausted. Positively drained. I'd be surprised if I got a wink of sleep, but at least I have to try."

And with that, she got up and closed herself into Amelia's bedroom.

Amelia sat a moment, realizing she had expected more. She could easily have pictured them breaking open a bottle of champagne and dancing frantically all night. Instead the author had simply gotten tired and retreated. Again Amelia had set herself up for disappointment.

Then she remembered Leon, and picked up her phone.

"It's better than *Labyrinth*," she texted him. "It's actually better."

She figured he'd read it in the morning, but his typing bubble appeared without delay.

"That's the best news I've heard in . . . my life," he texted back.

"What are you doing awake? It's 2:30 in the morning."

"I wasn't awake. I just put the phone on my pillow so a text would wake me. I wanted to hear."

"And now you've heard. It's better. It's the only way I know to describe it. I have no words for how good it is. I have to sleep. I'm going to fall over and die. I have to get some sleep."

"Do that," he typed. "We'll talk in the morning."

She got up and took the manuscript with her into Jaden's bedroom. She set it between the air mattress and the wall, and then settled under the covers.

She never slept.

When she got up in the morning, she picked up the manuscript and carried it into the kitchen, where she carefully loaded it into a cloth tote bag in preparation for driving it to a copy place.

She had expected to find Ella in the kitchen drinking coffee. Because the door to her bedroom had been wide open as she'd walked by.

She stuck her head out into the living room. Jaden was eating cereal in front of his cartoons.

"Where's Señora Steinbach?" she asked him.

"Don't know," he said. "She was gone when I got up."

"What do you mean, 'gone'?"

"I mean she didn't seem to be around anywhere."

Amelia trotted back down the hall to her bedroom. The bed was neatly made. The wild mess that had been Ella's claim stake on the room was gone. The silk scarf no longer hung over the lampshade to dull its light. The two big suitcases were no longer poking out from under the bed. The closet doors stood open, revealing a gap that the author had made to hang her clothes, now empty.

She walked back to the living room.

"Now how did she even get herself and her things out of here?" she asked, more or less of herself.

"Don't know," Jaden said.

"She didn't have a phone to call a cab or an Uber. And the bags were so heavy she couldn't carry them herself."

She looked down and saw her phone sitting on the coffee table, where she had left it the night before.

She picked it up and opened the phone app.

She pressed the little green phone symbol, then pressed it again, to bring up and dial the last number called.

It rang three times, and then an officious-sounding woman answered.

"Yellow Cab Company."

"Never mind. Sorry. Wrong number."

She clicked off the call and texted Leon.

"You're not going to believe this," she said.

Chapter Twenty-Four

Two Weeks Without E. L. Swann

It was maybe eleven p.m., and she was lying in bed beside Leon. In her own room, which she was just getting used to having back again.

They hadn't spoken in a long time, but it was clear that neither one of them was sleeping.

"Tell me the truth," she said. "When you said she'd call. Or write, or whatever. All hundred times or so you said that. You didn't really mean more than two weeks later, right? You thought she would have by now."

"Yeah. I thought she would have by now. Then again, this is Ella we're talking about. She's not the most predictable person on the planet. Still, even with her, that can't just be the end of it."

"I wish I had your confidence."

He seemed to think that over for a few minutes.

Then he said, "Is the publisher getting nervous? How are they even supposed to send her a contract? How will they get through the editorial process?"

"The publisher is not nervous," Amelia said. "That's only me. Her new agent told me she emailed the publisher so they could contact her electronically."

"But you don't have her email."

"No."

"Or her phone number."

"No."

"But you know where she lives."

"But I don't know a mailing address for the place. And, honestly, I'd be very surprised if there is one. The road had no name that I could see. There was no house number. No mailbox. She told me Marta picks up her royalty checks at a private mailbox in San Felipe. And I don't have that address, either. No, if I wanted to talk to her I'd have to literally show up at her house again. And that's no small trip."

"And why would you?" he said. "To do what? To say what?"

Amelia sat with that for a moment, something boiling inside.

She really, *really* wanted to go find Ella at her house. Part of her wanted to get out of bed in that moment, and start packing for the trip. She wouldn't, of course. But it was a hard impulse to resist.

"If she wants to leave without saying goodbye to me," she said, "without saying a word to me, I suppose that's her prerogative. She's like that, and I'm not going to teach her better manners after all her years. But nobody does that to my son."

"Oh," Leon said. And it was a big word, filled with all kinds of knowing, and sudden glimpses into the future. "That will not stand," he added.

"No, that will not stand."

"If you really feel the need to do it, maybe after the interview is done and submitted."

"Oh, it's done. It's not submitted, but it's done."

"You didn't tell me."

"Well. It's not *done* done. For me to tell you it was done, that would pretty much mean I wasn't changing a word of it. I'm still polishing here and there. But substantively, I have it. It more or less wrote itself. I just wrote an opening that was all bald-faced lies. About how she tracked me down and showed up with a manuscript. And then I wrote a wrap-up for the end about how I delivered the manuscript to the publisher. The whole middle section, probably four-fifths of the piece, was my questions and her answers, word for word."

"Sleep on it," he said.

"You don't think I should go."

"I think there's an element of weirdness in trying to talk to someone who isn't choosing to talk to you. Especially if that someone is E. L. Swann. But if it's something you really feel the need to do, I'll support you on it."

"Thank you," she said.

She kissed him briefly on the lips.

Then she rolled over, and did not sleep for hours.

In the morning she walked Jaden down to his carpool driver, and rejoined Leon at the breakfast table. She opened up her laptop, scanned the headlines, and began *The New York Times* crossword puzzle.

When the thought hit her, she really had no idea where it had come from. She hadn't seen it approach. In a rare moment, she hadn't been thinking about Ella in any way.

She looked up at Leon over her laptop monitor, and he looked back.

"What?" he said, seeming to catch that it was something big.

"I have Marta's phone number."

"And you just now realized it?"

"Yes. I just now realized it. Because she never gave it to me. I just remembered that Ella and Jaden had a FaceTime call with the donkey while she was here. Which means they called Marta's phone with my phone. Which means the number should still be in there. Assuming FaceTime saves recent numbers the way it does with regular voice calls. I don't know. Does it?"

"I think so," he said. "I think they show up with your other recents in the phone app."

She got up and fetched her phone from its charger in the bedroom and carried it back to the kitchen. As she walked, she opened the phone app to recents.

She sat down at the table with him.

"That's too bad," she said, "because it means I'll have hundreds of numbers to go through."

"Don't you ever clear your recents?"

"Obviously I'm bad about that."

She scrolled and scrolled, trying to remember how many months ago that call had been made.

"Wait," she said. "Do you need a country code to call Mexico?"

"Probably. I'll look it up."

He turned her laptop around to face him and clattered on its keyboard.

"Okay," he said. "Here we go. You have to dial what's called an exit code. It's 011. Then the country code for Mexico is 52. And if you're calling a mobile number in Mexico, which they were, you have to dial a 1 before the area code. So Marta's number is going to look entirely unlike anything else on that list."

"That's really helpful."

She scrolled a few more times, and there it was. Looking entirely unlike anything else on the list. It also clearly said "FaceTime Video" underneath, which made it jump out.

"I've got it!" she shouted.

She said it as though she had just triumphed over something daunting. Clawed her way to the summit of a mountain, maybe.

She tapped the number, and it rang as a FaceTime call.

Marta's cheerful face appeared on the screen.

"Hola," she said. Her face fell when she saw who it was. "She said not to be disturbed. Very important to her not to be disturbed."

"Just tell her it's me. Please. And that I want to talk to her. Two minutes. That's it. I promise."

Marta sighed.

A moment later Amelia found herself looking at the stucco ceiling of E. L. Swann's living room.

Not thirty seconds later Marta was back.

"She says not now. She says it's too much. It's all too much. Too much people, too much everything. She says she need to rest. She says just let her rest, and when she's ready she'll call you."

Amelia opened her mouth to say something, but Marta had already clicked off the call.

It was the following afternoon, after school, and Amelia was in the car with Jaden, driving him to his therapist appointment.

"How would you feel about my coming in with you today?" she asked him.

"Coming in where?"

"Dr. Walker's office."

"Oh," he said. He squirmed uncomfortably in his seat, and for a few seconds did not elaborate. "I guess it sort of depends. On . . . you know. What you want to talk about. I don't really like talking about the other kids at school except to Larry."

"That wasn't what I wanted to talk about. I thought maybe we could talk about Señora Steinbach."

"What about her?"

"The way she left so suddenly, without even saying goodbye to us. I thought you might want to talk about that."

He seemed to think that over for a time.

"I think it's just sort of how she is," he said. "But if *you* want to talk about it, I guess that's okay."

Amelia shifted nervously on the couch next to her son, who seemed quite relaxed. Then again, he'd been coming here for a while.

She looked up at Dr. Walker and he smiled a warm smile that was clearly intended to put her at ease. It worked, but only to a relatively small degree.

"I'm not sure how much Jaden has told you about our houseguest," she said.

"You told me not to say anything to anybody," Jaden hissed.

"Right, but I told you more recently that it's about to become very public that she was at our house. So it's okay for people to know that. Just never tell anybody that we were at her house, and especially not where her house is."

"But you just said we were at her house," he said, his voice heavy with complaint. "And right in front of Larry."

"I guess I forgot to explain to you about therapists, and how anything you say in their office, in a session, has to be kept completely private."

"Oh," Jaden said.

Then, for a minute or two, nobody said anything.

It was the therapist who spoke up.

"You don't need to tell me any more than you want to. But I don't know the story behind why there's secrecy surrounding your houseguest. It's none of my business, of course, unless it's related to what you wanted to talk about."

"It's the famous author E. L. Swann," she said.

The doctor's eyes went wide.

"Oh," he said. "Wow."

"It's about to hit the news in a very big way that she came to our house and gave me a fairly in-depth interview and left the manuscript of a second book."

"That's going to change your life a lot," he said.

"Yes, I'm getting previews of that. The secrecy part is just about making sure that she can stay in seclusion if she chooses to. We have to be very careful not to give away her whereabouts."

"I don't know her whereabouts," he said. "So there's no danger there. And even if you did tell me, as you pointed out, it would be covered by doctor-patient confidentiality. And I take that very seriously. But I'm still not clear on what aspect of this you wanted to discuss."

"I thought Jaden might need some help with the way she left."

"How did she leave?"

"In the night, and without even saying goodbye. They had a very deep friendship, Ella and Jaden, but toward the end he was beginning to doubt whether she genuinely cared for him. I figured it must have been hard on him, the way she just ran out on us like that. Without even saying goodbye," she added, though she knew she'd said it before.

She also knew she wasn't giving her son much chance to speak.

Dr. Walker turned his attention onto Jaden.

"What do you think, Jaden?"

Jaden only shrugged.

"How did that make you feel?"

"I think it's just how she is," he said.

"I'm not sure if that answers how it made you feel."

"It makes me feel like that's just how she is. We left *her* house without saying goodbye."

"We left her house without being *able to* say goodbye," Amelia interjected. "She slept in that day and left instructions not to be disturbed. Remember?"

"Maybe," the doctor said, "this is a woman who's simply not good with goodbyes."

"Yeah," Jaden said. "Maybe that."

Amelia looked up into the doctor's face, and he returned the gaze.

"Do you have issues getting him to open up often?" she asked.

"Who? Jaden?"

"Yes, Jaden."

"Not at all. He's very forthcoming."

"So why now, I wonder?"

"I'm not sure why you perceive it that way," he said. "You seem to be assuming he won't open up about how he feels, and I'm assuming he feels what he says he feels. That it's just the way she is."

"Right," Jaden said. "If it's just the way she is, then it isn't about us. It's just the way she is."

"That can't be all," Amelia said.

"Why can't it be?" the doctor asked.

"Because it was a big thing. It was a slap in the face. We turned our lives inside out for months for that woman. And believe me when I tell you, she was not the easiest person to have around. I put up with things I'd normally never put up with from anybody. I thought we'd gradually come to mean something to her. And then she just slipped away in the night and we haven't heard from her since. It was a terrible way for her to treat us. It was a very big deal."

The room fell silent, and some kind of waiting took place. Maybe Jaden and Dr. Walker were waiting to see if her rant had fully run its course. She wasn't sure.

While they all waited, she suddenly remembered Leon telling her that she might want to talk to a therapist too. At the time she had felt it was a good idea. But then she hadn't thought about it since. She wasn't sure why not, though her time with Ella could certainly knock all other thoughts out of a person's head.

"I hope you won't mind if I tell you what I'm hearing," Dr. Walker said.

"No, of course not. That's why I'm here."

"I don't want to challenge you, or make you feel like you're on the spot. But it feels to me like Jaden is doing well with her unceremonious departure. And you're struggling."

"Oh," Amelia said. "I . . . okay."

"Maybe this is something you'll want to talk about one-on-one at some point."

"That might be good," she said, feeling suddenly defeated and very tired.

"I can make an appointment for you before you leave today."

"Yeah," Amelia said. "I think I'll take you up on that."

She waited three months, and sixteen sessions with Dr. Walker, before breaking down and making travel arrangements to fly to San Felipe and rent a car.

During those three months, Ella did not call her.

Chapter Twenty-Five

Three and a Half Months Without E. L. Swann

When Amelia arrived in Santa Rosarita, it was after ten o'clock at night. She had no intention of surprising the author at that hour, so she parked in the lot of the same hotel where she'd stayed last time, hoping they had a room.

The desk clerk was a young woman she had not met on her last trip.

She was able to get a room, but it was not nearly as nice a room as last time. It did not have a patio letting out onto the beach, and its only windows looked out over the graded dirt parking lot.

Then again, what did it matter? The purpose of the room was only to hold her in until the morning.

She lay down fully dressed on top of the covers. Sometime around two o'clock in the morning she slept lightly and fitfully for a few hours.

In the morning she came out for the free hotel breakfast.

Guillermo was manning the desk.

"Good morning, señora," he said, and it was unclear whether he recognized her or not.

"You might not remember me," she said, walking closer to his desk.

"Ah, sí," he said. "Yes, of course I do now. You are the friend to the señora on the hilltop—the one we thought did not have any friends."

"I don't know if I'd say I'm her friend."

"Whatever you are to her," Guillermo said, "we thought she did not have any."

"Good to see you again," she said.

"And to you, señora. Enjoy your breakfast."

Over breakfast, Amelia toyed with the idea of calling Marta and asking her to drive down in the gator to get her.

She ultimately rejected the plan.

Marta might very well have said no. And even if she had said yes, it might have gotten her in trouble with her employer. And it might only have served to give Ella advance warning that she was coming, which could reduce her chances of being allowed in, and of having the conversation she'd come so far to catch.

No, she would walk up. She had done it once, in much hotter weather. She could do it again.

She walked to the front lobby and stood staring through the glass insets of the big, heavy wooden front doors. She could see the estate on the hill in the first slant of morning sunlight. It was dauntingly high over the town. It might have looked higher based on the fact that she knew she was going there on foot.

It also filled her with a flood of memories. Some good, some not.

"No one will come to get you in that big machine?" Guillermo asked her, knocking her out of her thoughts.

"No, I'm going to walk up."

"Here," he said. "Wait."

He hurried into an employee-only back area and came out a moment later with four bottles of water in his arms.

"You take plenty of this," he said. "You will need lots of water to drink for a walk like that one."

—

Amelia stood at the painfully familiar gate, and looked up at the bell. And, just for a few seconds, she allowed herself to admit she was scared. Deeply scared.

She had rehearsed what she would say to Ella interminably. Obsessively. On the plane ride, on the drive. And she had gone over it again as she'd lain awake for most of the previous night. And all the way up the strenuous road.

And yet now her mind felt blank, and the logic of coming here seemed to have cracked and fallen away.

Still, she was here.

She reached up and pulled the rope hard, putting all of her frustrations into that one motion. It let off its usual mighty clang.

As she waited, she could hear the roar of blood in her ears, and the world went white at the edges.

The gate opened and Ella stood there, looking preemptively angry.

When she saw who it was, the look changed. Though . . . changed to exactly what, Amelia could not have said. The anger calmed, but her face became closed and guarded, and it was unclear what she felt about this sudden development.

"I didn't expect this," she said. "But now I see I should have."

She stepped out and looked around, as though Amelia might have brought an army. Satisfied it was just the two of them, she looked straight into Amelia's eyes.

"Where's Jaden?"

"With his father."

"You couldn't have left him with Leon?"

"I could have. But Leon works nine to five, so he would have missed a couple of afternoons of work. And if Mark had found out for some reason, he would've been very upset. He always wants to spend more time with Jaden. Now he gets a little extra time."

Ella scanned around again with her eyes, but this time her gaze was aimed more at the path around Amelia's feet.

"No luggage. At least you know you won't be staying as long as last time. Well, you've come all this way," she said. "So I suppose you'd best come in."

Amelia sat on the terrace for a long time, looking out over the town and the sparkling gulf. Long enough that she had begun to worry that Ella was not coming back.

In time, though, the author appeared, carrying two glasses.

"Marta made us fresh lemonade."

She set a glass down on the table by Amelia's lounge, and sat.

"Thank you," Amelia said.

"Your career as a journalist has hit the stratosphere," Ella said. "Don't think I don't follow it. Why, I've even seen three or four big media interviews with you, and they're actually *about* you."

"No, they're really about *you*," Amelia said.

"That will become less true as time goes on."

"I get a lot of requests for television interviews, but I turn them all down. I'll only do interviews in writing. Interviewers can be wily about getting what they want."

"So I've noticed."

Amelia chose to let that dig go by.

"I worry they might trick me into saying something that could be a clue to your whereabouts. I'm sure you read the interview. I hope you were okay with it. You initially said you wanted editorial approval, but then you weren't around to give it."

"I didn't trust you as much back then. Look. I have no idea what you came all this way to say, but I know what it should be. You should have come to say thank you."

"Thank you," Amelia said. "But that's not all."

"*Of course* it's not," Ella said, dragging the first two words out into something long and sarcastic. "Well, I know I won't like it, but go ahead and get it off your chest."

"I want to know if you ever cared about me. And, more importantly, if you ever cared about Jaden. Or if you just used us as stepping-stones to get from point A to point B."

"Oh, and you're a fine one to talk. You got to some pretty desirable places by stepping across me."

"I'm not denying that. I'm only saying that in the course of all that, I started to genuinely care about you. And I just want to know if you ever returned that favor."

"You want to know why I left? Fine. I'll tell you why I left. And don't think I'm going to sugarcoat the truth for you. *This* is why I left. This. What you're doing right now, right here. I told you I needed a rest and I would call you when I was ready."

"That was three months ago."

"So? Who gets to decide how much rest I need? Me? Or you?"

"Okay. Let's say I'd waited a year. Would you have called? And don't *you* sugarcoat the truth for *me*."

Ella sat back on her lounge. Amelia felt a measure of the author's fire drain away in the pause before her answer.

"Probably not. But that still doesn't give you the right to violate my life without my permission."

"I notice something," Amelia said. "I notice that the question I asked was whether you cared about us. And that wasn't the question you answered."

"Of course I cared about you!" Ella shouted. "That was just the problem, don't you see? I cared about all three of you. Your whole little family. You seemed more worthwhile than the other people I encountered, so I let my guard down a bit, and I let you in."

For a time, she did not go on.

"And . . . ?" Amelia asked.

"And then you were in! And I don't want anybody in! I've told you and told you and told you, and you won't listen to me."

"I listen to you."

"Well, if you do, then you don't believe me. How many times have I told you I just want to be left alone?"

A pause, which Amelia did not fill. She had assumed it was a rhetorical question.

"No, I'm seriously asking you, darling. How many times did I tell you I just want to be left alone? That it's all I've ever asked?"

"I've lost count," Amelia said.

"Then why won't you believe me? I'm telling you who I am and you won't believe me!" She was shouting again now. "One of the first things I ever told you was that my readers felt I'd given them something with that first book. And that all I wanted in return was to be left alone, and I didn't think it was too much to ask. But I gave *you* far more than just a chance to read my debut novel, Amelia. I gave you more than I give anyone. And in return I told you I wished to be left alone. You want to know if I care about you. But a better question might be: Do you care about me? You claim to. But if you really care about me, why won't you honor that simple request? I keep telling you who I am, but you're either not listening or you won't believe me. You came here to tell me how I hurt you. Well, that's how you hurt me. Let's see if you can hear that for a change."

She stopped ranting, and Amelia did not start.

She only sat for a minute or two. Her stomach jangled, and her brain felt slightly disconnected from the scene. It struck her how far this conversation had fallen from the one she'd expected. The one she had rehearsed.

As Ella had correctly pointed out, Amelia had come here feeling she was right, to tell Ella how right she was. And she had expected to maintain that position of rightness.

Now she had some major recalibration to do.

"You're absolutely right," Amelia said.

"I am?" Ella asked, sounding surprised.

"Didn't *you* think you were right?"

"Yes, but I didn't expect *you* to think so. This is not a trick, is it? Some kind of reverse psychology?"

"No. It's not. I hear you, and I think you're right. I shouldn't have come here. You told me and told me how you wanted to live your life, and I just kept expecting . . . I don't know what. To be the exception to that rule, I guess. Or for you to see things differently. And then to cap it off I show up here demanding you care about me just the way I want you to care. But you never signed a contract promising you'd care about me any special way. Or at all."

"Nobody ever does, darling."

"I think marriage is supposed to be that kind of contract."

"Maybe. But it ultimately proves nonbinding. Every now and then one might get very lucky and find someone lovely, like your handsome beau, who's willing to work without a contract."

"Anyway," Amelia said, unable to pause to take in that rare compliment, "it wasn't fair to you. I'm sorry I hurt you."

She purposely did not look at the author's face as she spoke.

"Likewise, dear."

"I'm going to get out of your hair."

She stood, and Ella quickly stood with her.

"You don't have to leave *this* soon. You came all this way."

"It was my choice to come all this way. And I'm not leaving in anger. I said what I came here to say and you told me what I wanted to know. I'm going to go away and leave you alone now."

"At least finish your lemonade."

Amelia raised the glass and downed it in a few long gulps.

She walked to the gate, Ella following behind.

"Let me ask *you* a question," Ella said before Amelia could let herself out.

Amelia stopped. Turned. Allowed it.

"You thought I would come back to the world," Ella said, "and that once I did, somehow I'd be inclined to stay."

"That's not really a question."

"The question is: Why did you think so? Did you think I would find I had been entirely wrong about the world?"

"Not really, no. I see what you see about people. It's real."

"Did you think I would find that the world had changed?"

"I thought you might find that *you* had changed."

Ella snorted her famous, derisive snort.

"People don't change, darling."

Amelia only stood a moment. She was thinking, *No, they don't if they're so sure they won't.* But, more, she was thinking, *People do change, sometimes, but I accept the fact that this person never will.*

She didn't say any of that.

She said only, "Enjoy your quiet life."

"Oh, I will," Ella said. "Enjoy your fame and fortune, if such a thing is possible. Don't you want me to have Marta drive you down in the gator?"

"No. That's okay. I'll walk. It's not the way down that hurts."

She walked away, and, unlike the first time she had left that place, this time she did not look back.

On the way down the hill, she picked up the empty plastic water bottles she had left on the grueling hike up.

Then she took her phone out of her pocket and texted Leon at work.

"Do you think people change?" she typed.

"Where are you?" he texted back.

"On my way home."

"That was fast."

"It was long enough. I said what I needed to say. She said what she needed to say."

"Are you okay?"

"Yeah. I'm okay." And it was true, she realized. She was okay. A little shocked and sad, but okay. "You didn't answer the question, though. Do you think people change?"

She walked twenty or thirty steps before his answer came in. For some unknown reason she was counting.

"I think they can," his reply said.

"Yeah, sure. They can. But do you think they ever actually do?"

This time fifty steps. Then sixty. Then seventy.

"Yes," Leon typed. "But not nearly as often as we hope they will."

Chapter Twenty-Six

One and a Half Years Without E. L. Swann

Amelia was typing on the couch when Leon came in from work.

"You didn't bring in the mail," he said.

"Sorry. I got caught up in this piece I'm working on."

He dropped a package onto the coffee table in front of her. A thickly padded envelope containing something the size and shape of a hefty book.

She picked it up and looked at it more closely.

"From Ella's publisher," she said.

Leon was sorting bills on his lap in the big chair Ella had used to favor.

"I couldn't help seeing that," he said.

"Must be a finished copy of *Moratorium*."

"Sounds about right."

She tore it open. It was a beautiful finished hardback with a smooth, shiny dustcover. She opened it, and flipped through the leaf page and the title pages.

"It's not even signed," she said. "I thought at least she'd inscribe a copy."

"But she's not at her publisher's. They're in New York and she's in Mexico."

"But she must have copies. *She* could have mailed us a signed one. But . . . you know what? Never mind. I'm doing it again. She is the way she is."

"She certainly is," Leon said.

Amelia found a small note card inside, and pulled it out, swelling with anticipation.

But it said only, "The author requested that we gift you an early copy." It did not say whose desk it was from, and it was unsigned.

Then she flipped another page, and her eyes fell on the dedication.

"I'll be damned," she said.

"She did something good after all?"

"She dedicated it to Jaden."

"Really? That's great. He'll be thrilled. Read it to me."

"It says, 'To the young Jaden Booker, my muse. You are one of a very few people in this world I care about, though even that is in my own admittedly insufficient way.'"

"That's beautiful."

"It really is," Amelia said, her voice just at the edge of cracking.

"You think she meant to hint that we're among the very few?"

"Maybe. I don't know. Probably so. But either way, I kept telling her that I cared much more about her loving Jaden than I did about her loving me."

"Yeah," he said. "Too bad it's not true. I mean, you cared more about her loving Jaden. But maybe not as much more as you let on."

"You know me too well," she said. "Anyway, at least it means she listened, and she believed me. Even if she shouldn't have. Cover your ears." She cupped her hands around her mouth and shouted toward the far bedroom. "Hey, Jaden! Come see this!"

"I'll be out in a minute!" he shouted back. "I'm on level four."

"Video game?" Leon asked.

"What else?"

She went back to what she was writing then, because she had sentences she was holding in her head, and she didn't trust them to stay. And Jaden's version of a minute could be an hour, depending on whether he made it to level five.

When he finally stuck his head out of his room and yelled, "What?" down the hall, she was far too enmeshed in what she was doing to allow a break in concentration.

"Show it to him, please," she said to Leon, "would you?"

He picked up the book and walked down the hall, closing himself into Jaden's room.

It was maybe fifteen minutes later when he came back out. Maybe twenty. And by that time she felt safe taking a break.

He no longer held the book.

"Thank you," she said. "I was too much in the middle of that. What did he think?"

"It was kind of funny and sweet. After I explained what 'admittedly insufficient' meant, his voice went up about a full octave, and he started walking around the room in these jerky little movements like he'd been plugged into a wall socket."

"Ah yes," she said. "Level-six Jaden."

"He wants to borrow the book to show to his therapist. I hope that's okay."

"Of course it is."

"And then he wants to take it to school for a sort of show-and-tell. He's about to be the big man on campus at school, and he knows it. My phrasing, not his. I don't think kids say that anymore."

"I don't even think grown-ups say that anymore," Amelia said, half suppressing a smile.

"Fine. Have a laugh at my expense. But his status among his peers is about to shoot up by several levels, and since the book is not published yet, he wants to speed up the process."

Amelia mulled that over for a minute. She almost said something out loud about how Ella had potentially solved his bullying problem, and without ever coming out of hiding. But she wasn't sure exactly how to say it, and besides, Leon was undoubtedly thinking exactly the same thing.

It really did not require saying.

All she said was "Every now and then she gets one right."

Epilogue

Eight Years Without E. L. Swann

Amelia was driving home from a work meeting—an interview for the *Chronicle* with a local debut novelist.

Her phone rang, and it clearly read out across her car's information screen as Leon. Her phone was somewhere in her purse, but she answered the call hands-free.

"What's up, honey? I'll be home in fifteen or twenty minutes."

"You got a letter," he said.

She felt it in her gut immediately. Heavy, like a lead fishing weight. Pulling her down. It was partly something in his voice. Partly the fact that he normally didn't call to tell her about mail.

"It's from an attorney," he added.

"Crap," she breathed out loud. "Someone is suing me?"

"I don't know," he said evenly. "But of course that's the worry."

"Open it."

She could hear the sound of paper tearing on his end of the call.

She wanted him to hurry, but she didn't say so. She just kept telling herself, silently, *Breathe*.

"No one is suing you," he said at last.

"That's good to hear," she said on a long outbreath.

"It's from an attorney who says he was retained several years ago to revise the will and handle the estate of Ella Lynne Carmichael."

"Oh, it's about Ella."

"Yes."

"But you're sure Ella's not suing me?"

"I'm sure."

He didn't say more. Somehow Amelia got the impression that he was waiting for her to catch up. It took a few beats, but then it rose up and hit her over the head. And she got it.

"Oh. She died."

"Yes," Leon said. "She died."

"Wait. I need to find a place to pull over."

She was on the 1, the Shoreline Highway between the Sunset District and Golden Gate Park, but it wasn't a highway, really. Not that part of it. It was a very busy city street, simultaneously 19th Avenue, with a stoplight every short block. And no available parking, to understate the case.

She pulled in at a red curb, a loading zone, and shifted into park. If she got a citation, she just did. In that moment she couldn't bring herself to care.

"You okay?" Leon's voice asked.

"Yeah," she said. "Pretty much." Then, nearly half a minute later, she said, "Why do I find this shocking? She would have been ninety-two. Why does this feel so surprising?"

"I think it's always a shock when someone dies, if they meant something to us. No matter how inevitable it is. No matter how much we know that. Somehow we just never really expect it to happen."

"No, it's more than that," she said. She breathed for a minute and tried to find the "more."

Then she saw a police car several blocks behind her in her rearview mirror, and she pulled back into traffic, taking advantage of a very small space—small enough to prompt an angry honk from the driver she cut off in the process.

She shook it off and kept talking.

"I think . . . it's weird to admit this, but I think right up until this very minute I thought there would be more to the story. You know. The 'E. L. Swann meets Amelia Booker' story."

"Why is that weird to admit?"

"Because I haven't spoken to her in eight years. I mean, take the hint, Amelia. But I still thought there would be more. Or that there could be, anyway. And now I know. That was it. The whole story. The End."

"Are you still pulled over?"

"No, I'm driving again. I'll be home soon. And I think I want to get mildly drunk this evening and feel very sorry for myself. I promise I won't feel sorry for myself forever. Or even for too long. But definitely tonight."

"Sounds like a plan. See you soon."

"Wait!" she shouted. "Don't hang up."

"What?"

"If we got a letter from the attorney handling her trust . . . does that mean she *left* us something?"

"Looks that way," Leon said. "He wants us to call and make an appointment to come into his office. And he wants Jaden there too."

"I'll bet she left us some little thing that other people wouldn't value properly. Like for some reason I'm thinking maybe that first-edition copy of *Labyrinth*, the one she marked up in blue pencil."

"That would be nothing to sneeze at. I'll bet if that thing went on auction it would go for a small fortune."

"Except I would never sell it," Amelia said. "Anyway. We'll see. We'll see what she had up her sleeve this time."

Jaden was bouncing his knee, and had been since they sat down in the attorney's office. In fact, he had been doing it since he was thirteen.

His legs were too long to be his legs now. Maybe too long to be anybody's legs. His lankiness seemed without bounds these days, and he never seemed to know what to do with his limbs.

She reached across Leon and put one hand on her son's knee to still it, and he shot her a very dark, very teenage look from under a ridiculous amount of curly brown hair.

"How old is your son now?" the attorney asked.

"Fifteen," he and Amelia both said simultaneously.

The attorney's name was Lucius Grey, he was well into his eighties—if not older—and he spoke with a British accent and an oddly formal tone. It was clear why this would be the one Ella had chosen. In fact, someone could have lined up twenty attorneys and she could have picked Ella's out of the crowd.

"And you are Amelia Booker but you are Leon Rice?" he asked, turning to Leon. "But you two are legally married."

"We are," Amelia said.

"All right. You kept your maiden name. That's common enough."

"Actually . . . it's not my maiden name. It's an older married name, which I'm not entirely comfortable with, but I've been advised that it's probably too late in my career to change my name and expect to keep the recognition."

"Yes, I'm familiar with your work," Grey said, "and that's not an entirely uncommon situation. And of course no judgment is to be inferred. It's only that there will be a lot of paperwork and my goal is to see that it's made out correctly the first time. Now to get into some specifics, and there are quite a few."

"I hope you don't mind," Amelia said. "I know you do this for a living, and you have a way you like to do it, and an order to things. But if you could just jump ahead for a minute, and then I promise we can go back and I'll listen to the details. We're on pins and needles to know. How much of her estate are we talking about here?"

"I'm afraid we're getting into numbers I don't have here at my fingertips. The novels are quite successful and I'm sure the royalties are substantial. They'll probably jump even higher now, owing to the author's death. But I don't have access to the publisher's statements. Before too long you and your son will be able to access them as the rights holders."

"No, you misunderstood me," Amelia said, not yet able to process the sentence about being the rights holders. "Or maybe I didn't make myself clear. I wasn't asking what the estate is worth. I was asking what portion of the estate was left to me and my son."

For a moment, Lucius Grey only looked at her and blinked. He seemed not to understand the question.

"All of it," he said. "There was no one else. You knew the author. Did you think there was anyone else?"

"People bequeath to charities."

"Ms. Carmichael did not."

"And I would think she left something to Marta."

"We discussed Ms. Hernandez. At length. My client cared for her, of course. In her own way. But she also drew a line between employees and personal connections—of which she had few. The final decision was more of a stipulation for Ms. Hernandez. She is to stay on to take care of the house and the property, and the animals who call it home, and you will pay her from the very generous estate you have inherited. Now. If you don't mind, the details. To your son, Jaden, the rights to both novels, meaning of course that all royalties will be paid to him. But until he's eighteen that money will go into a trust. When he turns eighteen, it will pay for his education. It will provide tuition to the best, most prestigious university to which he can gain acceptance. And she left you a note here. It's a little off the cuff, and I wouldn't say it myself. I'm only reading her words. She says to tell you, 'If his grades aren't the best, try giving a very large donation to the university that seems most inclined to accept him. That tends to open doors.'"

"His grades are good," Amelia said.

"Excellent," Grey said, apparently with no humor or sense of irony whatsoever. "That will save you some funds. After he's graduated college, the rest of the money and all future royalties will be released to him to spend in any way he chooses."

She glanced over at her son, but he seemed lost. In full retreat. As if none of this could possibly be happening.

"Oh, and in addition to the rights to the books, she's left him one other thing. It's a bit unusual. Not something we see every day. It's a . . . donkey."

At that, Jaden's head snapped up.

"Francisco is still alive?" he asked in that deep voice that made him sound even older than fifteen.

"He is. I have his veterinary records here. He seems to be in fine health. Of course he doesn't have a stud book or a pedigree the way finely bred horses do, so we don't know his exact date of birth, but they take him to be about twenty."

"Is that old for a donkey?" Amelia asked.

"Apparently not. My assistant researched online a bit, and it seems they often live to be thirty-five or even forty. But that leads me to another stipulation. The house and surrounding property she is leaving to you, Amelia Booker. But it's the home of the donkey and five cats, and she has made it painfully clear that until each and every one of them lives out its full lifespan and dies a natural death, the house belongs more to them than it does to you. In other words, it may not be sold. When the animals are gone, you may do as you wish with the property. But she hoped you would keep it. She left a note about that, and I had to promise to read it to you word for word."

He flipped pages in his folder for a moment, then pulled out a scrap of paper roughly torn from a pad.

"'Tell Amelia if she has an ounce of courage, she'll keep it, and she'll hole up there as often as possible, and write those novels she claimed she wanted to write. Because, darling, if you can't do it there, you can't do it. And once Jaden is in college, you are fresh out of excuses, my friend. Take it from one who knows about excuses.' Sorry. Her words. Not mine."

He dropped the note onto his desk again.

Amelia only sat a minute, not sure what to feel or what to say.

Then a wholly inappropriate bark of a laugh burst out of her.

Everyone turned and stared at her. Everyone.

"I'm sorry," she said, feeling her face grow hot. "I know it's not funny. Nothing about this is funny. It was just so Ella. I just felt like she was sitting across the desk from me. It was just so completely her voice and her attitude. Just so . . . Ella."

Then, with absolutely no warning, she was crying.

"Wow," she said. "I'm just a roller coaster today, aren't I?"

"Are you okay?" Leon asked her, slipping an arm around her shoulders.

"I'm fine," she said, through some slightly hiccupy sobs. "It was just so Ella." She turned her attention to the attorney again. "I'm sorry. I didn't mean to get so emotional. I didn't think I'd get emotional in your office."

"People get emotional in my office all the time," he said, sliding a box of tissues across the desk in her direction. "I'm an estate attorney. I wasn't sure if *you* would, because I'm aware that you didn't know the author all that well. Though, frankly, you seemed to have known her better than anyone else did. No matter. I'm very sorry for your loss."

"Do we know how she died?" she asked, trying to compose herself. "I mean, of course she died of old age, but usually there's some complicating factor. I just wondered if she died at home or in a hospital, and if she suffered."

"There was no autopsy performed, due to her advanced age. Ms. Hernandez said she'd had a bad cold and a cough and had been characteristically stubborn about accepting medical attention. Her doctor thinks it probably went to pneumonia and she simply stopped breathing in her sleep. So most likely she didn't suffer, no, and we can take comfort in that. What we do know for sure is that she died the way everyone assumes she would have wanted to die. Alone, at home, in her sleep."

Amelia blew her nose hard and tossed the tissue into a metal trash can beside the desk.

"She wasn't alone," she said. "She had Francisco, and the cats."

Grey chortled slightly. He seemed uncomfortable, and unsure as to whether she was serious.

"Right, yes," he said. "Some people would count that, wouldn't they?"

"Ella would count that."

"Yes," he said, seeming to have found his footing again. "Yes, I suppose she would."

"I can't believe I don't get to go," Jaden said. "He's *my* donkey."

He was in his room, sorting through some dirty clothes that Amelia had insisted he clean up off the floor before Mark came to pick him up.

"We're not going to see the donkey. I mean, we'll say hi. But we're going because Leon has never seen the house. It's our house now. At least to the extent that Francisco and the cats allow it to be. But we own it, and he's never even seen it. He's dying to see it. And you know why you can't go. You have school."

"Write me a note," he said, his voice whiny for one with such a deep register.

"Oh. Write you a note to get you out of school for a week."

"Yeah!"

But he seemed to know this was not going to go his way.

"Now how would that go? Let's see. 'Dear principal of Jaden's high school.'" She spoke haltingly, as if dictating a note. "'Jaden will be missing school for a week. You see, he inherited a donkey. The donkey lives in Mexico, and Jaden is very anxious to see him again. I trust that when you hear this explanation you'll understand perfectly and excuse him from his classes. Sincerely, The Worst Mother on the Planet.'"

Jaden rolled his eyes theatrically.

"Okay, okay, I get it. I don't get to go."

"When school lets out for summer we can go spend the whole summer there if you want. Leon is talking about getting a leave of absence from work, or even quitting."

"He should quit," Jaden said. "We're so rich. Tell him he can have some of my royalties. I've got more money than I know what to do with. Hey. You think I'm too big to ride Francisco now?"

"You're so thin," she said. "I doubt you weigh any more than Ella did. And besides, he's a very big donkey."

"Yes," he said. "*My* donkey is a very big donkey. Tell him I said hi."

"Still five cats," Marta said on the noisy gator ride up the hill. "But three of them you don't know. Some who were here when you were here, they got old and died now. Some are new. Two you know."

"Which two?"

"Soolie. That one is seventeen now. And Bybee."

"Which one is Bybee?"

"The beauty one. With the green eyes. The one she called her sable lion."

"Oh, yes," Amelia said, straining her voice to be heard over the engine. "I remember him. He *is* a beautiful cat."

"He knows, too," Marta said. "He definitely knows."

Amelia reached over and took Leon's hand, and gave it a squeeze.

"That's so Ella," she said.

"Francisco," Amelia called. "I've brought somebody I want you to meet. Also, Jaden says hi."

The donkey's head popped out of his stucco shelter, long ears swiveling at their bases. He opened his mouth, showing his yellowing teeth, and let out that shocking bellow of a bray. And let it out, and let it out. It was long, and modulated, and just went on and on.

"You think he remembers me?" she asked Marta.

"Maybe," Marta said. "But he says that same thing to everybody."

They were sitting on the terrace in the evening, after Marta had gone home, more or less watching the sun go down. They were looking out over the gulf, so of course the sun was setting behind them. But the colors of the sunset reflected orange and purple in the few thin clouds hovering above the Sea of Cortez.

"This place is amazing," he said, his voice a reverent whisper. "It's so quiet."

"Oh, it's all of that."

"After having been in San Francisco all my life . . . of course I've been camping a few times. But, you know, even then, I could still hear voices from the neighboring campsites. Up here I don't hear *anything*."

"She wouldn't have had it any other way."

"I can see why she said what she said. That if you can't write a novel here you can't write a novel. Which leads me to a huge question."

"Yes," Amelia said. "I'm going to hole up here and write a novel. I don't know if it'll be any good, but there's only one way to find out. I'll probably have to wait till Jaden goes away to college. But that's okay, because the novel is not the first book I'm going to write anyway."

"Okay. That was an intriguing sentence."

"I'm going to start with a nonfiction book. About Ella and me. But the real story, not that fake thing we came up with about her showing up at my place with a finished manuscript. I mean every twist and turn, all the good stuff and the heartbreaking stuff, from the day I got that tip about an old woman in Santa Rosarita right up until . . . well . . . now, I guess. Right up until this moment when I brought you to see the house she left us, and we got to sit here on the terrace and try to absorb the fact that this is ours now. Because now she's where nobody can find her, and I get to tell the truth. The veil of secrecy is lifted."

"That's going to be a great book," Leon said, his voice brimming with an intensity that only rose up on the most special of occasions.

"I'm going to try to sell it more or less right away, on proposal. And then I'll do my best to knock it out over the summer."

"*Try* to sell it? Are you kidding? The publishers are going to be fighting duels to see who gets it. This is going to be *good*."

They sat watching the clouds turn darker.

Then he said, "Tell me the truth. How long did it take before it dawned on you that you get to tell the whole story now?"

"Longer than you would think. That old secrecy habit was really ingrained. How about you?"

"Oh, I thought of it immediately . . . after you mentioned it just now."

Amelia popped awake, unaware until she did that she had ever dozed off. She was still on the lounge on the terrace, and Leon was still beside her. But now it was dark and cool, with a riot of stars above their heads. And Leon had thrown an afghan over her.

"I waited for you," he said.

"For what?"

"You'll know if you think about it."

"The thing with the stars?"

"I looked at them, but only like they were a flat mural. I was waiting for you."

"Thank you. That was sweet."

"It's so clear tonight, too," Leon said. "I've never seen so many stars in my life. I never knew there were this many to be seen. You ready?"

"When you are."

For a silent moment or two, Amelia struggled to see the sky above her as three-dimensional deep space. It wouldn't come, and it wouldn't come. And it wouldn't come.

And then, just as she had ceased to expect it to, it did.

She said, "Wow," and Leon said, "Whoa," at exactly the same time.

"Ella's spirituality," he said. "Another thing she left us."

"The list just keeps getting longer, doesn't it?"

She looked up again, but it was gone. And it was no easier getting it back than it had been to find it in the first place.

So in the great scheme of the universe, it was only that one second. But some seconds are more impactful than others.

BOOK CLUB QUESTIONS

1. Amelia is a journalist who believes that if she could only write an incredible book like the one by E. L. Swann, she'd never doubt her purpose in life again. Is creative or career achievement essential to a person's sense of identity or fulfillment? Or do you believe one's worth as a person is inherent, regardless of their output?
2. Now that Amelia is divorced, she must share custody of their son, Jaden, with her ex-husband. In what ways does that influence the decisions she makes as a mother and how she balances parenting with her career goals?
3. Jaden and Ella build a strong bond after spending time together in Mexico. When Jaden opens up to her about being bullied at school, Ella says, "They're only trying to make you feel small because they're afraid it's really themselves who are small." What role does internalized self-worth play in overcoming emotional abuse?
4. Jaden doesn't think emotional pain "counts" because he hasn't been physically hurt by the schoolmates. Do you think emotional wounds have the same legitimacy as physical ones? In what ways does society tend to downplay psychological harm?
5. Ella says her fans have no idea how they make life "unlivable" for an author who is thrust suddenly into the limelight. Do the rewards of fame outweigh the loss of privacy? What are the

dangers of idolizing artists, authors, or celebrities? Can one ever truly separate the art from the artist?

6. Were you surprised by the evolving relationship between Jaden and Ella? Why do you think Ella came to think of Jaden as her muse? In what ways did this bond serve both the writer and the young boy?
7. Amelia believes that people have the capacity to be kind and good, while Ella believes people are self-serving and fear-driven. Which view resonates more with your experience of humanity? Can both be true?
8. In regard to people having the capacity to really change, Ella strongly feels that people never will. Amelia believes that sometimes they do, while Leon states, "People can change, but not nearly as often as we hope they will." What's your stance on the possibility of personal transformation? How do you balance optimism about change with realism?
9. At the end of the book, Ella passes and leaves Amelia and Jaden her estate in Mexico. She tells Amelia to write those novels she claimed she wanted to because she now has no more excuses for following her dream. What do you think making excuses is usually indicative of? What types of excuses hold people back from pursuing their dreams, and what does it take to move past them?

ABOUT THE AUTHOR

Photo © 2019 Douglas Sonders

Catherine Ryan Hyde is the *New York Times*, *Wall Street Journal*, and #1 Amazon Charts bestselling author of nearly fifty books and counting. An avid traveler, equestrian, and amateur photographer, she shares her astrophotography with readers on her website.

Her novel *Pay It Forward* was adapted into a major motion picture, chosen by the American Library Association (ALA) for its Best Books for Young Adults list and translated into more than twenty-three languages for distribution in over thirty countries. Both *Becoming Chloe* and *Jumpstart the World* were included on the ALA's Rainbow Book List, and *Jumpstart the World* was a finalist for two Lambda Literary Awards. *Where We Belong* won two Rainbow Awards in 2013, and *The Language of Hoofbeats* won a Rainbow Award in 2015.

More than fifty of her short stories have been published in the *Antioch Review*, *Michigan Quarterly Review*, *Virginia Quarterly Review*, *Ploughshares*, *Glimmer Train*, and many other journals; in the anthologies *Santa Barbara Stories* and *California Shorts*; and in the bestselling anthology *Dog Is My Co-Pilot*. Her stories have been honored by the Raymond Carver Short Story Contest and the Tobias Wolff Award and have been nominated for *The Best American Short Stories*, the O. Henry Award, and the Pushcart Prize. Three have been cited in the annual *Best American Short Stories* anthology.

As a professional public speaker, she has addressed the National Conference on Education, twice spoken at Cornell University, met with AmeriCorps members at the White House, and shared a dais with Bill Clinton.

For more information, visit www.catherineryanhyde.com.